HUNTRESS CADET

HUNTRESS CADET

HUNTRESS CLAN SAGA™ BOOK 3

JAMIE DAVIS

DISRUPTIVE IMAGINATION

Copyright © 2020 Jamie Davis
Cover Art by Jake @ J Caleb Design
http://jcalebdesign.com / jcalebdesign@gmail.com

LMBPN Publishing
PMB 196, 2540 South Maryland Pkwy
Las Vegas, NV 89109

First US Edition, February, 2020
eBook ISBN: 978-1-64202-767-9
Print ISBN: 978-1-64202-768-6

THE HUNTRESS CADET TEAM

Thanks to the JIT Readers

Dave Hicks
Diane L. Smith
Larry Omans
John Ashmore
Kelly O'Donnell
Dorothy Lloyd
Deb Mader

If I've missed anyone, please let me know!

Editor
The Skyhunter Editing Team

Quinn sat at the high-top table, scanning the crowded nightclub for vampires. After weeks of random night patrols around Baltimore and its suburbs, Clark had brought them to this club in Glen Burnie just south of the city. The electronic dance music pulsed through the crowded space as the DJ executed smooth transitions from one song to the next.

The huntress picked up her glass of cranberry juice and soda on the rocks, sipped the non-alcoholic cocktail, and peered through the flashing lights of the darkened club to try to pick out her mentor from among the crowd. He should've been easy to spot. A guy his age didn't fit in with the twenty-something crowd filling the bustling dance floor and clustered around the bar.

She wouldn't have been allowed entry into the twenty-one-and-up club since she was only eighteen, but Clark knew the bouncer. The guy at the door barely glanced at her and didn't request ID when she passed by. He merely nodded at Clark and turned to the next person in line.

When she couldn't find Clark, Quinn decided he'd shifted into the shadows, using the hunter magic in his amulet to hide from all but the most exhaustive and magically enhanced searches. The dark club, with its shadowy nooks and corners, was the best environment in which to use that skill.

Her hand drifted up to her chest, touching the spot between her breasts where her amulet should have been. Or at least, where it would have been if she hadn't melted it into a lump of slag almost three months before. It had been necessary to save herself and most of the others from certain death. She had been unable to stop vampire lord John Handon from killing a member of her new clan. She had missed Miranda and her abilities with magic and spellcraft ever since.

Quinn's fingertips traced the fabric of her black t-shirt above the scar that was a reminder of that night and her losses. The injury bore the imprint of the amulet. It stood out like a brand, the image of a tree on her chest. The melted charm was in a drawer in their hideout, nothing but a useless lump of silver on a chain.

"Are you paying attention?"

Quinn jumped at Clark's voice in her ear, startled from her drifting thoughts back to the present. Her head snapped around, her left hand reaching reflexively for the Bowie knife slung under her right arm, hidden beneath her leather jacket.

"Dammit, Clark! Stop sneaking up on me."

"I wouldn't be able to if you were paying attention. You can see through my illusion if you try hard enough."

The grizzled fortyish hunter turned away from her and

stared at the crowded dance floor. "Have you spotted them yet? There are two of them, a man and a woman. They'll be working in tandem to separate someone from the crowd so they can attack."

Quinn searched the crowd with renewed interest. "You're sure they're here? I know you said the disappearances around this area trace back to this club, but I haven't seen anything."

"Try using that tracking thing you do. Maybe that'll help us spot them. I'm surprised you haven't done that already."

Quinn groaned. The loss of the amulet hadn't meant the loss of her magical huntress abilities. What it *had* done was make accessing them difficult and spotty, and even reaching for the magic caused headaches. It was as if the destroyed amulet had provided a conduit that protected her from all those side effects.

However, the huntress realized someone's life was potentially on the line, and she shifted her mind to access the heads-up display her brain could show her. As she scanned the club's patrons, she concentrated on activating the tracking ability she'd gained from her time inside the magically enhanced VR training simulator that had gotten her into all of this.

Her HUD popped into view, although it was dim and flickering. A dull, throbbing ache started at the base of her skull.

Ignoring the pain, Quinn selected the tracking skill from the menu inside her head, and a faint overlay fell into place over the crowd. Now all the people had a sort of lime green outline around them, with the other colors muted.

All the people, that is, except for the two now outlined in pale red amidst the gyrating dancers.

"I see them," Quinn said, squinting to see them well enough to describe them to Clark. "Uh, it's the black-haired woman in the leather pants and silver blouse and the guy in the jeans with a gray sport coat. They're in the middle of the dance floor right now."

Clark nodded. "Good, I was hoping you'd still be able to do that."

"You mean, without my amulet?"

"I've told you before, Quinn. A hunter's amulet is only an assistant for using magic. The power comes from within. The charm has some inherent protections, but the rest is all you."

Quinn resisted the urge to snap at him. He *had* told her this before. He thought that since she'd grown up with the amulet from early childhood, she'd come to rely on it too much. The amulet had been left with Quinn when her parents abandoned her as a baby. She'd discovered early on that she could sense certain dangers around her. She had accessed the simple protections carried by the amulet, even though she had none of the proper training. Clark believed that accounted for her challenges in accessing her power now, without the charm.

Changing the subject, Quinn kept her eyes on the vamps and asked, "How do you want to do this? Should we attack them here or wait until they leave and try to catch them outside?"

The pair of vampires was dancing with a trio of young women, although Quinn could see they were focusing their attention on one of them. Of the three potential victims, the tall blonde was the most intoxicated of the group. She stumbled, bumping into the others as she danced.

"We need to get them alone so we can question them. They can tell us where Handon has gone to ground," Clark said, "That these two are out and hunting makes me believe they're part of his coven."

Quinn and Clark had been searching for the where-abouts of the powerful vampire lord ever since they'd forced him to flee. Clark had inquired among the peaceful members of the mystical community living in and around Baltimore, including a few vampire families who now fed only on animal blood. The vamps he'd met with were noticeably uncomfortable talking to the two of them. They all claimed to know nothing about Handon or his rogue vampire followers. It was apparent he had them all scared.

"What makes you so sure these two are working with Handon?" Quinn asked. "They could just be a couple of transients passing through."

Clark shook his head. "From what I hear from my police contact, the disappearances in the area have been going on for some time—perhaps several months. That fits within our time frame since that's when Handon went to ground. Also, no transient would be that careless, sticking to one location for so long, unless they had protection from the local vampire community."

Quinn watched the pair, growing more concerned as the male vamp separated the blonde from her two friends and started helping her toward the exit. The female vampire excused herself from the others and fell in on the girl's other side.

"They're taking her, Clark. We need to get to them before they get her outside."

"They won't get far with her. They're probably just taking her to the alley behind the club." Clark pointed to an emergency exit nearby. "We can go out this door and meet them in the parking lot."

Quinn shook her head. "We don't know that's where they're going. I'm going after them before it's too late," she said. She stood up, avoiding Clark's hand as he tried to hold her back.

Using her natural huntress speed and agility, Quinn ran through the crowded dance floor weaving through the gyrating patrons with ease. As she neared the front entrance, Quinn accessed her stamina. A green bar appeared in front of her, as if she were inside a VR game.

Ignoring the headache that continued to throb in the background, Quinn drew upon the stamina bar and supplemented her strength and speed. She'd need it as soon as she caught up to the pair of vampires. About a quarter of the green stamina bar drained, turning faint yellow-green.

The surge of energy filled her muscles, and Quinn burst through the club's front doors, scanning the sidewalk and street for her quarry. She spotted them not too far away, pushing the hapless woman into a green hatchback parked on the street in front of the club. Good thing she hadn't gone with Clark to the rear parking lot.

Rushing forward, Quinn grabbed for the nearest of the two vampires, the male. He appeared to be in his twenties, with shoulder-length brown hair.

He spun on her, saying, "Hey, what are you doing? We're helping our friend here get home."

"You're not fooling anyone, vamp." Quinn's Bowie flashed in the streetlights as she pulled the blade out from under her jacket and brandished it at the undead pair.

The black-haired woman stood, having finished pushing the drunk woman into their car. "You're her, aren't you? The one who thinks she can resurrect the dead hunter clans all by herself."

Quinn smiled. A part of her was proud they'd heard of her. If the word was getting around, it might mean they'd back down and let her have the girl without a fight.

"I'm Quinn Faust, if that's what you mean, and I'm a huntress. I'd rather not have to kill you both. All I want is the woman's release and information," she replied.

The man laughed, his fangs showing. "Oh, is that all?" he jeered. He glanced at his partner. "Well, then, Karla, maybe we should let our dinner go."

"Hell, no!" Karla said. She glared at Quinn. "We could grab some huntress for dessert, though."

Before Quinn could answer, the black-haired woman sprang at her, her extended hands reaching for Quinn's neck.

Glad she'd thought to charge up before coming outside, Quinn dodged to the left, barely avoiding the talon-like fingernails.

The move avoided the woman but brought her closer to the male. It felt like a steel clamp latched onto her upper arm, and it yanked to pull her off-balance. The male vamp leaned forward, mouth open and fangs bared to sink into her now-exposed neck.

Quinn knew she couldn't avoid him, so she used the momentum to her benefit. She twisted her arm in the vampire's grip and swung her elbow up and around to smash it into the guy's mouth. The powerful blow connected with shattering force, and blood and tooth fragments flew from his mouth.

He went to one knee with a cry of pain, letting go of Quinn to clutch his ruined mouth and jaw.

Quinn didn't wait for him to recover; she slashed at his neck with her Bowie knife. She either had to pierce his heart with the blessed silver-alloy blade or sever his head. The neck was the only option within reach of her knife, and she'd only half-connected.

The blade slid part of the way into the vampire's neck before coming free without completing the cut and decapitating him. The anguished gurgling shout indicated she'd done some damage, but he'd heal in no time if she didn't finish him off.

Quinn couldn't do that because the vampire's partner had other plans.

The one named Karla dove in, catching Quinn behind her knees. The huntress's legs buckled under the surprise attack, and she went down on the pavement with the female vampire on top of her.

Quinn rolled onto her back and brought up her free hand, catching the woman's neck as she bent forward to bite down on Quinn's shoulder. At the same time, the vamp's talons raked her abdomen.

Flashes of burning pain from her injured belly threatened to overwhelm her as the razor-sharp fingernails dug deep into skin and muscle. Quinn forced herself to focus, drawing on her stamina again to increase her strength and agility even more.

Her knife came around in an arc. Before the raven-haired vampire could stop her, Quinn drove it into her side. She twisted the blade as it slid between the ribs, seeking to push it home into the vampire's undead heart.

Quinn knew she'd struck home when the woman atop her stiffened and let out a gasping cry before slumping to one side.

Shoving the dead vampire off of her, Quinn rolled to her feet. She ignored the pain in her wounded belly to focus on the male vampire. He'd dragged himself into the driver's seat of the green hatchback and fumbled with his keys to start the car. The near-decapitation twisted his head at a funny angle, making it hard for him to see what he was doing.

Quinn darted forward, snatched the keys from him, and jammed her knee into his ribs as she pinned him against the car's front seat. She grabbed a handful of his greasy brown hair and yanked his head to one side. She held the shining silver alloy knife blade where he could see it.

"Stop struggling, or I'll finish the job and cut your freaking head off."

The man went still, his eyes wide. His voice was gruff and strained from the injury to his neck and the destruction she'd wrought on his mouth. "Wh-what do you want?" he asked thickly.

"A little information, and maybe I'll let you leave with your life."

"What do you want to know? I don't think I know anything you'd want. Take the girl and let me go."

"Oh, the girl is coming with me either way. The only thing up in the air right now is whether I kill you. Well, that and how much pain I can cause you if you don't answer."

"Okay. Ask me what you want."

"Where's Handon hiding? We know he's still around running things here in Baltimore."

The vampire's eyes widened for an instant, then he tried to shake his head. It wasn't very effective, given that his neck muscles had been severed on one side. "I don't know what you're talking about. Who's Handon?"

"Wrong answer," Quinn replied. She pressed the tip of her knife against the guy's chest and he shrieked.

"Help, help! Please don't kill me."

"Hush, no one is going to rescue you, and my partner should be here any minute. Believe me, you don't want him to take over. He'll do things I would never think of."

Clark spoke from behind her. "That I will."

Quinn avoided jumping in surprise at his silent arrival. "I was right. They weren't heading for the parking lot out back."

"Yes, you were right, but this isn't the time to gloat. Someone's bound to come out of the club any second. We need to wrap this up and get these bodies out of sight."

Quinn glanced at the female vampire lying on the sidewalk. The woman's sightless eyes stared at the night sky. "What do you suggest?"

"Slide him over to the passenger seat. We'll put the girl they were after on the sidewalk and replace her with the woman's body. She's passed out. They must've drugged her drink."

"You think she'll be safe, passed out on the sidewalk?"

Clark nodded. "Safer than she was five minutes ago."

Quinn nodded and pushed the vampire in the driver's seat. "Slide over. We're taking you somewhere to finish our talk."

"You promised not to kill me. Just let me go. I don't know anything. I swear I don't know this guy you're after."

Clark's fist flashed past Quinn to smash into the vampire's face.

The guy's head snapped back, and his eyes rolled up in his head. He slumped, unconscious.

"Get him into the passenger seat and then help me get the blonde out of the back."

Quinn wrestled the man's limp form over the center console. By the time she was finished, Clark had pulled the unconscious girl out of the back seat and laid her on the sidewalk.

He lifted the dead vampire's body from the sidewalk. Quinn came over and took her legs to help him shove her into the back seat.

"You drive," Clark said. "I'll get my car, then you can follow me back to our place."

"We're going all the way back there?" Quinn asked. "Don't you think that's risky? What if he figures out where we've taken him and gets away?"

"We're not going to let him get away. He made his choice by trying to take this woman against her will. There's only one penalty for that in my book. Get the car started and wait for me to pull out."

Quinn nodded and climbed into the car. They'd been lucky no one had come out while the brief but violent fight had occurred. It was time to get away from the puddle of dark vampire blood and the unconscious girl on the sidewalk.

Clark drove out of the lot at the rear of the club and pulled onto the main road. Quinn slid the green hatchback in behind him, and they headed for the interstate out of the city.

A glance at the full moon above reminded Quinn of Taylor back at the hideout. She hoped her friend had been all right on her own tonight. The tech witch had a lot going on, too. It was only her second full moon since she'd become a werewolf.

CHAPTER TWO

Taylor concentrated. Pain wracked her as her body attempted to shift from its human to its werewolf form. Only her intense concentration had held off the change so far. Even so, she could feel the occasional ripple of shifter magic threatening to break her body so it could change.

She sat cross-legged on the floor, her gaze on the locked steel door. She avoided staring out through the barred window set high in the wall to her right. The moon was calling to her wolf-self.

Another wave of lunar energy surged through her, threatening to overwhelm her control. For the previous two months, she'd been unable to resist and had spent both nights out of her mind as a howling, angry werewolf in this cell. It had been horrifying to be trapped inside that feral version of herself. Taylor was determined not to repeat that terrible, painful experience.

Clark had tried to help. Soon after she'd been bitten, he'd brought in the alpha from a nearby friendly werewolf pack. That senior werewolf, named Dameon, had told her the ability to resist the shift on the full moon would come in time, along with the ability to shift at will and to remain in control of herself while in wolf form. He'd even kindly offered for her to join his pack. He would take her under his personal care while she learned to deal with this massive change in her life.

"You're not alone," Dameon had said. "Living among the pack with me, and the others will help you realize this is just a new beginning for you. Your life doesn't have to change all that much."

"Thank you," Taylor had told him. "I have a pack and a family here with my friends. I appreciate the offer, but for now, just tell me what I need to do to control this thing."

Dameon smiled. His sad expression told her he didn't expect her to have much success, at least in the short term. "You won't be able to resist shifting the first time, or probably the next few after that. Don't despair, though. Everyone learns to control it eventually. Plus, there's an upside. You'll regenerate from most injuries that don't immediately kill you unless the injury is caused by something made of silver. Plus, you'll rarely get sick from common viruses and infections that affect normal humans."

"Great, so I get to be a man-eating monster who won't catch a cold."

Dameon's eyes had narrowed at her words. "Mark me, girl. Even if you don't come with me now and gain the help of the pack, you'll still be held to certain standards. Should you decide to give in to the animal instincts within you, I'll come back and end you myself."

Taylor remembered the matter-of-fact way he'd talked about killing her as if she was a rabid animal or something. That had been over two months ago, before the first full moon after she'd been bitten. Her flippant comment had been in jest, and she'd been shocked by the angry reply. Now that she'd spent two nights as a brand new werewolf, she didn't think her offhand words were so funny anymore.

All the more reason for her to learn to control this thing sooner rather than later. Dameon had told her it was unlikely she'd learn to control it by even the third full moon. She refused to accept that.

A surge of energy sent a ripple of pain through her bones and joints as they tried to accept the lunar magic and transform her. Taylor's head rolled back, and she screamed at the ceiling. The sound that came out was more howl than scream, and she stomped on the feeling that she fought a losing battle.

There was no way she was spending another night like the last two times. She'd raced around the room, torn at the walls with her claws, and repeatedly rammed into the steel door in an attempt to break free. She'd been sore for days afterward, even with the ability to regenerate.

The worst part of it was being trapped inside her rational mind, held captive by the wolf that had taken over. She could understand why some werewolves had to be put down. The change and loss of control in the early shifts drove them mad. Once they could no longer control their rational minds, there was no hope they'd ever be able to manage their wolf identities.

That wasn't going to happen to her.

She held onto her need to help Quinn and Clark, her family. They were her pack now. They all needed to fight back and avenge the death of their friend, Miranda, at the hands of that vampire. Taylor bit back a growl at the thought of what he'd done to the witch, and then she had to struggle to regain control. Thinking of Handon made her want to give in to the animal urge to shift and hunt. Taylor shook her head. No. There would be a time and place for that. She would be in total control when she did it.

Instead, she focused on remembering Miranda's face, calling to mind the time the two of them had worked closely together to build the VR rig Quinn had used to track down the slayers. The two of them had become close, and Taylor missed the older woman's companionship and advice.

She smiled at the memories of happier times with Miranda that flowed through her mind. As she did, the witch's face became clearer. Taylor felt like she could almost reach out and touch her. It was as if Miranda stood there in the cell with her, and the witch's spirit presence soothed her and helped her hold onto control over her lunar change.

"Thank you," Taylor said, expressing gratitude to the memory her mind had constructed.

"You're welcome, Taylor. You have the strength to resist. You just needed someone to encourage you."

Taylor's eyes opened at those words. They sounded real, as if the woman was in the room with her. Her eyes widened as they fell on the hazy, transparent apparition hovering a few inches off the floor in front of her.

"You're not real," Taylor said. "You can't be."

The apparition before her smiled. "Why not? Don't you believe in ghosts?"

Taylor started to say no but shut her mouth. She hadn't believed in vampires or werewolves either, and look where she found herself now.

Fighting back another wave of the moon's tidal forces passing through her, Taylor gritted her teeth and asked, "Is it really you, Miranda? How can you be here?"

The spirit nodded. "I'm not sure how, but yes, it's me. I was somewhere else for a time, although I can't remember much about it. Then I was here tonight, watching you struggle with your new reality, and I knew I had to help you in some way. Something about your pain called out to me."

"It was me. I tried to remember your face to help me focus on something that would give me a reason to retain control."

Taylor stopped talking and hugged herself as the shifting power within her threatened to retake control. Her bones started to crack and bend and begin shifting.

She cried out, "I can't stop it. It's starting."

Miranda came closer until she knelt right in front of where Taylor sat rocking back and forth, fighting to hold onto her human body and her sanity.

"Taylor, open your eyes and look into mine. You can do this. We'll do it together, okay? I won't leave until the moon sets. I promise."

Taylor forced her eyes open. Miranda's face hovered right in front of hers. The sad eyes held hers, and the ghost nodded. Something about having her close by helped

Taylor resist the lunar surge. She held onto that added strength, forcing her shifting body back into its normal form. It took a few minutes, but with Miranda's reassuring presence, Taylor felt like she could remain in control for the first time that night.

The peak of the moon's tidal power began to wane after a while, and Taylor slowly regained full control, no longer needing the witch's strengthening presence to help her.

Taylor lifted her eyes and looked around the room. Exhaustion gripped her. Strands of sweat-soaked hair were plastered to her head and face. Miranda's ghost sat next to her now, leaning toward her, with spirit arms wrapped around her.

"Thank you, Miranda. Thank you for coming back and helping me."

"I think you're right—it was you who brought me back. Somehow you've gained magic of your own and not just the internal body-magic of a shifter."

"I doubt it. I've been trying to find a way to cast the spells you used. We haven't been able to send Quinn into the VR world since you died. I've searched for ways to do the magic myself and tried just about everything I could, without success."

"And yet you summoned me here to this place to help you."

"I'm not sure how. You know I don't have any magic, not like you."

"Sometimes great need can unlock powers within a person. I think the desire to control your change, coupled with everything else you've been trying to do, might have opened a conduit within you to access the natural magic all around you."

Taylor wasn't so sure, but she couldn't argue that Miranda had appeared here somehow. Either that, or she'd gone bat-shit insane over the course of the night. There was only one way to be sure.

"Quinn and Clark will be so glad to see you're back. They've missed you as much as I have."

Miranda shook her head. "I don't think they'll be able to see me, at least not right away. We'll have to find out. I'm as new to this existence as you are to yours."

"So, there's no proof," Taylor said, her shoulders sagging.

"No proof of what? Me? That's silly. I'm here. You're not going crazy."

"That's what a crazy person's imagination would say."

"Stop feeling sorry for yourself. It's not a good look on you. If you were crazy, you'd have shifted. You didn't. You retained control. That means your mind is just fine."

"So, what do I tell the others?"

"Nothing. Everything. I don't care. It doesn't matter if they aren't able to see me. It's up to you what you tell them."

Taylor thought about what Miranda had said for a few minutes, sitting in silence in the cell with the ghost of her friend beside her. Then she said, "I think we'll keep it to ourselves, then. For now, at least. I'll tell them about you when the time is right—if it ever is."

"That might be best," Miranda agreed.

Taylor nodded. "Now that you're here, you can help me with more than my monthly shifting issues. You can help me find a way to send Quinn back into the VR world. If I have opened a way to tap into magic as you said, I should be able to find a way to cast the spells needed to activate the tech-magic interface."

"I can try. Those spells are very advanced. It might take you a while to master them."

"I'm willing to work hard, especially if you're here to help me."

Miranda looked down at her transparent arms. "I'm fading right now. It takes a lot of energy to manifest like this. I have to go back and regain my strength. Will you be okay if I go?"

"I will. Thank you for coming to me. I feel hopeful now in a way I haven't in a few months," Taylor said. She paused, thinking of something. "Before you go, how do I bring you back?"

"I think the barrier between the worlds has been broken for me at this point. I should be able to find my way back. In the meantime, when you need me, just call out to me. I'll hear you, and I'll come as soon as I am able."

"Then you go rest. I'm going to try to sleep, too. It'll be a while before Quinn comes and unlocks the door. I don't think she'll be back from her patrol until at least sunrise."

"Goodnight, Taylor. Rest well."

"You, too."

Miranda faded from view, and Taylor smiled. She lay on the padded floor, using her forearm for a pillow. The exertion of resisting the shift meant it didn't take long for sleep to come, and it was the first peaceful rest she'd had in a long, long time.

CHAPTER THREE

Quinn followed Clark's car as it left the interstate about fifteen minutes west of Baltimore. She soon found herself on back roads on the way to the old abandoned state psychiatric facility, Spring Grove. Most of the grounds had been closed years before, and the buildings boarded up. They'd chosen a clinic building in the back corner of the sprawling facility. It was surrounded by trees and accessible from an overgrown gravel utility road no one used anymore.

She stopped in the road while Clark got out of his car and opened the rusted chain link gates for her to drive through. While she waited, Quinn checked on her unconscious passenger. She knew vamps could regenerate, but usually, that meant they had to feed. This one had nearly been killed by her Bowie knife, so Clark's blow to his face was apparently enough to keep him knocked out until they could revive him.

Clark finished pulling the gates open and waved her through. She passed where he'd pulled up as he climbed into his car and followed her. She continued toward the building they'd settled into for their current safe house while the elder hunter stopped and closed the gates behind them.

Quinn got out and stood by the green hatchback with her hands on her hips. She stared at the unconscious vampire, trying to figure out what to do with him. Clark pulled up behind the building next to her.

He got out and pointed at the male vampire. "Take him inside and secure him to one of the tables in the main examination hall. I'll take care of this other one's body."

Clark reached into the back and pulled the woman's limp body out by her ankles. Quinn winced when her head hit the ground beside the vehicle, even though she knew she was dead.

"What are you going to do with her? We don't have a shovel or anything."

"We don't need to bury her. I'm going to take her body to that field out back and leave her there."

"Why would you do that? What if someone finds her?"

Clark stared at her in the dark for a second before he said, "Think, Quinn. What's going to happen as soon as it gets light?"

It took her a second, but she nodded. "Oh, yeah. The sun. That'll burn her to ash and take care of cleanup for us, won't it?"

"Exactly. That's also why we'll interrogate him in the examination hall. The windows there are completely shuttered, so if we're still chatting with him when the sun comes up, we don't have to worry about him being fried. At least, not until we want him to be."

"Gotcha." Quinn leaned down and pulled the vamp out until she could get him situated over her shoulder and back. She used a fireman's carry to get him into the building. It probably would've made sense for her to draw on some of her stamina so he wouldn't be so heavy, but she had a lot of natural strength from her huntress genes.

Once inside, she secured him to the primary leather-topped exam table in the center of the circular hall. It had leather loops at intervals to secure arms and legs. Then, for good measure, she applied a final pair of straps around the guy's neck and forehead. At least they would keep his nearly severed head from flopping around while they talked to him.

When Clark didn't show up immediately, Quinn considered checking on Taylor. There was a sliding panel in the steel door to Taylor's room, where you could look in on a detained patient safely. She decided against it, though. Clark would be angry if she wasn't here when he finally decided to show up. Besides, Taylor was self-conscious about her transformation, and Quinn figured she'd want some privacy.

Quinn didn't stop worrying about her friend, though. She hoped Taylor didn't have too hard a time of it tonight. Dameon had explained to them that each subsequent change from human to werewolf and back again would be less painful than the last until it was only uncomfortable. He hadn't let on how long that would take, but Quinn figured the third time around would be almost as painful as the first two.

Last month, Taylor had walked around with a vacant and hollow look on her face for several days after the full moon. She didn't talk about it, but Quinn could tell that what had happened haunted her.

Clark came in while she was lost in thought, once again catching her by surprise. He called to her several times before she answered. "Quinn, what's got you all wrapped up in yourself? You should be paying attention to make sure our guest there doesn't get loose."

"Sorry, I was just thinking about Taylor. I wish I could help her in some way."

"You're still blaming yourself for her getting bitten?"

"Well, yeah."

"Stop it. She knew what we were up against, and she decided to come with us and not stay in the car. In the end, she knows she's damned lucky."

"Lucky? How can you say that?"

"Why not? She could be dead like Miranda. You know as well as I do it was pure dumb chance that Handon chose to kill Miranda and not Taylor."

"I should have done something to save both of them."

"You did, at least for Taylor and me. Miranda was dead before you could have done anything to change it. As it was, you managed to do right by her. We got her body out of there so she could be buried decently and not just dumped in a landfill or the harbor by Handon's goons."

Quinn shook her head. No matter what Clark said, she wouldn't stop blaming herself and wishing she could've done better. She knew at some level he was right, but that didn't take away the guilt she felt inside.

"What about this guy?" Quinn asked. "He hasn't moved since I got him out of the car."

Clark smiled. "I'm about to teach you a little vampire first aid. Pull out your knife."

Quinn paled, thinking he was going to ask her to finish cutting the guy's head off or something. She did as she was told, though. Holding her knife, she walked over to join him beside their prisoner.

Clark was doing something with his hands by the side of the vamp's slashed neck. Then he reached up and used his hands to open the vamp's mouth. "Take your blade and cut your palm, just deep enough to draw some blood."

"Ew, why?"

"Because you're going to feed him just enough that he heals a little and wakes up."

"That's gross. Why don't you do it?"

"Because I'm the boss, that's why. Besides, you're probably more his *type*." He chuckled at the pun. "Don't worry. It won't take much. Hunter blood is supercharged, as far they're concerned. A little should go a long way to getting him to wake up enough to answer our questions."

Quinn looked at her knife. She knew the blade was sharp. She'd gotten good at putting a razor's edge on it, and she worked at keeping it perfect. Holding up her right hand, she laid the knife against her palm and drew it down in a single quick stroke.

She hissed in pain as the blade painted an instant line of red, the blood welling up in the shallow gash. Closing her fingers into a fist, Quinn turned her hand and squeezed while she held it over the vampire's face. Several large drops fell into the open mouth.

Clark nodded and pulled out a rag out of his jacket pocket. "That's enough. Here, use this to stop the bleeding."

Quinn pressed the makeshift dressing against the wound as she stared at the immobilized vampire. A few seconds later, the tongue moved inside the open mouth and reached out to flick the single drop of her blood from his lower lip.

The mouth closed and curled into a smile as his eyes opened. He looked at her. "Thank you, girl. You taste particularly delicious. I'd always heard hunter blood was a delicacy. I guess I'm lucky enough to get to sample a little of what everyone assumed was lost to the ages."

"Don't get to like it too much," Quinn said. "I promise you won't get the opportunity to have any more."

"A pity. Your blood is energizing. I'd love to know what sampling more than a few drops would do for me. Will you promise to save a little for me when my master and his demon-kinder come for you?"

Clark stepped forward and slapped the vampire hard across the face. "That's enough of that. You don't have to worry about that, vamp. Your boss isn't going to end either of us anytime soon."

The vampire's tongue flicked out again, this time to moisten his bruised lips following Clark's blow. "If you're just going to kill me anyway, Hunter, this is going to be a short conversation. I'll not give up any information under those circumstances."

Clark smiled and turned to Quinn. "Do you want to know the real reason I gave him a taste of your blood, Quinn?"

"Uh, sure, I guess so," Quinn replied.

"It's because our blood is so tasty that his kind gets a hankering for it after the first taste. Once they taste a hunter, they can't go back to ordinary human blood again, at least not without powerful magic to break them of the addiction."

The vampire's eyes widened, and he said, "That's not true, Hunter. It's just an old wives' tale."

"Maybe. Then again, maybe not. You know any of your kind who claims to have fed on us during the purges?"

When the vampire didn't answer right away, Clark continued. "No? Of course, you don't. Don't worry. Maybe it *is* just a myth. I guess we'll see when we let you go."

"You're not going to let me go. You'll stake me before I take two steps."

"No, actually, I want you alive long enough to take a message back to your master, Handon. I want you to live long enough to tell him that we're back. A new clan is here in Baltimore. It's time he moved on and found a new city to terrorize."

"What's to keep you two from chasing us when we go somewhere else?" the vampire asked.

"We're just one clan. By the time we're ready to expand to a new city, he'll have what he needs, and he can go anywhere else he wants."

Quinn had no idea what Clark was doing. She didn't think he was going to let the guy go. Why do that when they'd decided to bring him back here? This whole turn in the conversation puzzled her.

The vampire caught the quizzical look on her face. "See, Hunter, your girl here doesn't believe you, either."

Clark turned toward Quinn and smiled. "She doesn't know everything I do. She's just getting started. She doesn't understand why we all have to make allowances for coexistence."

"Why didn't you tell me all this back at the club, then?"

"Because I wanted you to know that we could have killed you. You have to know how serious we are. That's why I only needed one of you. Your companion was extra, and we've already taken care of her."

"Fine, I can pass along that message for you. I don't know how much good it will do. My master isn't the kind to run scared just because a few humans threaten him."

Clark looked Quinn's way and winked. "Tell him the huntress who nearly killed him wants to finish the job. Tell him I'm the only one who can keep her from doing it."

The vampire shot Quinn a glance. "Okay, I'm in bad shape, though. I might need a little more blood to get me all the way back to the city."

Clark leaned forward. "Looks like the wound on your neck has closed up enough for you to make it back to your lair in one piece. You can feed when you get there. You agree to deliver the message?"

The vamp paused for a second, then nodded.

"Good, then I'll take you to the nearest stop on the city metro train. You can take that downtown. Tell Handon he's got two weeks to clear out and relocate. After that, I let her loose on him."

Quinn tried to cover her confused look as Clark loosened the straps on the vampire and helped him sit up. The wound on his neck had closed, although there was a broad, nasty scar to mark the injury halfway around his throat. He was still weak, and Clark steadied him while putting a black bag he'd pulled from his pocket over the vampire's head.

Clark turned to Quinn. "You stay here. I'll take our friend to the metro station and leave him somewhere he won't fry at dawn."

Questions filled Quinn's mind, but all she said was, "I'll be here when you get back."

"Good. I should be back before breakfast. You take that stolen car of theirs way back in the woods on that old farm trail. Park it there in thick cover so no one will see it from the road or the grounds. Then come back here and wait for me."

Quinn nodded, and Clark led the vampire by the elbow toward the lecture hall doors.

Quinn watched him leave, and a minute later, heard the engine on Clark's old sedan fire up outside. She shook her head and decided she'd just have to wait for answers.

She checked the time and sighed, fishing the keys to the green hatchback from her pocket. She had to check on Taylor too, as soon as she was sure the worst of the moon's magical pull had passed. First, she had to dump that car in the woods and walk all the way back here in the dark. The thought angered her, and Quinn became sure of one thing: Clark was going to do a whole lot of explaining once he got back.

CHAPTER FOUR

By the time Quinn got back after hiding the car, Clark was pulling in following his trip to the metro station.

The hunter spotted her walking from the woods as he got out of his car. "You made sure it's well hidden?"

"Yes, I did exactly what you told me to do. Now tell me why you let that guy go without getting any information out of him?"

"We got some of the information we needed, and we'll find out the rest in due time."

"How?" Quinn asked.

Clark pulled out his phone and opened an app with a map on it. A blinking flag appeared on the screen as he showed it to her.

"What's that?"

"That is the location of our friend at the metro station. A few weeks ago, Taylor mentioned she found some random cell phone components mixed in with the gear we took from the old VirSync building. I asked her if there was any way she could create a tracking device with them.

She used a GPS chip and cellular transmitter to create a small one that could be concealed in a car or a coat pocket."

"So, you put one in his clothing?"

Clark smiled. "Better. He would have found it in his clothing. I hid it somewhere he'll never find."

Quinn's quizzical expression made Clark chuckle.

"That massive gash in his neck gave me the idea. If you hadn't nearly cut his head off, I wouldn't have been able to do it."

"You hid the chip in his neck?"

Clark nodded. "When I repositioned his head and opened his mouth for you to feed him some of your blood, I slipped it inside the slash. I hoped he'd heal enough to seal the edges of the skin around the wound, at least. It worked like a charm."

Quinn pointed to the phone. "So that's him. What's next?"

"We wait for him to go back and deliver the message to Handon. I'll get Taylor to track his location over time. One of his destinations has to be the master's lair. Then we'll decide on what to do next."

"You could've told me. It would have been nice to know what you were planning."

"I didn't know I was going to do it until I saw him cut open outside the club. Then there was no time to do it. Besides, I'm telling you now. Come on, let's go inside and get some breakfast. It's almost sunrise. I stashed the vampire in an out of the way storage closet at the station. My bet is he's not going anywhere until tonight, when it gets dark again."

Quinn followed Clark, irked he'd kept his plan from

her, even if his explanation kind of made sense. She hated not knowing what was going on. The last few months had left her out of sorts in many ways.

When they entered the building, Clark turned toward the kitchen. Quinn paused and then headed up the stairs toward her room.

"Where are you going?"

"I'll be right back. I have to get something. I'll be there in plenty of time to help make breakfast," she said as she continued up the stairs and Clark went to the kitchen.

Quinn's room was built to house a patient. The furniture was obviously from an institutional supply source. It had a metal bed frame with a single thin mattress, and beside it was a small night table and a bookshelf in the corner. The only window opposite the door had a metal grate across the outside. It let light in but prevented anyone from escaping.

The room was small, but it was more than enough for what little she had to call her own at this point. The bookshelf held all her clothes and personal items. She kept her most prized possessions in the nightstand. Sitting on the bed, she pulled open the small drawer in the nightstand and reached inside.

The silver necklace she pulled out had a single ovoid lump of melted silver dangling from it. It was all that remained of her magic huntress amulet, left with her by her parents when she was a baby. It had lost its power to protect her, burned out when she abused her unique ability to draw magical energy through it.

Ever since it had been destroyed, all she could think about was how she could restore it. She felt naked and helpless without it. She knew it made no sense but didn't care.

Quinn held up the necklace, watching the misshapen lump as it swung back and forth. There had to be a way to make it whole again. She'd brought it up with Clark on several occasions, but all he'd said was she didn't need it. He reminded her that she had found ways to use her magic and special skills without it.

It wasn't the same for her, though. Even if accessing the power didn't give her massive headaches when she used it, the amulet was her only connection to her family. Her mother and father were long dead, killed in the purges that had destroyed the hunter clans twenty years before. This was all she had left of them.

Quinn slipped the necklace into her jeans pocket and started back downstairs. On the way, she diverted to a different stairway at the opposite end of the building so she could check on Taylor. It was morning, and she should be ready to come out of her isolation cell. Hopefully, her experience with the full moon last night hadn't been as bad as the first two times.

The other stairs led down to the area with treatment rooms for the psych patients housed here. It included the single padded cell they'd found to help Taylor through her shifting on the full moons. Quinn stopped beside the gray metal door and pressed her ear to the cool surface. She couldn't hear anything.

The change, if it had happened, should have passed by now. The moon had been down for a while. Quinn lifted the keyring from the peg in the wall nearby and slid open the panel that covered the viewing slot in the door.

Peering through, she jumped back, startled to see Taylor's eyes staring back at her from the other side. Her friend's muffled laughter sounded from the other side.

"Scared you, did I?" Taylor asked with a chuckle. "I heard you coming and figured you'd open the peephole before you unlocked me. This super-hearing thing I've got now is cool."

Quinn unlocked the door and pulled it open, hanging the key back on its peg. She hugged her best friend and asked, "How'd it go last night? Your outfit seems to have survived."

She referred to Taylor's sports bra and shorts. The last two times she'd faced the full moon, Taylor had worn the same outfit she'd had on all day. Everything had ended up shredded during the transformation to wolf-person. They'd talked about how to handle that, and Taylor had come up with this combination. It looked like it had worked.

Taylor smiled and shrugged. "I don't know. I didn't shift."

Quinn stopped and held Taylor at arm's length, staring at her. "You did it? You controlled it?"

Taylor nodded, smiling.

Quinn pulled her into another hug as the two of them laughed.

"T, that's awesome. Dameon had told you it could take months before you'd be able to do that."

"I think I'll still need at least one more month in there on the full moon, and I'm nowhere near ready to try to shift on command yet. Still, I held it off. It hurt like hell, and the shift started up a couple of times, but I wrestled it under control and reversed it."

Quinn smiled as she released her friend. "Come on, let's go tell Clark. I know he's been wondering how you did, too."

"Old Grumpy Guts? Worried about me?"

"You'd be surprised," Quinn replied. "The more I work with him, the more I'm sure his rough outlook on life is just a cover for all the stuff he's seen and had to endure. I think he worries a lot about both of us."

The two of them continued chatting on their way down the hall to the end of the building where the large kitchen was located. Quinn noticed that Taylor paused a few times during the description of her night as if trying to find a way to say something and then changing her mind. Quinn didn't want to pry. She figured the whole werewolf thing was a personal, private hell for her friend, and she would be supportive in any way she could to get Taylor through it. Taylor would share what she wanted to when she was ready.

When they entered the kitchen, they found that Clark had fired up the gas stovetop and was mixing up eggs in a metal bowl. He nodded to the large refrigerator set in the wall. "Get the juice and milk if you want it. You can start some toast, too. I already made the coffee."

Quinn and Taylor did as he asked, getting them all drinks for breakfast. Most of the institutional kitchen was operational once Taylor hacked the power supply to the building. She managed to switch everything back on, along with the natural gas line.

Clark finished cooking the scrambled eggs while the

women got the toast and put the coffee pot on the table with mugs for all of them. He brought the hot pan of eggs to the table, setting it down on a folded towel in the middle.

He sat down and glanced at Taylor while he reached for toast. "You look none the worse for wear. This time was better, less painful? Dameon said it would get easier over time."

Quinn didn't wait for Taylor to answer. "She did it, Clark. She held off the change and remained human last night. That's huge, right?"

Clark didn't hide his surprise. "Yeah, that *is* a big deal. You didn't start shifting?"

Taylor shrugged. "No, I did, but I managed to reverse it each time. I never lost control of myself. Dameon told me holding onto my humanity would be the hardest part of the change. It would start with me resisting the change, or reversing it if it started. I did that, so I guess it's a step in the right direction."

Quinn shook her head. "It's way more than that. Tell her, Clark."

He finished buttering his toast and took a bite, gesturing with the piece still in his hand. "It is, but there's still a long way to go before you should trust yourself on the night of the full moon."

"I know, but maybe it won't be six months like Dameon warned. And I'll be able to shift on my own sooner, which means I won't be helpless in a fight anymore."

Quinn knew that was something Taylor wanted more than anything else. She wanted to be able to pull her weight, even though no one expected her to be part of the action that way. She was way more important on the computer behind the scenes.

"Taylor," Quinn said, "Clark and I can fight for all of us. No one else here is a tech witch."

Taylor smiled. She liked the nickname she'd gotten from Clark, and she wore it like a badge of honor. "I know, but there've been times where I could've helped more. Now I'll be able to. I'm already stronger than I've ever been before, and my hearing and sense of smell rock!"

"It's better to take it slow, Taylor," Clark said. "If you want, though, you can join Quinn and me for training, especially the meditation on healing. That could be especially useful for you in learning to have more control for next month."

"I'd like that, thanks," Taylor replied.

Quinn smiled. Clark had made an extra effort to try to include Taylor in stuff since Miranda was gone. He recognized how she could feel like the literal third wheel in the team. This wasn't the first time he'd extended such an invitation to her.

"Hey, how'd the patrol go last night?" Taylor asked.

"We finally found some of Handon's coven."

"You did? That's great," Taylor said, leaning over her plate as she shoveled a forkful of eggs into her mouth. "Tell me everything."

Quinn shared the story of their run-in with the pair of vamps at the club and what had happened after. She left it to Clark to share the end since he'd been the one to take the male vampire to the metro.

He finished with a mention of the tracker. "We'll need to keep an eye on where he goes. I was hoping you could create a map of his travels for the next little while until we find out where their lair is located. I don't know how long the internal battery will hold out once it's turned on."

"It should last about a day and a half," Taylor said. "I had to set the chip to update continually, so it's going to use up a lot of juice accessing the GPS. Hopefully, it will track him long enough to get him back to Handon."

Clark didn't look happy about the battery life. He pursed his lips as if to say something but shook his head. "It doesn't matter. What's done is done. We'll just have to see if he goes where we want him to in time."

Taylor finished the eggs on her plate and reached out to get some more. It was clear the night's strenuous activities with her shifting or resisting it had worked up an appetite.

"I'll write a program that'll track his stops right after breakfast. I'll also set it up with a record search to compare it with property tax ownership databases. We should be able to narrow it down that way. Don't worry. This is a big break."

Quinn used the lull in the conversation to reach into her pocket and pull out her chain and amulet. She put the ruined talisman on the table and turned to Clark. "I want to get this fixed or get a new one made to replace it. I want to use the original silver, too. How do we get that done?"

Clark sighed and paused before answering.

Quinn could see him considering what he was going to say. "Look, Clark, you've put me off every time I ask about it. This is important to me, and I want to get it done. There has to be a way to do it. Someone made the amulet to begin with."

"It's not as simple as that," Clark replied. "I never had

anything to do with the crafting of the amulets. I only know it was a process that involved some of the oldest magic possessed by the clans."

"So, what's the holdup?"

"It's all gone, Quinn."

"What do you mean, 'gone?' Magic still exists. Your amulet is still working."

"I mean, the people and lore are gone. The ones who crafted the amulets and cast the spells on them to give them the old protections are all dead. They were killed in the purges with everyone else. I wouldn't even know where to begin."

Taylor finished a mouthful of eggs and interrupted them. "What about records, manuals, or spell books? There must've been some way the clans passed along knowledge besides word of mouth."

Clark shrugged. "The chapter house was destroyed in a fire around the same time. I always assumed everything was gone. The only thing that's left is the old keeper."

"The what?" Quinn asked.

"Old Joshua Dalton. He was the keeper, a person who worked with the clan in this area to organize their finances and keep their records. He used to work at the chapter house part-time. He was spared during the purges. I think it was because he wasn't officially a clan member, just a normal human who worked with us from time to time."

"And he's still alive?" Taylor asked.

Clark nodded. "I touch base with him several times a year. It's how I can afford to pay our meager expenses. He was able to salvage some of the off-shore accounts during the attacks. Most of the local assets were appropriated by the ones who took us out. That's how they financed starting companies like Handon's brokerage and VirSync, more than likely."

Quinn was confused. This was all new to her. "But there are other accounts? More money somewhere?"

"Yes, but not much. I try not to use more than the bare minimum we need to keep us fed and operating. Anything more might draw attention to us, and we don't want that."

"So," Quinn said, "this Joshua guy is the connection we need, then. He could have information on how we can make a new amulet from the old one. That's great!"

"Hold on, Quinn. Joshua is old, and pretty skittish since the purges. He only meets me in person on rare occasions when he needs a signature or to transfer physical cash to me. Most of what we do is handled electronically. I don't even know where he lives or works. I use an old-style internet bulletin board to contact him."

"But you do meet with him, and you can contact him when needed." Quinn wasn't going to let this go. This was the best possibility she'd heard about since her amulet had been melted.

"I can, but I caution you, he's not likely able to help us. As I said, the loss of everything in the fire affected him. He won't even talk about it. I've tried."

"But probably not recently," Quinn said. "I think it's worth trying again. Maybe he's relaxed some since you last asked about it."

Clark laughed. "There's nothing relaxed about Joshua Dalton."

"What's that mean?" Quinn asked.

"You'll see." Clark sighed. "Look, I'll try to reach him

after I get some sleep. I'll let you know if I can set up a meeting after I hear back from him."

Quinn scooped up the chain and amulet and returned it to her pocket. Then she smiled and went back to her breakfast, a sense of renewed hope filling her. They were closer to tracking down Handon than they had been in months, and now they had a lead on getting her amulet replaced. Things were looking up.

CHAPTER FIVE

Taylor sat behind her triple computer screens, staring at the code scrolling past in an open app. She'd set up her new attempt at assembling the VR rig in a large office that had probably once belonged to one of the doctors who'd worked here. The oak desk was so massive that she guessed no one had bothered to move it when they shut this building down. It had plenty of room for her screens and enough surface for Quinn to lie down in preparation for going into the VR world.

At least, it would if Taylor could figure out a way to get the system running again without Miranda. It had been a long day. She'd been up the night before fighting the full moon, and most of today. She noticed the darkening sky outside her window and sighed. Taylor stood and stretched her arms and back, then ran her fingers through her long blonde hair and secured it in a ponytail with the elastic band around her wrist.

She checked the time. Clark and Quinn had been gone for an hour or so. They were trying to follow the remote tracker Clark had slipped into the vampire. She'd hooked them up with a custom tracker app that should help them. They didn't have to go anywhere.

Clark had decided he and Quinn needed to be close by when the vamp started moving, in case the tracker battery failed sooner rather than later. That way, they could track him the old-fashioned way.

Before they left, Quinn seemed a little deflated by the lack of response from the keeper guy, Joshua. Clark had messaged him right after breakfast but hadn't heard anything back. Quinn grumbled about it before they left. Taylor hoped tracking this vamp would give her friend's morale a boost and they would get the information they needed.

Taylor sat down at the keyboard again and typed in a command that brought up the complex computer code used to initiate the VR rig. She stared at the screen for a few seconds, scrolling through the text, and sighed. There was little chance this attempt would be any more successful than the last time she'd tried to fire it up. She'd been seeking a way to use the technology without the magical component. It was no use, though. The system wouldn't work without the spells cast to supplement it.

"You should ask for help when you need it," Miranda said from behind her.

Taylor resisted the urge to jump and spin around. Her werewolf side had given her a powerful self-confidence that helped her resist the flighty nature of her former self. Taylor just smiled and said, "Nice of you to drop by again."

Miranda glided around the desk to the opposite side, so

she faced Taylor. "I told you I would help. Why didn't you call me?"

"You said it took energy to come here. I didn't want to ask until I'd tried one more time."

"That's silly. If you need help, ask for it. What would you tell Quinn if she acted like this?" Miranda put her hands on her hips as her transparent image stared down at Taylor.

Taylor grinned. "I'd tell her she was pig-headed."

"Exactly." Miranda leaned over so she could see the screens. "Do you have the system up and running?"

"Yeah," Taylor said. She pointed as the code scrolled by. "This is the part that jams me up. At this stage, you'd cast the initial spells to activate the VR's tech-magic interface. I've tried to work through the spells as I see them in the code's notes and logs. I even tried reading them aloud, but it doesn't work."

"That's because magic is more of an art than a science. Every spell is as different as the individual casting it. You can read the words in the computer notes all day long, and nothing will happen. They are nothing more than sign-posts to tell the caster what is needed. They aren't spells in and of themselves."

Taylor leaned back and stretched her arms out, palms up. "Well, I've tried everything I can think of. That's why I need you here to cast the spells."

"I can't do that."

"Why not?"

"I'm dead. I cannot access the energy of this world anymore. I can't even pick up a pencil. You have to be the one. I told you last night that you possess the ability. I sensed it, and I believe it was part of what allowed me to come back in spirit form."

Taylor shook her head. "If I possessed the ability, I think I would know it."

"Not if you're being a stubborn little girl."

Taylor growled low in her throat, heard what she was doing, and closed her mouth, silencing her wolf self.

Miranda nodded. "Now, stop telling yourself that you can't do it. Believe in yourself and try to relax. Magic is about feeling the power around you and opening yourself up to it. You can't do that if you're all tense. Let's try some relaxation exercises my teacher used with me when I first started learning to control my power."

Taylor started to shake her head but stopped. Miranda was right. If this was going to happen, she had to start believing she could do it. There wasn't anyone else who could, and Quinn needed her to suck it up and find a way. Taylor didn't think much of meditation and things like that. She was much more of a techie and needed to touch things to believe they were real. Still, it couldn't hurt to try. Quinn had to be able to track down the slayers and the rest of Handon's people once they were located.

"Do your thing, Miranda. I promise I'll try," Taylor said. She put her hands down on the arms of the chair and leaned back in the seat, letting the padded desk chair support her as she relaxed in a semi-reclined position.

"Good. Let's start with basic breathing techniques. Then we'll move on to trying to grasp some of the natural energy around you."

The pair spent almost two hours working together as Taylor went through different techniques to help her see what Miranda said was all around them. She was about to give up when the final method the ghost witch suggested worked.

Miranda had suggested Taylor bring up a sequence of meditation images online and play them on a loop while she focused on the deep breathing exercises they'd used earlier. The video had played through the third time and was about to start over when a flat ribbon of pure light floated across the screen. At first, Taylor thought it was a part of the video she hadn't seen before, but then the ribbon drifted past the screen and into the air beside the monitor. As she concentrated on it, fainter lines of different colors came into view.

"I see something, Miranda, like strings of light or energy. My God, they're all around us."

"Yes! That's what I've been telling you. The natural energy of the earth is everywhere, supporting everything. You just needed to break through your doubts and see it."

Taylor squinted at the threads and ribbons of energy floating in the air around her. "The magic strings seem pretty fragile," Taylor said. "It doesn't look like they can do much."

"Think about it this way," Miranda said. "You know how individual fibers are twisted to make a thread?"

Taylor nodded.

Miranda continued, "And then how that thread is woven into a pattern with others until it is a piece of fabric strong enough that it can catch the wind and propel a ship across the waves?"

"So, what? I have to weave the strings and ribbons together to make a spell? Where do I even begin?"

"That is where the art of magic comes in. Some of us are better weavers than others. Some even possess a sort of ability to use intuition to let the threads fill in the pattern themselves. It's up to you to find out what kind of caster you are."

"How do I start?" Taylor tried to touch one of the more substantial-looking ribbons with her fingertips. She didn't feel anything, but the light stuck to her fingers for a second before it drifted on.

"Were you able to touch one of them?" Miranda asked. "It's okay if you weren't."

"Sort of. It stuck to me for an instant and then let go."

Miranda smiled and clapped her hands, although no sound came from it. "That's wonderful. It took me weeks to reach that point. Before that, my magic came haphazardly and by accident. Okay, to answer your question, yes, you can touch them, sort of. Remember, though, you'll never be able to hold one for more than a second. The next part requires you to think about moving your hands and fingers while you pull the necessary pieces into place beside each other. Once you get them into the right order, you'll be able to create the spell. You have to work fast because they'll slip by otherwise. Let's try a simple spell. We'll create a light."

"Sounds good," Taylor said, rubbing her hands together in anticipation. "What do I do?"

"Think of a ball of white light about an inch in diameter. Then, focus on that image in your mind while you study the magical energy around you. Some of them should sort of highlight themselves. Those are the ones you need to create the light."

Taylor did as she was told, imagining a hovering light-bulb in the air over her computer monitors. As soon as she did, the ribbons of light changed. Some faded until they almost disappeared, while others grew brighter. She waved her fingers toward the most brilliant of them, one that pulsed with power, coaxing it in her direction. Another highlighted behind it, and she did the same with that one.

Soon she was waving her hands and fingers in the air like a symphony conductor, pulling the pieces together, forming a jumble of light strings in front of her. She pulled a final piece into the mess, and there was a flash as they all fell into a pattern and disappeared.

In their place hovered a marble-sized ball of white light. It flared very bright for a few seconds, then rapidly dimmed until it faded completely.

"I did it!" Taylor exclaimed.

"Yes, you did, and it was magnificent for your first try. As I said, it took me weeks, maybe months, to progress to that point."

"I feel so tired all of a sudden. Why?"

"Because it takes energy to hold onto the threads. Over time, you'll be able to do more. It's like building yourself up with exercise so you can run a race."

"That's a good analogy because I feel like I've run one. And now I know why spell casters have to wave their arms and wriggle their fingers as they do. It's part of the weaving."

"Exactly." Miranda smiled

Taylor noticed the ghost had become so transparent that she was little more than an outline. "You're tired, too.

Why don't we call it a night? We can try again tomorrow if you're willing to come again."

"I'd like that. Goodnight, Taylor. Get some rest."

"Goodnight, Miranda. Thank you again."

The ghost faded, and Taylor shut off her monitors and got up to start to her room upstairs beside Quinn's. Her legs shook and quivered beneath her as she walked into her room and fell onto the bed. She was asleep before she even kicked off her shoes.

CHAPTER SIX

Quinn checked the time and stared at Clark's phone, which was resting on the center console. "What's taking him so long?"

Clark's fingers drummed on the top of the steering wheel as his gaze shifted from his phone to look through the windshield at the dark sky. "I don't know. He hasn't moved, and the sun's been down for almost an hour now."

"Should we check on him? Maybe he died after all."

A low snarl came from Clark before he answered. "Yeah, something is up. Let's go into the metro terminal and see if he's still there. I'm worried he discovered the transmitter somehow and removed it."

"Could he do that and survive?" Quinn said, doubting Clark's explanation. "He'd need to find a knife of some sort, and it would have to be pretty painful."

"Sitting here speculating about it isn't doing either of us any good. Come on, let's go check."

Quinn opened the passenger door and climbed out. She

stretched her hands over her head. They'd been in the car for almost two hours.

Clark came around to her side and motioned for her to accompany him. Quinn fell in beside him as he walked across the parking structure to the stairs that led to the underground metro station.

She followed him down to the lowest level and into a broad hallway. A few late commuters were around, but not too many. Clark reached the end of the corridor and stopped at a door labeled Metro Staff Only.

"Be ready, Quinn. Tackle him if he makes a run for it."

She nodded and slipped her left hand under her jacket to rest on the hilt of her Bowie. She didn't want to draw it unless she needed it. Someone might see her and call the cops.

Clark tested the handle. It was locked. He knelt and waved a hand at the locked door while he muttered words under his breath.

"Was it locked when you were here last time?" Quinn asked.

"No, and that has me worried," he said as he stood up and gripped the handle again. "Ready?"

"Yes, and you need to teach me that one sometime. It could come in handy."

"When we get the VR open and working again, we'll try it. You seem to learn best there."

That didn't feel like a solution to Quinn. Taylor had been stuck on getting the VR system up again for several months and didn't seem hopeful about fixing her problems with it any time soon.

She realized Clark was still staring at her, making sure

she was ready for whatever lay on the far side of the door. She nodded. They'd solve the VR issue another time. The potentially missing vampire was the problem at hand.

Clark turned the handle and pushed the now-unlocked door inward. It opened about a foot and then stopped, blocked by something. Quinn looked at the floor inside as Clark put his shoulder to the door. An arm flopped to the floor in the narrow opening. Blood stained the hand.

"Dammit," Clark said. "The body is wedged against the back of the door. Quinn, see if you can squeeze through and shift it so I can open it the rest of the way."

"Is it him?"

"I can't tell for sure, but I don't think so."

Quinn moved up and slid sideways through the narrow opening made by the partially open door. She looked down as she did and saw the body wasn't the vampire. It was a woman wearing the light blue shirt and navy pants of a metro employee.

She bent down and lifted the body by the arms to shift her back and out of the way. As she did, something slid off the woman's chest to the floor. It looked like a small circuit board with a rectangular box at one end. It wasn't any bigger than the end of her little finger.

Quinn set the woman down so she leaned against the back wall of the dusty storage closet. The small room was nearly empty, containing only a broom and a few cardboard boxes. She bent down and picked up the circuit board. It was sticky with blood, so she held it by the edges between her forefinger and thumb.

"Come on in. It's clear."

Clark opened the door just enough so he could enter

and then closed it. He glanced down at the woman's body and shook his head. Quinn was sure he'd noted the puncture marks on her neck where the vampire had fed on her.

"Damn, I'd hoped no one would find him. This room looked like no one had been in here for a while."

"Maybe he lured her in and then attacked her?" Quinn suggested. She held out the circuit board. "Is this your tracker?"

Clark took it from her, cursing again.

"It was on top of her. He must have found it when he woke up after sundown. What do you think?"

"It doesn't matter. He found it, and that puts us back to square one, or worse, maybe. Now they're sure we're looking for them."

"You think they didn't know we were still around?"

"It was a possibility. Now they'll be waiting for us." Clark stood and turned to the door. "Come on. We need to get out of here. It won't do to be here when someone else comes looking for her."

"Shouldn't we call someone?" Quinn asked.

"We can do that after we leave. I want to be far away before we do. Let's get to the car and then head back to Spring Grove."

Quinn glanced at the dead woman leaning against the wall. She'd be found eventually, another random attack that would go into the unsolved murder bin at the local police station, forgotten by all but her family.

"I'll remember you," Quinn muttered to herself.

"What's that?" Clark asked.

"Nothing. Let's go."

Clark pulled the door open a crack and checked the corridor outside, then slipped through, followed by Quinn.

She pulled the door shut behind her and tried to assume an ordinary demeanor as she followed Clark back to the parking garage.

They almost made it back to Clark's car when his phone went off. He pulled it out and checked the screen, then put it to his ear.

"It's Clark. I'm busy with something. Can I call you back?" There was a brief pause, and Clark's expression changed from annoyance to concern. He looked at Quinn and pointed at the car with urgency. "Get to a room where you can lock the door if you can't get out of the house. Do you have a weapon? Anything?"

Quinn ran to the passenger side and yanked the door open. She jumped into her seat and slammed the door.

Clark was already behind the wheel, digging for his keys with his free hand. "Just hold on. Do whatever you have to, just hold on. We're on the way."

He threw the phone on the console and started the car, peeling out of the parking space and racing for the garage's exit.

"Who was that?"

"He's a Sylph, a kind of fae. He owns a corner grocery downtown and lives down the block. He says two people dressed in black leather are trying to break in. They're carrying swords."

"Slayers?" Quinn asked, knowing the answer already.

"Sounds like it."

"Can we get there in time?"

"It's not far, and we're right off the downtown expressway. Maybe ten minutes if we hurry. I hope he can hold on."

Quinn nodded and clicked her seatbelt on as Clark gunned the engine and accelerated up the ramp onto the expressway leading to the center of Baltimore. They'd been one step behind the slayers since they'd lost the ability to get into the VR system. This was the closest they'd come to catching them in the act.

She hoped they got there in time.

CHAPTER SEVEN

E ight minutes later, Clark slid to a stop at the curb in front of a small home in West Baltimore. The few people still out on the sidewalk took one look at the two of them as they got out of the car and bolted into their houses.

Quinn figured she and Clark looked scary, dressed in black and carrying bare steel. She had her Bowie in hand already. Clark had drawn his gleaming short sword.

He led the way, ignoring the rapidly retreating residents. Quinn followed as he raced up the steps to the front porch of the two-story brick home. Clark must've heard the crash of broken glass coming from inside because he leaned forward and didn't slow as he hit the wooden front door.

The door jamb had splintered under the force of a previous assault, so the door swung inward to slam against the wall inside. Clark pointed up the narrow stairs straight ahead. "Take the upstairs. Watch your back."

He kept going past the staircase to check the rest of the

first floor while Quinn bounded up the stairs two at a time. When she reached the top, she checked the first door she came to. It was a small bedroom, unoccupied. She backed out to continue her search.

A twinge of biting cold flaring in the amulet scar on her chest surprised her. She realized just in time what it meant and ducked. Maintaining her direction, she turned her dodge into a backward somersault.

The longsword blade passed through the air where she'd been standing a split second before. The black-clad figure behind her overbalanced when the swing didn't connect. Quinn used the stumble to take a swipe of her own.

From her crouched position, she swung her Bowie knife behind her, twisting so she jammed the blade into the attacker's thigh. The slayer recovered from their mistake and jumped back, although they landed awkwardly. Judging from her assailant's grunt of pain, coupled with a pronounced limp as they backpedaled away from her, she'd caused some damage.

Quinn rolled up to her feet, her blade held before her to counter an incoming sword strike. Her shorter blade gave her a distinct disadvantage against the longsword her opponent wielded in the present close quarters. She resisted the urge to charge in, instead holding her place, balanced on the balls of her feet, ready to dance away from a swing of the longsword.

This gave her a good chance to get a look at her opponent. It was a woman about her own age, but not anyone she knew. That meant Myles and the rest of the remaining

VirSync team had recruited new candidates to work with them in their twisted VR assassination program.

A thought occurred to Quinn. Maybe this woman didn't know it was real.

Quinn held out her free hand, palm out. "Hey, I don't know what they told you about the VR system. You need to know this is all real. You're killing people."

The woman sneered and a pinpoint of red light flashed in her eyes as she spoke. "It's too late to save this one, Huntress. We've changed the way we recruit now. You'll find we don't make the same mistakes twice."

The slayer was already possessed and had become one of the demon-kinder, their souls subverted by the invasion of a demonic presence brought to this plane by the vile magic Myles Hickman and the others from VirSync used, under the direction of the vampire lord, John Handon.

Quinn had to keep this one talking while she waited for Clark to hear her and come up to help. She put on an air of defiance. "You made a fatal mistake. You're still here, and we came to stop you."

"Oh, you're the one who made a mistake, foolish girl. We already killed the fae creature who lives in this place. We were waiting to see if you showed up. Where's your master?"

The woman followed up her statement with a careful lunge in Quinn's direction. It wasn't a complete attack since she couldn't put her full weight on her injured leg, but it was enough to make the huntress take a few steps back to avoid the longer blade.

"I have no master," Quinn countered. "My clansman

will be here soon enough. You won't be alive to see it, though."

Quinn took a chance and darted in before the woman began her return stroke. The huntress brought up her blade to counter the reversed sword swing. Sparks flew as the demon-kinder's sword met her blessed silver Bowie.

It was Quinn's turn to grunt as she realized her mistake. The demon-possessed woman was much stronger than she was, and Quinn hadn't taken the precaution of supplementing her strength before coming into the home.

The weight of the sword pressing against her blade knocked her backward. Quinn teetered on the top of the stairs for a second and almost managed to regain her balance, but her heel slipped off the carpeted step and she fell backward with a yelp.

She tried to catch herself as she tumbled down the stairs, arms and legs flailing as she tried to break her fall.

Quinn hit the floor at the bottom of the staircase hard enough to knock the wind out of her. She tried to get back to her feet while she assessed her injuries. It didn't feel like anything was broken, but she was battered and bruised. Worse, she'd lost her knife. She looked around in a frantic search to find her weapon before her opponent came down the stairs after her.

The other woman started to follow Quinn, but a male voice from somewhere upstairs stopped her. She smiled mockingly at the huntress lying at the bottom of the stairs, then turned and disappeared. There was a flash of reflected light from somewhere around the corner, out of sight on the second floor. Then there was silence.

"Quinn," Clark called as he ran back to the front of the home from where he'd been searching in the back.

Quinn climbed to her feet, still searching for her knife. She found it lying on the fifth step up and snatched it, then turned to face Clark as he raced up the hall to where she stood.

"What happened?"

"I found them. They were upstairs. There was a woman, and I heard a man's voice, too. She attacked me and forced me back until I fell down the steps. I wounded her, though. She won't be running marathons any time soon."

"What about Dizzy?"

"Who?" Quinn asked.

Clark dismissed the question with a wave of his hand. "It's a nickname, never mind. I meant, the guy who lives here?"

"I didn't see anyone else. The female slayer indicated they had accomplished their mission and were waiting for us."

Clark cut her off and raced up the stairs. "Dizzy, where are you?"

Quinn followed him.

They found Dizzy, a thin, gray-haired man, lying in a pool of blood in the front bedroom. The wooden door had been kicked in. It appeared they'd caught him hiding in the closet. One of them must've pulled him out by his feet while the other finished him off with several vicious sword thrusts to the chest.

Clark knelt and checked for a pulse, then shook his head. "He's still warm. They must've killed him just as we arrived," he said. The hunter stood and stared out the front window for a few seconds.

Quinn waited while her mentor gathered himself.

A siren wailed in the distance, which snapped Clark back to the present.

"We have to go. We'll have a hard time explaining why we are standing here with edged weapons next to a body with those wounds. Get back to the car."

"Where will you be?" Quinn asked.

"I'll be right behind you. Dizzy was holding something for me. I want to see if they got it from him before they killed him."

Quinn wanted to ask what he was talking about, but she knew this wasn't the time to do that. She headed down the hall to the stairs. She'd wait for him in the car out front. She paused only long enough to wipe the thick black blood from her blade. It had come from the wounded demon-kinder, and she knew from Clark it was caustic and could damage her blade if not cleaned off soon after a fight.

She spared a quick glance around the first floor, then walked out to the front porch. There was no one on the street, but she spotted curtains moving in several darkened windows and knew the neighbors were watching her. The sirens drew closer, and she decided it was better to wait in the car. Clark would be in a hurry when he came out.

As she sat in the car, she remembered the cold sensation she'd felt, warning her of the pending attack. It came from the spot on her chest where the amulet had left its mark. She didn't know how it had happened, but somehow a part of the amulet's power must have transferred into the mark seared into her skin.

It wasn't the same sensation as what she experienced when she'd worn the actual amulet. It was more like a memory of what it had been before. She wondered if that was why she could still access some of her skills, but with difficulty?

Clark walked out the front door and down the steps to the car. He moved quickly but didn't run.

Quinn looked over her shoulder down the street behind them. The sirens were much closer now.

Clark climbed in the car and started it, then accelerated to the corner and went right at the intersection. Behind them, flashing lights turned into the street, stopping in front of the home they'd just left.

"Cutting it a bit close, weren't you? Did you find what you were looking for?"

"No," Clark said, shaking his head. "I searched as long as I dared. He might have hidden it so they couldn't find it, but that's probably wishful thinking. I suspect they wouldn't have left without it. Did you see the person you heard at the top of the steps? Were they carrying anything?"

Quinn shook her head. "I only heard him. It sounded like a guy. Other than that, I couldn't say. What were you looking for?"

"It was an old clan talisman, an ancient silver dagger. I was able to salvage it after the purges, but at the time, I didn't have a place to keep things like that, so I gave it to Dizzy to hold."

"We have plenty of daggers, knives, and swords. Why do we need another one?"

"This one had secrets inscribed on the blade in old

runes. Some of them might have helped you recreate your amulet, or at least the magic it contained." Clark shrugged. "I wasn't sure, so I didn't say anything to you about it. I was going to get with Dizzy at some point to check it out. I didn't know I was running out of time."

A thought occurred to Quinn. "How are the slayers identifying these people to attack them? They aren't attacking random people who happen to be mythical creatures living here in secret. There must be a method to all this. Was there someone who knows which ones might hold ancient hunter knowledge, as this guy did?"

Clark drove on in silence, but Quinn could see him thinking through what she'd said. She waited for him to answer.

It was nearly two minutes before he answered. "I wonder if I somehow exposed them to danger without knowing it?"

"Was there a list somewhere of the people you entrusted with information and artifacts?

"The only person I told was Joshua, but he's the keeper. It's his job to keep all of those things safe. I can't believe he'd do anything to betray that sacred task. I guess there could be a security leak in his precautions he doesn't know about, though."

Quinn wanted to know more about the keeper. "Have you heard back from him regarding your request to meet? Maybe he can help expose the problem."

Clark shook his head. "He hadn't answered before we left tonight. I'll check online when I get back to Spring Grove. I want to talk with Taylor when we get back. It's even more important now to get the VR system up and running. If we can get to the slayers faster, we can stop them before they attack anyone else."

"Taylor is doing the best she can. She insists she can figure out a way around the magic needed for the program to run."

"I know you want to protect her, Quinn. She's got a lot on her plate right now, but I can't help thinking we're running out of time. It's time to consider breaking the rules and bringing another person into the group. We need a new spell caster. If we don't get that system up again soon, something is going to tip the balance in Handon's favor for good, and we won't be able to stop them in the last battle."

Clark was referring to the final conflict for the disposition of Earth between good and evil. If Handon and his minions won the fight here in Baltimore, it could open the door for the netherworld to take over other areas across the world. For centuries, the hunter clans had prevented that from happening. Now that they were gone, she and Clark were the only ones standing in the way of the netherworld taking everything over.

"Let me talk to her in the morning," Quinn said. "If she's not close to finding a solution, we'll go with plan B and get someone else."

Clark nodded and they continued driving back to the hideout. It was getting late, and it had been a long two days. Their hunter genes kept them going longer than most people, but even they needed sleep at some point.

CHAPTER EIGHT

Quinn got up early the next morning. It was just before dawn, judging by the faint light on the horizon. It had only been a few hours since she'd gone to sleep, but she'd never needed much sleep, even as a child. Her mind still churned through the jumble of issues facing her and their tiny clan. Foremost in her thoughts was the strange revelation that she still possessed a link to the destroyed amulet.

As she walked down the stairs and started toward the kitchen to get something to eat, she heard a grunt from the opposite direction. Changing course, Quinn went down the first-floor hallway to the large meeting room they'd cleared to use for training.

Clark stood in the center of the room, running through a series of moves with his short sword. His chosen blade, modeled on the Roman gladius, gleamed in the light of a single fluorescent fixture overhead. He slashed and thrust with it as he worked through the footwork that accompanied the attacks. Quinn waited by the door as he finished. He walked to where he had left the sword's sheath and belt.

He didn't turn around as he acknowledged her presence. "You're up early, Quinn. Did you want to train a little before breakfast?"

"No, we can do it at the usual time. I'm up because I couldn't sleep any longer. I can't shake the feeling that there's something I need to be doing."

Clark turned, a grim smile on his face. "Welcome to my world. There's never enough of me to go around. People are dying because of it."

"You can't hold yourself responsible for being unable to do the work done by dozens of hunters in the past."

Clark looked like he was about to say something but changed his mind.

Quinn kept going, trying to encourage him. "At least you're not alone anymore. There are two of us now, three if you include Taylor in our clan. If I can figure out how, we'll find others and expand the clan even more."

He chuckled as he gathered his gear and started toward the door. "I'll give you one thing, Quinn—you don't let go of an idea once you get it into your head. This huntress clan of yours is real to you."

"Of course, it is. I don't know why, but something feels right when I think about it. Plus, on the few occasions when we've had words with our enemies, the very mention of it seems to get under their skin, as if they know something we don't."

"There is that, I guess," Clark said as he left the training room and walked with her toward the kitchen. "Anything that gets them off-balance is a plus. Maybe I'll feel better once I eat some food. I smell something. Did you start breakfast already?"

Quinn shook her head. She smelled it, too. "I was heading that way when I heard you training and came down to see. It's Taylor," she said, chuckling. "She was out cold when we got back last night. The shifter thing and controlling her change two days ago must be taking a lot out of her."

They found Taylor standing at the large institutional stove, cooking bacon and eggs. She turned when they came in. "Hey, guys. I woke up super-hungry and had to get something to eat. I've got enough going here for all of us if the two of you want to get drinks and plates."

"Long night last night, T?" Quinn asked. "I noticed you fell asleep fully dressed with your door open. You're not pushing yourself too hard, are you?"

"I'm fine. I've got some things to talk to you both about but help me finish up first, and then we can talk while we eat."

Quinn nodded and helped Clark get the table set. She poured drinks while Clark stepped over to the stove to assist Taylor. Quinn had to give him credit; he didn't get locked into making them do certain chores just because she and Taylor were women. He lent a hand with anything that needed doing. She appreciated it.

Soon the three of them were sitting at the table and started their meal. Taylor waited until they'd all settled and said, "I've made a breakthrough. I think I'm close to getting the VR rig back up and running."

Quinn glanced at Clark. He was as surprised as she was. She asked, "What kind of breakthrough? Did you find a way around needing magic to enable the transfer into the system?"

"No, even better. I found a way to cast the spells."

Clark's jaw dropped. "How? You were getting nowhere with that the last time we talked about it."

Taylor paused and shifted her gaze between them before she answered. "Okay, this is going to sound weird, but I had help."

"From who?" Clark and Quinn asked together.

The voice from the doorway startled the pair.

"From me."

Quinn spun, staring in disbelief, unable to stop herself from gawking at the glowing form that stood behind them.

Clark handled it better, but Quinn could see he was a little rattled, too. He tried to laugh it off, saying, "I figured you'd find a way to come back and haunt us."

"Miranda, how?" Quinn asked.

"My work here wasn't finished, I guess," the woman said. The glowing image of the witch's ghost, dressed in a pale yellow dress with a floral pattern, drifted around to the other side of the table and sat beside Taylor. "Sometimes, the higher powers endow spirits with the ability to return to finish tasks left uncompleted. In my case, I think I am supposed to help you three."

Quinn shook her head, trying to process the emotions swirling through her. She opened her mouth to speak, tears welling in her eyes.

Miranda held up a hand to stop her. "Quinn, you don't have to apologize. There was nothing you could have done to stop what happened to me. It was my time."

"How can you say that?" Quinn asked. "You just told us you had unfinished business."

"I did, but the thread of my mortal life was only so long, and that was the end of it, at least in that form. I've returned in this form to continue my important work."

Clark smiled and nodded. "You're here to cast the spells again and help us activate the VR system. We could've used you last night, but better late than never."

Miranda shook her head. "I'm limited in how I can interact with your world. I cannot physically touch any part of the mortal realm. That includes the magic that is present here. What I *can* do is help Taylor realize the power within herself so she can do it in my place."

Quinn didn't understand. "Taylor, you can do magic now?"

The other girl nodded. "I made a big step in the right direction last night. It was why I was so tired. Using magic takes a lot out of you."

"I want to know more about how this happened, but in any event, that's great news," Clark said. "We'll need to get the rig up and running tonight. I want to take the fight to those bastards and get some payback."

Miranda shook her head. "Taylor's not ready for that. She only just learned to see the energy flows last night. I think she'll learn fast because of her programming experience since it takes that kind of analytical mind to do a complex spell, but she won't be ready by tonight. No way. It's not safe for her or for Quinn."

Clark grumbled something under his breath Quinn couldn't make out. She jumped in to let him work through whatever he was thinking. "It's still great news, both the magic and knowing you're still here with us, Miranda. At least in some form."

"I think Miranda's right about me picking it up fast. I have been thinking about the notes written by the VirSync developers in the program. I think I understand what they were going for and can't wait to start trying stuff."

Miranda held out a hand, cutting Taylor off. "But we're going to be careful because any mistakes can cause catastrophic consequences for both the caster and the subject of the spell."

"I get it," Quinn said. "We'll try to be patient. Right, Clark?"

"Uh, yeah," he replied. He pulled out his phone. "I need to check and see if Joshua answered my message. At least if we can meet with him, we won't feel like we're doing nothing. No offense, Taylor. I just lost a good friend last night. If we'd had the rig up and running, he might still be alive."

"I understand. I'll work hard and try to learn as fast as I can. I want this as much as you do. I have a score to settle on Miranda's behalf if nothing else. Plus, I've got this werewolf thing hanging over me now. They have payback coming for that too."

Clark interrupted Taylor, looking up from his phone. "Joshua got back to me. He wants to meet downtown at the public library. I'm supposed to come alone, but something about his reply makes me think he's in some sort of trouble," he said. He glanced at Quinn. "I want you to come with me. We need another set of eyes on this and he doesn't know you, so he won't know you're watching my back if he spots you."

"You're expecting trouble?" Quinn asked. "He's a book-keeper, right? How dangerous could he be?"

"Oh, Joshua's harmless. He wouldn't hurt a fly. I've seen him catch a spider in a cup and set it free outside rather than step on it. It's everything else that's going on right now. I worry about another slayer team catching him before we get there or showing up at the meeting."

Quinn grinned. "You know I'm in. When do we leave?"

"Now. I want to check out the library's surroundings and then drop you off to go in early and be in place before he arrives. That way, we can see if anyone is watching him. You'll have to look like you're doing research or some-thing. Can you look like a bookworm?"

Quinn paused, and Taylor laughed. "Don't worry, Quinn. I have an outfit that'll work for you, and even an old pair of plain-lens glasses. They just block screen frequencies, and they look nerdy as hell, so they'll be perfect to complete the outfit."

"If you say so. I've never been much of a student."

"You only have to look like you belong in the library," Clark said. "He wants to meet me in the basement where the antiquities section is located. That's where the moldy old books are kept, so you have to look the part, or he'll figure out you're with me for sure."

"I can fake it."

"Good, then go get changed. I'll tell him that I'll be there."

Quinn got up, as did Taylor. Miranda followed them from the room while Clark tapped his response into the phone.

CHAPTER NINE

Quinn stood in front of the mirror and shook her head. "No way, T. I look like a girl from a freaking private school."

"Exactly," Taylor said, smiling. "You look like someone who'd rather be locked in a basement with a bunch of moldy old books than be outside getting fresh air."

"If you say so."

Quinn stared at the image in the mirror again. She wore a gray wool skirt that came down to her knees. Black tights and flats completed the bottom half of the ensemble. She had a white button-down shirt with a collar, a plain cardigan and her hair braided in two pigtails that hung down her shoulders.

"Where do I keep my Bowie?"

Taylor handed her a backpack. "Keep it in here."

"How am I going to get it out if I need it in a hurry?"

"With this outfit," Miranda said, "I doubt anyone will consider you a threat, so you'll have plenty of time. Hopefully, you won't need it. This is supposed to be a peaceful meet-up with a friend, not a full-on fight with slayers."

"I hope you're right," Quinn said. "I can't run in this skirt, let alone fight anyone. It's too tight."

"You'll be fine," Taylor added. "Stop obsessing about it. You'll be back in no time, and you can change back into your ass-kicking gear then."

Quinn gave herself one last look and started toward the stairs. Clark was probably fuming at having to wait so long.

Taylor raced behind her. "Don't forget the glasses. They complete the outfit."

Quinn took the dark-framed glasses and slipped them on. "How's that?"

"Perfect. Completely non-threatening."

"Thanks."

Taylor laughed as Quinn continued down the steps and walked toward the entry. Clark was waiting in the car with the engine running. He checked his watch as she came out.

Quinn moved as fast as she could. She wasn't kidding about the skirt restricting her speed. It was going to suck if she had to get anywhere quickly.

She sat down in the passenger seat, not missing Clark's amused expression. "Don't say a word. I know how ridiculous I look."

"I wasn't going to say anything of the sort. You'll blend in perfectly. Knowing Joshua, he'd consider you the perfect woman."

"Ewww, I don't need some old guy drooling over me."

"Don't worry," Clark said as he drove out of the parking

area and onto the lane leading to the main road. "You just have to find a spot where you can see the meeting. There's no reason for you to interact with him."

"You'd better be right." Quinn paused and checked the backpack in her lap. Taylor had found some old medical textbooks somewhere in the building and stuffed them in with her Bowie knife and phone. She closed the backpack and set it on the floor at her feet.

Clark said, "Let's go over the plan and see if there's anything we're missing."

"What's to miss? It's a meeting, right?"

"Maybe. There's just something nagging at me. When I told Joshua I wanted something that contained information on how to fashion an amulet, he initially put me off and told me he didn't have anything I could use. Then he came back suddenly and requested the meeting, saying he'd found something he forgot about."

"You said he's old. Old people forget stuff."

Clark frowned. "It's not like him to forget. He's the freaking keeper. They don't forget anything left in their care. It's in the genes or something."

Quinn thought about it and asked, "Could it have been someone else answering? Maybe they've already gotten to him. It could be a trap."

"That's what you're there for. Watch my back and make sure." Clark glanced her way while he drove. "You've got that, right?"

"No worries. I can do that."

"Good," Clark said as he sped up and merged onto the interstate heading into town.

It took them half an hour to reach the main branch of the library downtown. Clark circled the block once and then pulled over to drop off Quinn. "Be careful. If you need to, use your hide in shadows ability to get to where you need to be."

"I'll be fine. After all, I'm wearing library camo."

Her comment made Clark laugh.

She laughed, too. "See you in a bit."

Quinn climbed out and grabbed her backpack, swinging it onto her back and slipping both arms into the straps. She figured that would look the nerdiest. She leaned down and looked into the car. "The meeting is supposed to happen in about an hour, right?"

Clark nodded. "I'll go find a place to park and walk back. The extra time will give you plenty of room to get settled in place before Joshua arrives."

Quinn nodded and shut the door, then headed up the broad steps out front as Clark drove away. To her amusement, on her way inside, she spotted two other women dressed in very similar outfits. She'd have to tell Taylor.

Inside, she followed Clark's instructions and turned just inside the main entrance and headed for the first stairwell. Taking the steps down two flights to a sub-basement level, she pulled open the heavy fire door and walked into a musty room with rows of tall bookshelves that nearly reached the low, dropped ceiling.

Clark was supposed to meet Joshua near a research area on this floor. Clark had met him here before and told her it had glass walls so she would be able to see into it from all around the tables and study cubicles situated facing the center of the room.

Quinn walked down a row between two floor-to-ceiling shelves filled with old books until she reached the end of the shelf and entered an open area. She spotted the small room in the center with its glass walls. As Clark had told her, there were many tables and a few low-walled study cubicles situated around the room. Any of them would afford her a view of what was going on in there.

Glancing behind her, Quinn decided to locate the other exits and entrances to the room before she found her seat. She didn't want to put herself in a position where anyone could sneak up behind her, and she also wanted to ensure she knew where the nearest escape route was.

She found another stairwell opposite the one through which she had entered. There was also a main entrance to the floor, with a bank of elevators. That was where both Clark and Joshua would probably arrive. She decided to pick a place where she could see the main entrance and also keep an eye on the spot where the bookshelves led to the stairwell entrances. This would give her the best option to keep an eye on things all around.

She took a seat in one of the cubicles and made sure she could look over the top of the cubicle wall to see the rest of the room. It was perfect, and would keep her mostly hidden from view.

She pulled out one of the two books Taylor had packed for her and opened it. Leaving the book open, she pushed her backpack to the side and made sure the hilt of her knife was right inside the pack so she could grab it in a hurry if she had to. She glanced down at the book. It was some sort of surgery guide with anatomy drawings, along with descriptions of medical instruments from a long time ago. The more she looked at it, flipping the pages, the more she realized it was interesting.

Quinn checked her phone for the time. The meeting was to take place in about forty-five minutes, so she settled in to wait with her book. Maybe she could learn something to help her cause more damage in her next battle.

CHAPTER TEN

The textbook drew her in as she thought about matching up the anatomy in the illustrations with the lessons on specific injuries caused by certain attacks. Before she knew it, twenty minutes had flown by. Because she had her nose down in the book, she missed the arrival of the others.

Her amulet scar warned her once again with a slight twinge of cold against her chest. Absently rubbing it to remove the dull ache the chill caused, Quinn looked up and scanned the room for trouble. The presence of four individuals she hadn't seen before surprised her. When had they come in?

Cursing silently, Quinn peered over the top of the cubicle and studied the newcomers. Clark hadn't arrived yet, which was good. None of them matched Clark's description of Joshua, either. That didn't ease her mind, though. Something had caused that twinge of cold.

The woman and three men all wore ordinary street clothes and stood in different places around the room. The men pretended to look at books they'd pulled from the shelves nearby.

She could tell they were pretending because the one closest to her hadn't bothered to check what he was looking at. From the book's cover, it was obvious it was upside-down. He held it open as if he was reading it up close so he could peer over the top in the direction of the elevator.

They all seemed to be waiting for something or someone. Quinn figured it was either Clark, Joshua, or maybe both of them. She grabbed her phone and swiped to open the messaging app. Then she saw the notification at the top —*No Signal*. She couldn't warn Clark to stay away, or even give him a heads up as to what he could expect.

She started running down a list of options but stopped when the elevator chimed. A tiny elderly man in a dapper suit and bowtie stepped into the area. It had to be Joshua. He looked precisely like Clark had described the keeper.

Joshua Dalton carried a slim black wood cane with polished silver metal at both the tip near the floor and forming a stylized L-shaped grip for his hand. He tapped on the tile floor with each step but didn't appear to need it other than for show. He walked farther into the room, to the glassed-in area. Joshua opened the door and entered, stepping up to the large table inside and sitting down. If he noticed the four people standing around the room, he gave no indication.

Was she wrong, and the presence of the others was coincidental? She brought her hand to her chest and rubbed the scar. No, she thought, the warning had been real. There was something about them. Calling up her huntress abilities, the HUD appeared, along with the ever-present headache. Ignoring the pain, Quinn engaged her tracking ability, which enabled her enhanced sense of hearing, smell, and sight.

The distinct odor of wet dog greeted her, and her nose wrinkled. At least some of the newcomers were shifters, probably werewolves. While that didn't automatically make them evil and working with Handon, it gave her a reason to be careful. If they were friendly and here at Clark's bidding, he would have warned her. Maybe Joshua had hired local muscle for protection.

One of them, the woman, glanced her way. Quinn quickly returned her gaze to the anatomy book on her desk while she tried to come up with a solution that wouldn't scrap Clark's meeting with the keeper. She needed the information from Joshua.

Quinn stole a glance over the top of the cubicle. The female shifter had returned to pretending to scan the titles on the shelf beside her while she watched the elevator foyer. There was something oddly familiar about the woman, although Quinn was sure she had never seen her before.

Shaking off the feeling, Quinn thought about trying to sneak away from her spot and work her way to the stairs. If she could get to the first floor before Clark got there and stepped on the elevator, she could warn him.

She started to rise but stopped when the elevator chimed again. All four of the watchers moved at the same time, stepping back between the bookshelves to hide from whoever was coming.

Quinn reached into the backpack and gripped the hilt

of her Bowie. Pulling it free but keeping it near the surface of the desk so no one could see it, she craned her neck to look around. She couldn't see any of them anymore. The wet-dog smell had grown stronger, though. To her, that meant only one thing. They'd shifted form in anticipation of what was coming next, and that made them enemies, not friends.

She stood as Clark appeared from the opening elevator. He stepped into the entry and turned toward the glass room. Joshua rose from his seat and nodded at Clark.

Quinn waved to get the hunter's attention, but he kept walking toward the meeting room's entrance. Realizing he couldn't see her, Quinn ducked out of the cubicle into the nearest row of books and started toward the room's perimeter.

Before she reached the wall, a large partially shifted werewolf in jeans and t-shirt turned the corner, nearly bumping into her. It was hard to say which of them was more surprised.

The huntress was prepared for him and ready to fight. He'd clearly expected to find the harmless little girl still seated in her cubicle. Quinn stabbed up with her blade. She aimed to bring it up into the hairy belly of the beast, angling the long knife up under the ribs to the vital organs beneath.

Surprise was in her favor, and the Bowie plunged into the creature's heart. The only sound he made was a soft sigh as he collapsed to the floor.

Quinn didn't wait to see if the others heard. She kept moving to the wall and began walking around the perimeter of the room. The stupid skirt kept her from going as fast as she wanted. Quinn considered pausing to cut the sides with her blade to free her legs, but she opted to continue around the wall rather than take the time to fuss with the skirt.

As she moved, Quinn tried to remember which row of shelves held the next closest werewolf and slowed as she passed the last few rows.

Peeking around the bookshelf to check each row, she spotted one of the werewolves crouching and trying to peer between the bookshelves to see the front of the room.

Quinn held her knife in front of her and whispered "mist" as she started forward. The hazy outline around the edge of her vision indicated her shadow-hiding ability had engaged.

She snuck up behind the werewolf and yanked his elongated snout up, exposing his throat. At the same time, she plunged the Bowie in from the side, burying it to the hilt in the beast's neck until the tip protruded from the far side. The silver sizzled as the shifter's blood poured from the wound, spraying the books in front of him.

He struggled to clutch his throat for a second, then went limp as Quinn twisted the knife, severing the spine. She lowered him to the floor, careful to avoid the spreading pool of blood as she stepped away.

That took care of the two on the right side of the room. She was about to try to work her way around to the far side when an earsplitting snarl ripped from the front of the room. Quinn jumped over the werewolf's body to see what was going on so she could lend Clark a hand.

She miscalculated her hop over the body, in part because her tight skirt hampered her movements. She landed on one foot, stepping in the edge of the bloody puddle she'd created. Her ankle twisted as her foot slipped out from under her, and she fell over the body of the shifter. After death, he changed back to a man.

Turning her fall into a tumbling roll, Quinn came back to her feet toward the middle of the row. The snarling had changed in the other end of the room, and Quinn knew another battle raged there.

She started forward again, drawing on her stamina bar in the HUD to increase her strength and agility. There were still at least two more of them out there. They could be ganging up on Clark right now.

She usually figured he could handle himself in situations like this, but he had Joshua to protect as well. She stepped around the body again, more carefully this time. Blood smeared her tights and skirt.

Quinn had almost reached the last section of shelving when the woman who'd come in with the shifters stepped into the aisle at the end of the row. She hadn't shifted into a werewolf, which puzzled Quinn until she realized the woman wasn't a shifter like the others. She was a vampire, which became evident when the woman smiled, exposing her elongated canines.

The woman didn't advance or move in any threatening way. Instead, she cocked her head to one side and nodded. "You're the huntress, aren't you?"

Quinn nodded. "I am. You've heard of me?"

She pointed at Quinn and chuckled. "Nice outfit. I went through a Brittney the naughty schoolgirl phase too. It looks good on you, although that blood'll be hard to get out of the skirt and tights."

Quinn didn't answer. This woman's fashion choices or how she got blood out of her clothes didn't interest her. Quinn considered seizing the initiative and charging forward, but something told her to hold back. The vampire knew Quinn was dangerous. After all, Quinn had killed at least one of her companions, as far as she knew. Even with that, the woman wasn't attacking her and didn't seem to feel threatened. As long as she was here with Quinn, Clark could hold his own against the remaining werewolf.

"Do I know you?" Quinn asked, feeling a vague sense of familiarity when she looked at the woman.

The vampire broadened her smile and shook her head. "Probably not, but I know you. I have to say, you're not what I expected, based on everything I've heard. I expected you to be taller or something."

Quinn glared at the woman. "What you see is what you get. Anyone who's complained isn't around anymore."

"No offense was intended, Huntress. Despite my misconceptions, you appear to be every bit as formidable as I was told."

The fighting continued toward the front of the room. The woman glanced in that direction before turning back to Quinn.

Pointing with her knife toward the sound of the struggle, Quinn said, "I'm not going to let you kill the old man."

"Oh, my dear," the vampire said with a chuckle. "I'm not here to kill him. Just to make sure he comes home from his little meeting. He's far too valuable to kill."

The woman's answer puzzled Quinn. What did she mean by 'come home?'

The struggle near the elevators ended in a gurgling snarl.

It was impossible to tell who'd won until Clark's voice called from somewhere else in the room, "Quinn, are you all right?"

"I'm good," Quinn replied. "I'm just having a chat with someone."

The woman shook her head again, the smile not leaving her face. "Looks like the day's outcome has been decided for me. Do me a favor, would you?"

Quinn wasn't sure why, but she nodded.

The woman continued, "Tell dearest Joshua that there will be no hard feelings. We know he's not responsible for what happened here. All he has to do is return home, and all will be well."

"Why don't you tell him yourself?" Quinn asked.

"Oh, no, dear, I'm leaving. I have no desire to cross blades with you at this time. I would have killed Clark. He has had it coming for any number of reasons, plus, he was supposed to come alone, which proves he still can't be trusted. That is something you should keep in mind, Huntress," the woman said as she took a step backward. She smiled as she raised her hand and waved. "TTFN, my dear."

"What?"

The woman rolled her eyes. "It means 'ta-ta for now.' Don't they teach you kids anything?"

Before Quinn could answer, the female vampire leaped backward, twisting in mid-air to land on the opposite side of the room. Then she bolted for the exit stairs, running faster than Quinn had ever seen anyone move.

Quinn stood gawking at the place the vampire had been just a second before. She considered what fighting her would be like, given how fast she could move.

On impulse, Quinn started after the woman, but she had to catch herself when the skirt tripped her again. Grabbing the nearest shelf, Quinn barely kept herself upright. When she looked up, the exit door was swinging closed, and the vampire was nowhere to be seen. Quinn would never catch her now.

Clark called again, nearer this time. Before Quinn could answer, he came around the corner to stand where the vampire had been only seconds before.

He glanced at the body on the floor and then at her. He pointed at her clothes. "You all right? That's a lot of blood."

Quinn nodded. "Yeah, it's not mine. I'm fine."

"Why didn't you come out after you answered me? Who were you talking to?"

She realized he hadn't seen the vampire leave. "I was talking to someone who came in with the shifters—a female vampire. She said some very strange things."

"Like what?" Clark asked.

"I'll tell you later." Quinn needed to process what the woman had said, especially about Clark. She'd acted like she knew the hunter personally.

Clark shrugged, looked to his left, and cursed. "Dammit, Joshua's trying to run." He turned and sprinted back toward the elevators.

Quinn followed as fast as she could, hampered by her skirt as she was. Finally, she stopped and bent down, gripped the fabric in both hands, and ripped the skirt open at the seam running up the side.

There, that would enable her to move better if there was any more fighting down here. She straightened and walked over to Clark. He and Joshua were arguing in front of the elevators.

"Who were those people, Joshua, and how did they know we were meeting here today?"

"There's so much you don't know, Master Clark. I have long sought to protect you from it. You've been through so much over the years. I thought I had shaken off any who were tailing me. I was wrong."

Quinn jumped into the conversation. "They weren't following him, Clark. They got here a good fifteen minutes ahead of him. They knew about the meeting and set up a trap to capture or kill you."

"How do you know that?" Clark asked.

"Because that's what the female vampire told me before she ran off. She thought you were going to be here alone."

Clark glanced around. "How many were there? I only saw the werewolf I fought and the one you killed."

"Two I killed," Quinn corrected, holding up two fingers. "I got another one near where I was sitting at the back of the room. The woman was watching from the other side. After I finished off the second werewolf, she confronted me. She said some very strange things and then ran off. One of them was that she had only expected you. That worked in our favor."

Clark turned back to Joshua, who'd paled during their conversation about the woman and the werewolves. "Who's the woman, Joshua? How did she know about our meeting?"

The old man took a few seconds to compose himself

and said quietly, almost to himself, "They must have been monitoring my computer."

"Talk to me, Joshua," Clark said. "Who must've been monitoring you?"

"My employer, Master Clark—the vampire, John Handon."

Quinn and Clark stood there with their mouths hanging open.

Clark gathered himself first. "You work for Handon? For how long?"

"Since right after the purges. The clans were gone. I had to find work somewhere. I'd managed to save most of the clan records and salvage some of the financial resources, as you know. I'd not been able to save enough on my own to maintain my role as the keeper. There were no more hunters other than you, and John Handon showed up a few months later to offer me a job. He sought me out and offered to hire me, even to help me maintain the hunter collection in his private library. He's a well-known collector of rare books and documents."

"That's not all he is," Clark growled. "He was directly involved with the purges, Joshua. Maybe even led them."

It was Joshua's turn to be shocked. "I cannot believe that, sir. He's never been anything but supportive of my role as the keeper of the records."

"Of course he has, you crazy old man. He wanted them for himself after he killed the original owners. He even added you to his collection. You turned over most of the clan's financial assets, too, didn't you?"

"Oh, no, sir," Joshua exclaimed. "Once I realized someone had started confiscating the clan's financial resources, I salvaged what I could and moved them to secret off-shore accounts. I was only able to save a small percentage, as you know, but I did what I could. I've never told anyone but you about them."

Quinn's head spun as she tried to take it all in. This was her best chance at restoring her amulet, and he was working for their enemies. She struggled to find some way they could leverage the information to their advantage, grasping for anything that might help them.

She asked, "What about the woman, the vampire? She had a message for you. She spoke as if you knew her well. She told me to tell you there were no hard feelings and to come back home so all could be forgiven."

Clark turned back to Joshua. "Who is this woman to you?"

"Mistress Naomi is the one who's watched out for me over the years," Joshua said with a wistful smile. "She's protected me from the rougher sorts that follow Master Handon on more than one occasion. I guess you could call her the keeper of the keeper."

Clark stared at the old man for a second, then said, "We have to get out of here. We can't afford to be down here when someone discovers the bodies. Come on, we'll take you back to our place and finish finding out what we need there."

"I cannot go with you," Joshua said, crossing his arms. "I must return. Mistress Naomi is right. My place is with the collection, and I'm sure Master Handon will understand. He has always given me a certain latitude when it comes to my studies."

Quinn shook her head. "That monster would kill you without a second thought. You can't go back."

Joshua's sad smile told her what his answer would be before he spoke. "We're all monsters, young lady. Look at what you and Master Clark have done here in such a brief time."

"We were attacked," Quinn replied.

"Master Clark was. Were you as well?"

Quinn didn't answer. She'd killed her opponents by surprise on both counts. She closed her mouth and looked at Clark, hoping he had an answer that would convince the man to come along.

"Look, Joshua," Clark said. "We can't force you to come along, but we did come seeking information, and you can help with that before you leave. Will you do that much?"

Quinn gawked at Clark. If this man left, he was as good as dead. They'd never hear from him again.

"What do you need?" Joshua asked.

"I need anything you have from the records about creating new hunter amulets. Can you give us the information on that, at least?"

Joshua paused in thought and then nodded. "I'll try. There are several places to look. That is ancient magic, and requires components that might be hard to locate, even if I find what you are looking for in the tomes."

"You get the information. Leave the rest to us. Thank you."

"Think nothing of it. As the last of the hunters here, you are entitled to what little I can do as keeper these days."

"Be careful going back, old man," Clark warned. "Handon is a monster, and I think you know it. Just because he finds you useful now, it doesn't mean he won't kill you on a whim once your utility has passed."

Joshua just nodded, offering a sad grin as he poked the tip of his cane at the elevator button. He moved over to stand before the doors.

When the elevator arrived and the doors had opened, he said, "Watch the message board. I'll leave word on what I find there. I fear meeting in person will be too fraught with danger from now on. Goodbye, Master Clark, Mistress Quinn."

He nodded to each of them and stepped inside, disappearing as the doors closed.

Quinn turned to Clark and stared, unable to say anything. They hadn't gotten anything they came for, and the source of their information was likely a dead man walking.

"Don't say anything, Quinn. Grab your stuff and meet me upstairs by the front of the building. I'll go get the car. We can talk once we're back at Spring Grove."

He walked toward the nearest stairwell, leaving Quinn alone again with the old, musty books. She shook her head and went to get her backpack and the books. She had too many questions swirling in her head right now to make sense of what just happened. She wasn't sure Clark had the answers either.

She gathered her things and left the room, heading up the same stairs Naomi had taken when she left. As she climbed to the ground floor, Quinn thought about the strange woman and the things she'd said. Her thoughts ended in more questions and no answers.

CHAPTER ELEVEN

Taylor and Miranda ran the VR rig through another test so the tech witch could work on improving her spell-casting skills.

"Good work," Miranda said, staring at the status bar on the computer monitor. "The magic has engaged with the programming this time. Keep pulling in the pieces of the weave, based on what looks right to you. Trust your instincts."

Taylor half-listened to what the ghost said. Beads of sweat came out on her forehead and began to drip into her eyes. She couldn't spare even a second to wipe her brow. She needed both hands to continue gathering the floating threads and ribbons of random magical energy so they'd fit the puzzle she'd begun to fill in.

A single gold thread seemed to be perfect for the next in the weave she'd created. Taylor reached out for it with her right hand, forefinger extended to coax it closer, but the sound of a distant car door slamming and arguing voices broke her concentration, and she lost hold of the power. The rest of the weave began to unravel, and the pieces floated away to resume the random pattern nature initially intended.

Quinn's voice reached her as clearly as if Taylor had been standing beside her friend. "Fine, be that way, but you're going to have to answer the question eventually."

Clark muttered something Taylor's enhanced shifter hearing couldn't pick up.

"Damn," Taylor said, shaking her head as she turned to face Miranda. "I almost had it. I'm sorry I got distracted."

"Don't worry about it," Miranda said. "You've got to be exhausted. You only have so much energy you can expend before it takes a toll on you. Remember that."

"I had more energy. I was almost finished. I let something break my concentration. Quinn and Clark just got back. They're arguing about something. It sounds like they didn't have the successful meetup they expected."

Miranda spun in the air where she hovered beside the desk. She looked out the doorway at the empty hall beyond. "How do you know?"

"Wolf ears, remember?" Taylor said, pointing at her head. "They're on the way in. Quinn didn't sound happy."

"Stop eavesdropping on things that aren't your concern, T," Quinn said from the doorway. "It's not polite."

Taylor noticed the dried blood all over her. The faint coppery scent of it filled the room.

"Sorry, I can't help hearing things. You have to be more careful with what you say and where," Taylor said, pointing at Quinn's outfit. "That's a lot of blood. Are you all right?"

Quinn looked down, wiped one of the stains on the white blouse, and groaned. "Ugh, I'm fine. This isn't my blood, but I've got it all over me. No wonder the people in the library's entrance and on the street were staring at me as I left."

Miranda asked, "Where's Clark?"

"He walked off into the woods in a huff," Quinn said. "I asked him some questions he didn't like about what happened at the library. He told me it was ancient history, and I didn't need to know about it."

Taylor grinned. "This sounds juicy. What happened out there?"

"The long and short of it is that his keeper friend Joshua is the chief librarian for none other than John Handon."

"What? How is that possible?" Miranda asked. The already-pale ghost grew a shade paler, becoming more transparent at the mention of the vampire who'd taken her life.

Quinn shrugged. "Apparently, he's been working for the other side since just after the clan purges."

Taylor gawked at Quinn. "Wait, the whole time?"

"Yep," Quinn said. "Hold on, it gets better. Joshua has a vampire assigned to keep an eye on him." Quinn shared the details of the fight and the aftermath.

"So, Joshua isn't an option for us anymore?" Taylor asked. She knew Quinn was counting on the information he might have to restore her amulet.

"That's even stranger. He sees no problem with working for the enemy while sending us information on the side. He's going to get back to us with what we need."

"How can he go back, now that they know he's working with you? That's suicide!" Miranda exclaimed.

"He claims he is too valuable as the keeper to be killed.

It seems too crazy to be true, even though this Naomi character said there'd be no hard feelings if he came back to do his work."

"So, what were you and Clark arguing about?" Miranda asked.

"It started because of something Naomi said. She acted like she knew things about Clark. She said he still couldn't be trusted. When I asked Clark about it, he got upset and told me he didn't know any vampire named Naomi, and I shouldn't listen to anything she said. I could tell he was lying about something and pushed him, but he wouldn't back down. My questions got to him, even if he wouldn't answer me. That's why he stalked off into the woods just now."

"I hope he comes back soon," Miranda said. "We have news."

"What?" Quinn asked. She pointed to the computers and the VR headset hanging on the back of a chair nearby. "Is the system working again? That'd be a huge win for us. We could sneak into Handon's secret library and get the records we need for ourselves."

"Taylor is really close. She's able to draw in and hold the power necessary to cast the spells. It's a question now of putting that together with the right combination of magical energy and the programming at the same time. There might be one last piece of the puzzle we need, but we'll know for sure about it soon."

Quinn turned to her friend. "That's great. It's just in time since I think we're going to need the rig soon."

"Why do you say that?" Taylor asked.

"It's a gut feeling. I don't know why." Quinn shrugged and held out her hands.

"Don't worry, Miranda and I have got this. I need a little more practice. I think tomorrow night or the next, we can try it for real."

"Perfect." Quinn swiped a blood-stained hand at her skirt. "I'm a mess and need a shower to get all this shifter blood off me. Then I'd better go find Clark and apologize for yelling at him in the car."

"He's a big boy, Quinn," Taylor said. "He should come to you and apologize for hiding things from you."

Miranda held up a hand and said, "Don't forget, ladies, he's been through a lot. He watched his clan—his whole family—be slaughtered in the purges. He hid during them and afterward and survived against all the odds, losing everything. He's been hiding so long, covering up his past, I suspect he doesn't even know when he's doing it anymore. Give him some time. He'll realize the need to let us in on his secrets. Just don't expect him to tell you everything. We all have things we keep to ourselves."

Taylor nodded. Miranda was right. "Quinn, go get that shower. Everything will look better once you do that. Miranda and I have a few more things to try here. Then I'll start pulling dinner together."

Quinn stopped in the doorway and smiled at Taylor. "Thanks, T. You're right. I'll be upstairs for a while. Gah! I think there's blood in my hair, too."

"There is," Taylor said, trying not to laugh at the look on Quinn's face. "Throw the clothes in the cardboard box you use for your dirty stuff. I'm making a laundromat run tomorrow. I'll see about getting the stains out in case you want to wear the outfit again."

Quinn laughed. "Not on your life. There's no way. Besides, I had to rip the skirt so I could fight and run. Just toss it. I'll find a way to pay you back and get some new clothes for you."

"Ooh, sounds like we have a shopping trip in our future," Taylor said, clapping. "I could use a few new things. I hope Clark has extra cash for us so we can each get something."

"He'll come up with it if he knows what's good for him," Quinn growled. "He can ask his buddy Joshua to wire him some more."

Taylor snapped her fingers. "Really? I knew it! I'll bet he only lives like a homeless guy because he's all moody and stuff. He's probably secretly a millionaire or even a billionaire. He's definitely paying for a shopping trip now."

Quinn laughed and left Miranda and Taylor chuckling as she headed up to shower.

Taylor looked out the window at the nearby stand of trees that led into the woods behind the building. There was no sign of Clark. An idea came into her head.

"I'm going to go find Clark. I get the feeling he needs to talk to someone who isn't Quinn."

"What makes you say that?"

"Just a hunch. Something is going on here that he can't tell Quinn, but maybe he can tell me."

"What about the rig?" Miranda asked.

"We've almost got it. Besides, you're getting transparent. You go sleep or whatever it is you do to recharge so you can appear in the real world. We'll hit it again tomorrow."

Miranda smiled. "It's about gathering more spiritual energy so I can manifest again. Come to think of it, I guess 'recharging' is the right word for it. I'll check in tomorrow morning. There aren't clocks where I am, so I can't say when."

"That's fine. Thanks for all your help."

Miranda nodded and floated away, fading into nothingness.

Taylor grabbed her jacket against the chill outside and headed for the building's rear exit. She wasn't sure where Clark had gone in the woods, but it was time to put her wolf senses to the test and see if she could track him down.

CHAPTER TWELVE

Taylor was surprised by how easy it was to pick up Clark's scent. She knew he could mask himself if he wanted to, but this time he hadn't bothered.

She started through the stand of trees behind the clinic and worked her way to where it merged into a natural forest that backed up on the old psych hospital's grounds. As she walked along, Taylor wondered how many of the people confined here years ago had run into these woods to escape whatever the doctors thought was the right treatment for their mental illness.

She shivered, not from the cold, but from the stories she'd heard once about how they used to lock up and essentially torture people here. It had made the first few nights she'd spent here creepy as hell, wondering whether the place was haunted. Now that one of her best friends was a ghost, she wasn't as freaked out about it. She still wondered if she was being secretly watched by un-manifested spirits in her room.

As Taylor made her way deeper into the woods, she

realized the initial trail had dissipated. She walked a little farther and realized she'd lost it. It had disappeared. She backed up to the point where she'd lost the scent and started examining the surrounding forest floor.

Taylor tried different things to see if she could determine which way Clark had gone. She crouched to examine the dried leaves covering the forest floor. Try as she might, though, she had no idea what to look for, and no visible footprints or anything stood out to her. Had he detected her coming to look for him and turned on his hunter mojo to hide from her?

The voice directly behind her startled her and answered her question at the same time.

"Why are you following me?" Clark asked.

Taylor stood. "I thought maybe you needed to talk to someone who wasn't Quinn."

He snorted a chuckle. "And you think it should be you?"

"We've never really talked, Clark. There are things about Quinn that nobody but me knows. Honestly, I should've come to you sooner. Maybe you'd have had an easier time with the earlier training sessions."

"I managed just fine, thank you. I didn't need any help to break through the outer layer of BS she puts on. She's a tough girl. Instead of settling for letting her actions prove it, though, she wears it like armor."

"That's because of all the things she's had to deal with, including growing up in so many different homes and families."

"She's not the only person to have a hard life, Taylor. That doesn't excuse the way she acts sometimes. She won't let me be in charge, and I'm afraid it's going to get her killed before she can grow into the person she was meant to be."

Taylor paused and wondered how far she should go with this. She nodded and decided she'd come this far, so she might as well go all-in. "She can't let anyone be in charge of her. Giving up control isn't the way she's wired. She grew up in foster families, moving from place to place in the system. Some people were decent enough although not really homes, but a few of them were outright monsters, and the only way she could survive was to be tougher and stronger than those who tried to take advantage of her."

"Why didn't she report them when she got the chance? Surely some caseworkers monitored her."

"You have a lot to learn about how people cope with trauma. Some become victims. They retreat inside and hide their real selves from the world. Quinn's another sort altogether. The lesson she learned early on was that she could roll over and let things happen *to* her, or she could stand up and make things happen *for* her."

Clark nodded. "That makes sense. She's a hunter through and through. There's no way I can see her rolling over and taking abuse, even as a kid."

"She's a hun*tress*," Taylor corrected with a smile. "And you're right—she never let anyone lay a hand on her without permission. The earliest story she's ever shared with me was when she was seven. A foster mom's boyfriend tried to force his way into her room. She pulled a bookshelf on top of him and broke a snow globe over his head. Then she ran away. I have no way of knowing for sure, but my guess is she spent half her life living on the street on her own. She always said she felt safest there. The street people told her the shadows protected her from harm."

Clark chuckled. "I wish I'd been there to see that. Her amulet let her access her hidden strength even then, although she didn't know it. If only she'd been able to train in her skills from the beginning!"

"There are skills, and then there are skills, Clark," Taylor said. "She brings something different to the job, but that doesn't make it wrong. You've said yourself that she can do things no one else can. I don't think she'd be able to if it weren't for what she went through."

"I know that, and I figured out some of it from my research into her background. I even tried to find out who her parents were. I thought maybe she was related to me somehow. I don't think she is, though. None of the hunters I know had babies at the time of the purges." Clark paused for a second, then said, "Why follow me to tell me all this now?"

"Because you need to know why it's not a good idea to keep secrets from her. She has a hard time trusting others as it is. If she thinks you aren't telling her something she needs to know or that you're lying to her, she'll never listen to you when you need her to."

Clark's brows lowered, and his eyes narrowed. "What makes you think I'm hiding things?"

"Quinn said something came up while you two were out. Also, your reaction just now kind of confirmed it."

Clark started to say something, but Taylor stopped him.

"You don't have to tell me anything. I don't care what

you're hiding as long as you treat Quinn right, but you need to be willing to come clean with her at some point."

The two of them stared at each other in silence for a few long seconds. The chirp of Clark's phone interrupted them.

He pulled it out and scrolled through a message before glancing toward the hospital grounds.

"What is it?" Taylor asked.

"How close are you and Miranda to getting the rig up and working again?"

"We think we can do a test run tomorrow night. Why?"

"Make it happen. Joshua just sent me a message, but it wasn't from him."

"How do you know?"

Clark turned his phone around so she could see the screen.

Hunter, the keeper is no longer your lackey. He works for me. The life tome of the clans which you seek belongs to me now, too. That magic is lost to you forever.

Come seek me out, though. I captured you once, and I relish the rematch.

JH

Taylor let out a long slow breath as she finished reading the message. "Wow, he's a cocky bastard, isn't he?"

"He has a right to be. He nearly ended us all the last time we went up against him. Vampires get stronger the older they are. He's positively ancient and that gives him the power to be almost god-like in his abilities."

"Yeah, I was there," Taylor said, fighting back the sadness she'd felt after Miranda was killed. She cleared her throat and got her voice back. "I also remember how Quinn kicked his ass and sent him running away like a scared little baby."

Clark's grim smile showed he remembered that, too. "There's no guarantee she can do the same trick again. She lost her amulet doing it. Now she has to fight to access the least of her powers. We can't count on that."

"True, but we're also all stronger now. Hell, I'm a freaking werewolf. Once I learn to control my change, I'm gonna be badass. I'm already twice as strong as I was before. He tried killing Miranda, and she came back as a ghost. You know what we're up against now, so you'll be able to help us prepare, and Quinn…"

Taylor paused and smiled, showing her teeth. "Quinn is still the biggest baddie around town. At full power or not, remember that seven-year-old girl. She will fight back. She will find a way to win. Handon might think we beat him by a fluke. We didn't. And when the time comes, Quinn will figure out how to win again."

"I wish I had your faith in her," Clark said.

"Give it time. It'll come," Taylor said, glancing back toward the hospital grounds. "I'm supposed to be getting dinner ready. I've got to get back. You coming?"

"I'll be along shortly. I've got some things to work out."

Taylor nodded and turned to leave.

"Taylor, thank you. Quinn would never have shared those things with me. I'll keep them in mind when I decide what to do next."

She smiled and returned along the forest trail to the hospital. It was dinnertime, and they had plans to make.

CHAPTER THIRTEEN

Quinn headed downstairs wearing sweatpants and a t-shirt. She pulled her hair over one shoulder and used a towel to wring more of the water out of it. Her thick hair took forever to dry, even with a blow dryer, and she was almost always in too much of a hurry to use one anyway.

Walking into the kitchen, Quinn took a deep breath and smiled. "Wow, T, it smells awesome. What is it?"

Taylor stood by the stove, stirring a saucepan. "It's just gravy, using the drippings from the chicken. Go ahead and sit down. It'll be ready in a minute or so. I'm just finishing up."

Quinn sat down. Taylor had already set up the table for them.

She looked around. "Clark's still not back? It figures."

"You two need to come to an understanding, Quinn. You aren't giving each other any breaks or trying to see things from the other person's point of view. Clark's been through things none of us know about. If he's keeping stuff to himself, there's a good reason."

Quinn rolled her eyes. Taylor had been a peacemaker back in high school. This sounded a lot like something she would've said in the middle of some girl-drama situation.

"Why are you defending him, T? Wait, you didn't talk to him about what I said, did you?"

Taylor glanced over her shoulder at Quinn and turned back to her cooking.

"Oh, my God. When are you going to learn you don't have to be the great problem solver? I suppose I have to go and apologize to him now?"

"No, not at all. Miranda had to leave, and I needed some fresh air after being cooped up in here all day. I went for a walk to tell him when dinner would be ready. He seems really upset about your fight. I just suggested that he needed to understand a little about where you were coming from and why trust is important to you."

"Taylor, you shouldn't have said anything. He doesn't need to hear about my issues growing up. None of that matters anymore. I survived, and now I'm here. I'm more than able to take care of myself." Quinn gestured at herself. "None of this could exist without all of that."

"Exactly," Taylor said, turning around holding the saucepan. She used a large serving spoon to drizzle the gravy over the platter of chicken on the table. "He has to understand what went into the super-powered Huntress Quinn Faust of today."

"Taylor, if Clark—"

"If Clark what?" Clark asked from the doorway.

Quinn sat back in her seat and closed her mouth as he came in and sat down across from her.

Taylor set the now-empty saucepan on the stovetop, then came over to sit at the head of the small square table with Quinn and Clark.

She started dishing up while she said, "Clark, tell Quinn about the message you received from Joshua."

The announcement excited Quinn. She was surprised he'd gotten back to them so soon. "What did he say? Has he found the records we need for the amulet already? When can we go pick them up?"

"Yes and no," Clark replied. "The message was on the channel Joshua and I use, but it wasn't him. It appears to have been from Handon."

"Oh, no, they killed him!" Quinn exclaimed.

"I don't think so," Clark said, shaking his head. "It was more like a challenge, daring us to come and do something about them having the keeper."

Clark pulled out his phone and opened the screen before sliding it across to Quinn. He pulled off a bite of chicken and pushed it into his mouth. He watched Quinn's reaction while she read.

"What's this clan life tome thing?"

"I think it's the location of the ceremony and magic to create an amulet like the one you wore. The life tomes hold the birth records of each hunter clan. In this case, it holds the records from here in this region."

Quinn sat up straight at Clark's words. "That book could have something about me in there."

"Yes, it could. It'll have a lot of records, but the thing we want the most is the part with the old rituals and magic spells used by the clan's mages over the centuries to create the amulets and other tools used by the hunters."

"We have to go get it, Clark," Quinn said. "I don't know why Handon even wants to have something like that. He can't use it."

"No, probably not, but it doesn't mean much. There aren't more than a handful of people around the world right now who can make use of one of the life tomes."

Taylor swallowed a bite and poured herself some water from the aluminum pitcher in the center of the table. "He's probably like a serial killer."

Quinn and Clark looked at Taylor. What she'd said didn't make sense to either of them.

Taylor laughed and continued, "You know how a psycho killer has to keep something from the people he's killed as a trophy? This is probably the same thing. He orchestrated the killing of all the hunters in this region. Why not keep their records and ceremonial books as a reminder of all you destroyed?"

Clark nodded. "It makes sense."

"Yeah," Quinn said. "If you're a psycho-killer type. The question is, why did you think of it, T?"

Taylor laughed and shrugged. "I dunno, probably because of those true crime shows I like so much. The killers always get caught in the end because of all the evidence they kept from each crime."

Clark laughed. "I didn't take you as someone who likes that sort of thing, kid."

"You have no idea," Quinn said. "She likes autopsy videos, too."

"Really? You don't have any bodies buried we should know about, do you, Taylor?"

"Not that either of you knows about," Taylor replied with a big grin on her face. She looked at her companions.

Quinn suppressed a groan. Taylor was enjoying that their little family squabble was working itself out with inane conversation. Sometimes it irked her that the other girl was right about those kinds of things more often than not. She seemed to have good intuition about how to fix people and relationships.

Clark smiled and pulled his phone back over by his plate.

"Oh, sorry," Quinn said as he took the phone back. "So, when are we going to try to get the book?"

"That's what they want, Quinn," Clark replied. "It is a trap, for sure."

"Not if I can get in and out using the VR system. Taylor said she was close to getting it back up and running."

"But we don't know where he has it," Clark said. "There's no way to find it."

Taylor cleared her throat. "Not necessarily. I mean, Handon lived completely out in the open until we came in and screwed things up for him. A guy like that is full of pride and hubris. I gotta figure he'd brag about his rare book collection and stuff."

"You're not wrong," Clark said. "Vampires his age develop a taste for high society along with blood. What are you thinking?"

"Let me do some searching. I'm finished eating so I'll go get started. You two good to clean up?"

"Sure," Quinn said. "Go start digging. Do your tech-witch thing."

Taylor smiled and skipped out the door.

Quinn laughed after she left. "She loves the title you gave her. It makes her so happy."

Clark chuckled. "Honestly, when I said it, I thought it would annoy her. Now, though, I'm glad it didn't. She deserves it."

Quinn stood and gestured at the dishes on the table. "You clear, and I'll clean?"

"Sounds good."

It didn't take the two of them long to clean up from dinner and set the dishes beside the sink to dry. They headed down the hallway to Taylor's office. She sat behind the large desk, hunched over the wireless keyboard in her lap while she tapped away and stared at the center screen of the three-monitor setup.

Taylor didn't look up when they walked in, just held up a finger in the air and said, "I'm on to something."

The two of them came over and stood by the desk while she continued to tap away at her keyboard. Quinn asked, "What did you find?"

"Handon's brokerage company had a foundation set up for charitable donations. It funded numerous programs and events around town, including several small museums."

"What do you think, Clark?" Quinn asked. "Would he be dumb enough to have the hunter records out in the open in a museum open to the public?"

"Before you showed up, what did he have to be scared

of?" Clark replied. "All the hunters were gone. His stolen goods were safe and sound."

Taylor looked up and smiled. "Until now. Look," she said as she swiveled the right-hand monitor around to show a color photo of a collection of old leather-bound books with gold lettering.

Quinn leaned forward and squinted at the screen. "I can't read the titles."

Me, neither," Taylor said. "But this museum collection has to be the one we're looking for. The description on the museum website calls it a collection of records from a medieval paramilitary order. Sounds like the hunters, right?"

Clark smiled after checking out the screen. He straightened and said, "The reason you can't read it is it's in Latin. All of us had to learn it in school. I wasn't very good, but I can read enough to know those are the right books. Taylor, good work."

The tech witch beamed at the two of them and said, "I knew it as soon as I saw this." She used her trackpad to scroll to the bottom of the museum website. She highlighted some text with the cursor. "Didn't you say Joshua's handler was named Naomi?"

"That's what he told us," Clark said.

Quinn leaned forward to read the blue highlighted text.

Museum Director - Naomi Rodriguez

She smiled. "It can't be a coincidence. Her name isn't common."

"No, It isn't," he said, turning to Quinn. "You got a good look at her when she talked to you in the library earlier today. Describe her to me."

"*Now* you want to know more about her?"

"Just describe her."

"About my height, maybe a tad shorter. She was wearing boots with heels, so it's hard to judge. She had shoulder-length dark-brown hair. Her skin wasn't particularly dark, but I guess she could have been Hispanic."

Clark paled and shook his head. "It's got to be her, and she's a vampire now. I can't believe it. She should have died rather than succumb to…"

"What's wrong, Clark? Tell us who she is. She's obviously someone you know."

"I had a distant cousin named Naomi. She'd gone to train in Europe among the master hunters with her parents when she was young. She grew up in the old country, even married some guy she met over there. I always assumed she'd remained there at the end, but maybe during the purges, she came back to try to defend the clan at home."

"She's a hunter?" Taylor asked.

"Not anymore. Any decent hunter would have died or killed themselves rather than become a vampire. It's an abomination for one of us to even consider it."

"Maybe she didn't have a choice," Quinn said. "That could be why she didn't attack. Her hunter background might have been why she chose not to fight me."

"Everyone has a choice to become a vampire," Clark said. "You have to drink a vampire's blood to complete the transformation before he drains you. She couldn't have done that by accident. She *let* him turn her."

"And now she's guarding the last records of the

hunters," Quinn said. "It's a strange twist to all this, don't you think? Probably Handon's idea of a joke."

"I'm not laughing." Clark's face had turned dark. "She's a traitor. She needs to be put down."

"You can do whatever you want," Quinn said. "As long as we get that life tome thing first. Will you know it when you see it?"

Clark nodded. "I can read Latin, remember?"

"Taylor, the ball's in your court now. How sure are you that you and Miranda can get the rig up and running tomorrow night?"

Taylor leaned back in the chair and looked at the ceiling for a few seconds. "I'd say ninety percent. There are a few things we haven't worked on yet, but I think I can master what's left before dark tomorrow."

Quinn smiled and clapped. "Then tomorrow night, we steal the book from Handon. It's time I got my amulet back."

CHAPTER FOURTEEN

Quinn hit the mat hard but smiled because Clark landed beside her a split second later. Her last-second counter to his attack had broken through his defenses and toppled him to the floor. It wasn't the first time, either. While Clark still bested her most of the time during training bouts, she had grown more consistent in landing successful attacks, connecting perhaps one in five or six times now. She laughed as she rolled to her feet, delighted her counter had worked.

"What are you laughing at, Cadet?"

"Aw, c'mon, Clark! You gotta give me that one. I came up with that combination on my own," she said, pausing as something sunk in. "Wait, 'Cadet?' I thought I was an apprentice in the hunter hierarchy. Is that a promotion?"

Clark did a poor job of hiding his smile as he climbed to his feet. "Don't let it go to your head. You have a long way to go before you get to master hunter."

"That's master hunt—"

"Yeah, yeah, I know. Huntress."

Quinn let out a brief giggle. This day had been full of hurry-up-and-wait moments, but it had been full of hopeful optimism, too. They'd found where the secret book was that held the recipe she needed to recreate her broken amulet. Tonight, she was going to go into the VR rig and bring it back.

She and Clark had discussed it, and they had decided that since she'd been out of the VR world for so long, the VirSync corporate slayers, Handon, and his vampire and werewolf lackeys wouldn't be expecting her to sneak in that way.

Quinn glanced out the training room door to the hallway beyond. Taylor's office was two doors down. "Should we head down and check in with her again? It's almost dark."

"No. A half-hour ago, she told us she'd come to get us when she was ready. Remember the last time we bothered her? She threw us out, followed by the contents of her dinner tray."

"She seemed a little frustrated with something," Quinn observed. "You don't doubt she's going to do it, do you?"

"You know her better than I do," Clark replied. "She is as solid as ever at the computer stuff, but magic is completely different. It might not be as easy as she thought it would be to solve the last few hurdles."

"Miranda seemed pleased, even when Taylor yelled at us. The smile never left her face. That's gotta be a good sign."

Clark shrugged. "We'll know when they figure it out. For now, let me try that new combination on you. If you're going to do stuff like that, it's important to learn how to counter it. If you can think of it, someone else can, too."

Clark crooked a finger at her, and Quinn sighed. He wouldn't let her give up until she learned how to stop him from using the same trick on her.

An hour and a half later, Quinn and Clark sat on a bench beside the training mats, rehydrating and taking a much-needed break from their workout. Neither of them spoke. Clark seemed as winded as Quinn for the first time ever in their training together. She took that as a definite win. The last round, she'd bested him three times out of ten, a new high point for her.

"You two look like you're too tired to do this," Taylor said. "Maybe we should reschedule."

Quinn sat up straight, her fatigue draining away in her excitement. Her best friend stood in the doorway with a huge grin on her face.

"Did you figure it out?" Quinn asked.

Taylor nodded. "I had to think of a different way to do it than what Miranda originally thought. Our brains work in different ways. That was what blocked me."

Clark stood, stretching his arms behind him for a few seconds. "You're both sure the system is ready this time?"

"Yep," Taylor said. "As soon as you two are ready to go, we'll fire it up."

"I'll go rinse off and change," Quinn said. She checked her phone. "I figure we'll go in at midnight when everything in the city has settled down for the night."

Clark wiped his face with a towel and said, "It's your call, Quinn. I'll be outside the museum until you let me in.

Remember, midnight is as good as noon to a vampire, so if Naomi is there, she'll be wide awake."

"She had no problem getting to the library during the daytime yesterday. Maybe she's on a different schedule."

"Probably came in a car and parked in the underground garage beside the building. Vampires don't need sleep like we do, so it's not surprising she was up in the daytime. When a vampire isn't doing anything and wants to rest, they settle down somewhere and go into a trance."

"No sense borrowing trouble, right?" Quinn said. "We'll cross that bridge when we come to it. First, we need to get in there. If we play our cards right, we should be able to find the collection, get the book, and get out again without alerting anyone. Taylor's got the bypass for the alarm system figured out. Plus, the online brochure gives the layout of the museum building, so I know where I'm going. This should be a piece of cake."

"Many a botched mission started out with a statement like that, Quinn," Clark said. "Stick to the plan, pay attention to your surroundings, and don't freelance. Got it?"

Quinn saluted but couldn't hide the grin on her face. "Yes, sir. Permission to change, sir?"

"Get outta here. Be back down and ready by ten-thirty so we can do a run-through of what the plan is one more time before we go live."

Quinn nodded and bounced out of the room. Ever since the amulet had been destroyed, there'd been a cloud hovering over her. It kept her from believing anything could ever be normal again. Now, in one day, her hope had been restored. The VR system was up now, giving them a way to stop the slayers again. Now they were going to get the book that would help her restore her amulet. Everything had fallen into place in a way that on most other days would have alerted Quinn to possible trouble ahead. In this instance, she wouldn't let anything banish the hope filling her.

CHAPTER FIFTEEN

Just before midnight, Quinn stared at the ceiling. The VR goggles rested on her forehead as she listened to Taylor and Miranda going over their checklist again. Clark had left a half-hour before so he could be in position outside the museum to help if she needed it.

Quinn let out an exasperated sigh. "You two have gone over the stupid list twice now. Even I know you've checked everything."

Taylor stood up and leaned over the table so Quinn could see her. "This is deadly serious, Quinn. I didn't know everything Miranda did on her end of things. It's a freaking ton of stuff, and now I have to do it on top of making sure the tech is working. If I screw up, you could get stuck somewhere in between where we can't get you back."

Quinn smiled. She wasn't letting anything break her mood tonight. "But you're not going to let that happen to me, are you, sweetie?"

"Not as long as you let me make sure everything is ready. Now I have to start the checklist all over again."

Quinn groaned and then saw Taylor's smile. "Hah, very funny. I take it that means you're ready to go?"

"Yes. I'm going to try to make the transition as smooth as possible. Because I'm working both ends of the equation, I found some places in the code that didn't match the magic. This will ease the process for you, I hope."

"I know you'll do the best you can. Let's get this over with."

Taylor glanced at Quinn's waist. "You've got the gear I made for you to bypass the security system, right? Just follow the instructions I gave you. Try to bring the gear back so we can use it again."

Quinn patted the pouch attached to her waist, then checked her Bowie just to be sure. She nodded, and Taylor sat back down behind the computer screens.

Miranda floated over her with a smile. "Put on the goggles. We'll see you soon."

Quinn nodded, lowered the goggles over her eyes, and situated the cups of the headphones in place. Everything went dark and silent for a few seconds, and then the wrenching backward sensation hit her. She fell into the familiar darkness.

When she woke up seconds later, Quinn lay completely still and stared into the darkness. She could just make out rafters in the ceiling above her. She strained to listen for anyone nearby. The plan Taylor had come up with placed her in the attic of the old home that had been converted into the museum. It was the only place they could be reasonably sure would be unoccupied, even at night. They figured any vampires or other guards would remain below, watching the building's entrances.

Glancing left and right, Quinn saw nothing until she murmured, "Dammit, I need to see." The darkness changed to greenish light that filtered things into shades of gray. All around were wooden crates and cardboard boxes sealed with packing tape. The sloped roof didn't leave a lot of space. Quinn would only be able to stand up in the very center of the room.

Rolling to her side, she searched for the opening in the floor that would be the stairs entrance leading to the storeroom below. That was her next objective.

"Quinn, can you hear me?" Taylor asked over the earpiece Quinn wore.

Quinn tapped her ear to open the radio connection. "Yeah, I'm in. The attic is smaller than it looked in the drawings you pulled up. It's pretty cramped up here."

Clark came on. "Can you find a way out?"

"I'm looking now," she said, chuckling. "If I can't, that would suck, and it would make this a very short trip."

Quinn crawled over and around boxes and crates until she located the rectangular opening framed in the floorboards.

"Got it. It's got a trapdoor and has one of those folding ladders attached to it. It ought to be fun, trying to open and extend it from this side."

"Be careful," Clark said. "Listen and make sure no one is down there before you go through."

A muffled voice said something Quinn couldn't make out, followed by Taylor saying, "All right, I'll tell her. Just wait."

"Are you talking to me?" Quinn asked.

"Sorry, Miranda is pissed because ghosts can't wear headsets."

Quinn stifled a laugh. "Tell her I know she's here in spirit."

"Hey, good one," Taylor said, laughing. She repeated what Quinn had said to Miranda, then said, "She wanted me to tell you to be ready for supernatural protections and spells. After your joke, she says, 'Never mind.'"

Quinn smiled. "Tell her I'll be careful," she said as she squared up to the opening and leaned over. "Okay, I'm going through."

Pressing her head to the wooden floor beside the opening, Quinn listened to the room below. She couldn't hear anyone.

Taking a deep breath, she moved so she could put her feet on the folded ladder and pressed down. The spring-loaded trapdoor opened and the ladder went down, locking into position. Quinn pressed her foot on the top until the base of the stepladder touched down below with a soft thump.

The shelves in the storeroom at the bottom of the ladder were full of papers and pamphlets in boxes, along with boxes of paper towels and toilet paper rolls. Other than that, the room was empty.

Quinn climbed down and turned to the door. According to the floor plan and what Taylor had been able to find in the planning and zoning database, she was now on the top floor of the museum. The map showed what looked like offices and a single exhibit of early handstamped printing presses. The area she needed was down on the second floor, just below her.

She keyed her mic. "Clark, are you set up outside?"

"I'm in place."

"Do you see any movement inside on the first or second floors? It's all quiet up here on three."

"I've been watching for almost twenty minutes. There are a few lights on, but I think they're just the ones they leave on at night since most of the windows are dark. I think you're good."

Quinn nodded. "Okay, let me check something else," she said. She mentally clicked on the map icon in her HUD, and a transparent overlay of the surrounding area popped up. She focused on her location in the center and searched outward for any of the telltale red dots indicating an enemy detected by the VR system.

Seeing nothing nearby, she was about to close the map when she spotted a green dot at the edge. Quinn concentrated on it, and her map moved over and centered on the dot. It showed up just inside the entrance of a building across the street. It took a few seconds for her to figure out what she was looking at.

"Clark, are you standing by the front door of a building across the street?"

"Yes," Clark said. "How did you know?"

"I have you on my HUD map."

"Oh, yeah," Taylor chimed in. "When I was going over the code to review places I needed to merge the magic, I found that function and switched it on. You can now see allies on the display, but only ones you've got a personal connection with. You have to have met them before for it to work."

"That's useful. Thanks, T." Quinn canceled the overlay and reached for the storeroom door. "I'm headed into the museum. I'll check in with you in a little bit."

Quinn tried the doorknob. It twisted with ease and she opened the door, stepping through into the museum's third floor. There were no lights on this level, but there was a sensor blinking on the wall across from her.

She froze, remembering the alarm system. She slowly moved the pouch at her waist around to the front, unzipping it as she did so. She pulled out a device a little larger than a cell phone, except this one had a mechanical keypad on it. Thinking back to Taylor's careful instructions, Quinn pressed the red on-button and waited for the red light at the top to turn on. It blinked to life, and she keyed in the six-digit code she'd memorized.

This was the moment of truth. She'd either just shut down the alarm system or ordered a pizza. Only Taylor knew how the hell the thing worked. All Quinn could do was stand there and wait for an alarm to sound, the cops to come, or the little light above the keypad to switch from red to green.

Five long seconds later, the light blinked a few times between red and green before staying a bright and steady green. Quinn realized she'd been holding her breath the whole time and let it out in a long, slow exhale. The sensor on the wall with the blinking red light had turned off.

"The alarm is off, Clark," Quinn said. "Taylor, the little box thing worked."

"Good," Taylor replied. "Don't forget to turn it back on

before you leave. If we're lucky, they'll never know you were there."

Quinn smiled. She'd love to pull off the perfect crime and stick it to Handon without him even knowing it. First things first, though. She had to locate the old clan's life tome.

Walking through the offices and into the exhibit area, Quinn moved to the open stairway. She started down, opening her huntress senses outward as a precaution. She had ways to hide from her opponents, and there was no reason the other side couldn't hide from her tech and abilities, too. It was best to be ready for anything.

Quinn activated her tracking ability, so her enhanced hearing and sense of smell kicked in. She continued down to the second level. In the background, she heard the steady drip, drip, drip of a faucet inside the bathroom at the bottom of the steps, but nothing else. She scanned the open space around her, looking for the correct exhibit.

She smiled at the small printed placard on a waist-high sign beside a pair of glass cases.

Medieval European Collection

After walking over to the cases, Quinn leaned close and studied the old leather books inside on glass shelves. She expected them to be beaten up and falling apart, but they didn't look that way. The leather shone in the single overhead security light. It looked as polished and supple as if it were brand new.

It so surprised her, Quinn straightened and scanned the room, trying to locate something more like what she expected. Her eyes kept returning to the books in the case.

"I think I found them. The lettering on them is in Latin

like we expected, but I'm going to need help. There are seven books here, and some of them are pretty large. I can't bring them all back with me."

"Send us a pic," Taylor suggested. "Clark can read the titles."

Quinn pulled out her phone, snapped a photo, and texted it to a group message thread. She waited while it went through the system until it showed as delivered.

"You should have it now in the group chat."

"Got it," Clark said.

Taylor followed with, "Me, too."

"Okay," Quinn said. "Which one is it?"

"Give me a second," Clark said. "It's been a long time, and I wasn't very good at Latin when I learned it."

Quinn smiled. She couldn't wait to bring this up with him when they all were back at Spring Grove.

After a few seconds, Clark said, "Um, I'm not entirely sure, Quinn. I never saw the book growing up. It was called the life tome by everyone in English. Nothing fits that."

"What would it be?" Quinn asked. She scanned the room again. "Maybe they took it somewhere else."

"It would be something like *Libre de Vita* or another combination of those words. Damn, I wish my Latin wasn't so rusty."

"I can't stand here all night," Quinn said. "Are you sure it's not one of the ones in these two cases? Damn, there's got to be an app for translation. Next time I'll load it before I come."

"None of them match what I expected," Clark said. "But I can't translate all of them, so I can't be sure."

Quinn walked around the cases and checked out the

tables and displays nearby. None of them had any books. They were all individual documents under glass.

"Hey, everybody *stop*," Clark hissed in alarm. "Someone just pulled up out front in a red sports car. It's a woman with long dark hair."

"What's she doing?" Quinn asked. "Maybe she's going to a neighboring building."

"Nope, she's going up the museum steps to the front door. Maybe I should try to take her out."

"Stay where you are, Clark," Taylor said. "I think I figured it out. Quinn can still get the book and get out of there. The image you sent is blurry, but one of the titles looks like it's *Narratio*. I did a quick search online. That could mean narrative or story, which would match its purpose for the clan—holding the clan's history. It's also the largest of them and has the most ornate leatherwork. What do you think, Quinn?"

She moved back to stand beside the first case. She saw the one Taylor described on the top shelf. The leatherwork depicted vines, leaves, and things growing, which could mean life or nature. It could also be an old gardening guide.

Clark's urgent whisper filled her ear. "The woman is going in the front door. She had a key."

Quinn didn't need the warning. She heard the door open on the floor below hers. She had to decide. The case was hinged at the back, and Quinn lifted the heavy glass lid, grabbed one of the smaller books, and used it to prop open the case.

She lifted the book with both hands and looked at it closely. A tingling sensation spread from her fingers to her shoulders, making her shiver for a second. Quinn smiled, taking it as a sign.

"Got it. This has to be the right one."

"Okay, Quinn," Taylor said. "I'm engaging the recall sequence now. Start back upstairs. The transition will be easier on you if you return from the spot where you started."

Quinn turned around, clutching the leather tome to her chest.

"Hello, Quinn. When I got the alert the alarm was off, I thought the idiot janitor had forgotten to turn on the security system again before he left."

Naomi stood between Quinn and the stairs, up or down.

Quinn glanced at the book. There was no way she could fight while holding it. If she put it down and transitioned out of VR, it would remain here. All she could do was play for time.

"I guess you got lucky this time, Naomi. Too bad you couldn't stay out on a lovely night like this. Someone like you must enjoy the Baltimore nightlife," Quinn said. Naomi looked only a little older than Quinn, maybe early twenties, but that could be deceptive. Vampires stopped aging when they were turned.

"Actually, I was looking forward to a quiet night at home with my cat and some binge-streaming. Instead, I'm here having to teach you a valuable lesson."

Quinn started to make a snarky reply but stopped when Taylor cursed over the connection in her earpiece. "Dammit, I missed a step. I have to restart the sequence. You'll have to do something to stall her, Quinn. Sorry."

"I'm coming in," Clark called.

"No!" Quinn exclaimed. "Stay where you are."

A puzzled frown crossed Naomi's face. "I don't think you are in a position to give me orders, Quinn. Now, hand me the book and come along peacefully. The master will want to have a few words with you before he decides what to do next. If you play your cards right, you might survive the night."

"What, and give up everything I ever fought for to become one of the enemy? I know you used to be a hunter. That's how you knew who Clark was, am I right?"

Naomi paused. She stared at Quinn as if searching for something.

"What?" Quinn finally said. She was grateful for the additional time it gave Taylor to fix things, but it was creepy, too.

"Nothing. For a moment, I thought... Well, that doesn't matter now, does it? You're right, of course. I was a member of the clans. In the end, let's just say I had my reasons to want to stick around. When Handon offered me the option, I took it. Who's to say the clan's version of what the world should be is any better than Handon and his cohort?"

"You can't be serious. You were raised to fight demonic forces and everything that entails. You've seen what power does to people. How could you trade sides so easily?"

Taylor whispered in Quinn's ear. "Get ready. Since you didn't make it back to the attic, this is going to be a rough transition. Sorry."

Naomi shook her head. "You have no idea what I've given up in my life or what drove me to make the decision

I did. I don't have to justify what I did to you of all people. Now, stop stalling and give me the tome. I have no qualms about teaching you a lesson about your betters. Do it now, or I'm coming to get it.

The familiar tugging at the back of Quinn's mind began, and she smiled as Naomi started forward. The vampire was about to be disappointed.

Quinn's smile disappeared when the gentle tugging became a gut-wrenching pull that sent her tumbling backward into darkness just as Naomi reached out to grab her. Quinn turned over and over in the dark, then landed on an unyielding surface hard enough that she banged her head and saw stars.

Her stomach churning, Quinn yanked off the goggles and headset and rolled to the side of the desk in Taylor's office. Taylor was ready for her and handed her a plastic trash can. Quinn grabbed it from her and proceeded to empty her stomach as waves of nausea struck her.

Taylor keyed her headset. "I've got her, Clark. Come on home."

"What about the book?" Clark asked.

"That's here too, and she didn't throw up all over it, so we're good."

Taylor knelt so her head was level with the tabletop. "How ya doing, hon?"

Quinn handed Taylor the trash can and sat up, wiping her mouth with the back of her hand. "That was the worst one yet. I thought you said you'd worked out the kinks for the return trip?"

"I did if you were able to get close to the point of entry. I still don't know how VirSync's engineers and programmers got it to operate so smoothly. The transmission in their version of the system was usually silky-smooth."

"For you, maybe. I always had major headaches after going into the system for them."

Miranda floated over. "Maybe it means the issue is with you and not the programming. Your hunter blood could be resisting the magic and technology coupled together. I'll have to think about that."

Quinn looked around until she found the life tome. It sat at the edge of the desk behind her, where she'd dropped it as soon as she landed. She slid it over to sit beside it and tried to open it.

"No," Miranda said. "Don't open it. Magical seals likely protect it. Let Taylor and me examine it first."

Taylor took the book from Quinn. "You can't read Latin anyway. Go. Get cleaned up and get some rest. It'll still be here in the morning."

Quinn nodded. Taylor was right, of course. Nothing in the book would make sense to her. She slid off the desk and started up to her room. The trip had exhausted her, so maybe she'd wait to shower in the morning.

CHAPTER SIXTEEN

Two days later, Taylor checked on Clark to see how the translation was coming. He sighed and sat up, arching his back to stretch, then hunched over the book again and ran his finger down the text as he tried to read the Latin script. Taylor couldn't help but chuckle at his exasperation. When he said his Latin was rusty, he wasn't kidding.

She noted his phone sitting next to the book, open to a translation app. This was the third occasion Taylor caught him checking a word or phrase in his phone, so she called him on it. "Clark, if you're just going to have the internet to do the translation for you, there's a better way, and we won't take weeks doing it."

He looked up and blushed. "I really should have paid more attention when I was a kid, but I never saw any reason to learn it. I was not going to be a scholar or a mage, so what did I need it for?"

"And yet, here we are," Taylor said. "Look, I might have

another idea that will get this done a lot faster. Are you willing to let me have a go?"

"My God, yes. All I can think about is still working on this a month from now. There are a lot of more important things I have to do out there. We've got to track down Handon's new location in addition to blocking the things they've done when we couldn't track them."

"Well, go do that. If I need to check back with you for help, I will."

Clark pushed his chair back and stood, then slid the open book over to Taylor and left. She noted that in two days, he'd only made it to the fourth page of what looked like several hundred. She smiled, shaking her head.

Taylor took the book back to her office and cleared a spot on her desk alongside the triple monitors. She propped the book on the stand she usually used for her tablet, then turned to page one and pulled out her phone. Time to get to work.

Three hours later, Taylor flipped to the next page and held her phone steady, making sure the new page filled the frame. She tapped the button to take the picture and then moved to the other side to catch the opposite page. The laborious process took a long time, but it was exponentially better than trusting Clark's painfully slow and unreliable translation skills. Taylor had made it about a third of the way through the enormous book in just three hours.

That was just the page scanning process, of course. After that was completed, she could rely on an online scanning and translation app a hacker friend of hers had appropriated from a government server. It would take all the scanned pages and create translations for each alongside a photographic representation of the real page. The whole process with the app would take about an hour, and most of that would be spent in setting up the correct parameters.

Taylor stretched and then checked the book to see how many more pages there were in the section she was working on. The whole first part of the book was lists of what looked like place names and people's names followed by dates. The earliest time in the life tome was November 1st, 804 A.D. Beside it, someone had written two names. Taylor wondered if they were the original members of the clan in Europe.

There were only three more pages in the section, so Taylor decided to wrap them up and then take a break. She needed to get outside and feel the sunshine on her face and the cool autumn breeze in her hair. It drained her to be cooped up like this under ordinary circumstances, and it was worse ever since the werewolf had bitten her. She'd become even antsier to get outside and take in the richer sensory experience.

Taylor turned the page and took the picture, then moved on to take the next one and stopped. A name jumped off the page at her. Taylor leaned forward and scanned higher on the page so she could make out the full entry.

Clark had been able to interpret some of the symbols used with the names during his two days of studying the book. He'd shown them to Taylor and explained what little he knew. The first entry in the group that had caught her eye listed "Naomi Rodriguez." She had the tiny arrow sigil next to it, designating her a member of the hunter clan that had settled in Baltimore. Most of the entries in the book were from the same clan, designated by the tiny arrow.

Next to Naomi was the name "Brian LoFasso." It had no symbol next to it, which designated he was a normal human, or a mundane, as Clark put it. From what she'd seen so far, mundanes had married into the clan infrequently over the years. This was one such occasion. The date next to it Taylor took to be a wedding or betrothal date.

What had jumped off the page at Taylor and made her stop was the next part. Naomi and Brian were just the beginning of a family entry. The third entry in that grouping was what had caught her eye.

Below Naomi's and Brian's names, there was one more listing dated a little more than eighteen years ago.

Quintana Rodriguez-LoFasso

Quintana? Could that be Quinn? It could just be a coincidence. She would have been born right in the middle of the two years of the purges. Quinn was abandoned almost eighteen years ago as an infant. That put it in the right timeframe.

Taylor sat back and stared at the page, her eyes drifting back up to rest on the mother's name.

Naomi Rodriguez

What were the odds there were two Naomis who used to be part of the hunter clan in the area? Taylor would have to check the other modern listings, but she was willing to bet this was the same one. Maybe there was another reason she didn't attack Quinn on sight at the library.

This changed everything. She had to talk to someone about this, and it couldn't be Clark or Quinn. Both of them had too much emotion tied up in it. That left one other person.

"Miranda?" Taylor called. "You floating around some-where close?"

The ghost didn't manifest unless she was there to help with something specific, but Taylor had discovered she wasn't far away most of the time, at least in spirit-realm terms.

"What is it?" Miranda said from directly behind Taylor.

Taylor jumped and spun around in her swivel chair. "God, you scared me."

"You called me. Weren't you expecting me to show up?" Miranda smiled, enjoying the moment. "What did you want, anyway? You're not still working on that book, are you?"

"I am, and you're not going to believe what I found. Check this entry out."

Taylor stabbed a finger at the book, pointing out the listing. She waited while Miranda leaned in and looked at it.

Miranda's eyes widened as she hovered over the book, and she turned to Taylor, her mouth open. "You think—"

"I do." Taylor nodded.

"Do you think Naomi knows who Quinn is?"

"She'd have to, wouldn't she? Especially if she stayed here in the city the whole time. How many orphaned huntresses with superpowers named Quinn are there in Baltimore? Naomi would have been changed into a vampire pretty soon after her capture. It explains a lot, actually. She could've kept tabs on Quinn, watching over her daughter even if she couldn't raise her." Taylor held up a finger as an idea came into her head. "That's why she allowed herself to be turned!" she exclaimed.

"You think she managed to keep tabs on her daughter after she was changed into a vampire? Why would Handon allow her out of his sight?" Miranda asked.

"I don't know the answer to that, but possibly she did whatever she had to so she could gain his trust and loosen the leash a little bit. This explains something else Quinn told me when we first met. She always talked about her luck and how bad things happened to people who tried to hurt her. Some of that was because Quinn fought back, even as a little girl, but she tells stories from living on the streets about bad people who would just disappear. The street people told her the shadows watched over her. It could have been a vampire secretly guarding her while she slept.

Miranda glanced at the entry in the life tome. "We can't tell anyone. Not until we verify it."

Taylor nodded. "Don't worry about it. Quinn has big-time parental issues. I wouldn't know how to tell her about her mother even if we'd found out her mom was alive and working as a diner waitress. Telling her that her mom is a vampire who secretly followed her the whole time she was growing up? That's something I don't even want to think about."

"Think about what?" Quinn asked from the doorway.

Taylor spluttered, fumbling for an answer, but Miranda rescued her.

"We're looking at all the names of the hunter clan members at the beginning of the book. All of them are dead, except for Clark. It's kind of horrible."

Quinn nodded. "It's one of the things I'm looking forward to taking out on Handon, that Naomi chick, Myles, and all the rest. They've caused enough pain in this world. As soon as my amulet is restored, we will take the fight to them."

She walked in and sat down opposite Taylor at the desk. "Can I look at the book? I haven't had a good look since I brought it back."

Taylor picked it up from the stand where it was propped for scanning and slid it over to Quinn. She flipped a few pages as she did, making sure Quinn didn't see the page with her name on it.

Quinn took it and flipped forward, staring at each page as willing the words to make sense to her. After a while, she stopped and closed the book. "Any luck finding the spell to repair my amulet?"

"Not yet," Taylor replied. "I should finish scanning the pages tomorrow. Then I'll start the process of translating them. A wild guess would be a few days? I don't know for sure."

Miranda moved around and sat by the end of the desk. "Quinn, Taylor might not find what we're looking for. Even if she does, I can promise you it's not going to be a simple fix since the magic that goes into things like your amulet is as complex as it is powerful."

"I'm not a complete idiot, Miranda," Quinn said. "None of this has been easy. You, of all of us, are the proof of that. The problem is, I can't shake the feeling that the amulet, with its connection to my lost family and me, is important somehow."

Quinn closed the book and stood. "I have to go meet

Clark. He has a new training program planned for today," she said. She pointed at the book. "Keep looking. That's all I ask."

She left the room, and Taylor pulled the book back to her side of the desk. Flipping it open and finding the page where she left off, Taylor began scanning the pages once more while Miranda watched.

CHAPTER SEVENTEEN

The next day, Quinn and Clark sat in the kitchen at the table, working at the daily ritual of caring for their blessed blades. Clark had his short sword out on the table while he slowly used a cloth to rub a fine coating of oil on the knife to protect the steel and silver alloy from rust and tarnish.

Across from him, Quinn ran her Bowie knife across the sharpening stone with smooth, even strokes. She flipped the blade over and began working on the bevel on the opposite side. Once the metal had been honed to an optimal edge, she'd complete the work as Clark did with the oil. She took her time, finding the whole thing to be a sort of meditation where she could calm her thoughts and focus on something simpler to understand than her complicated life.

Clark smiled as he watched her work. "You're getting really good at that, Quinn. I remember when I first taught you. I didn't think you'd ever get the hang of adding a double angle to the edge to help maintain it in combat."

"I guess I appreciate my blade a lot more now. It's saved me enough times."

Clark laughed. "That's the whole *point*, right?"

Quinn groaned at his joke. He tried to work it into every conversation about their blades. She held up the Bowie and checked the edge with her thumb. It was ready, and she picked up the cloth to begin applying the oil.

Taylor came into the kitchen, a distinct bounce in her step and a broad grin on her face. Miranda floated along behind her.

"I found it," Taylor announced, holding up her phone.

"The amulet spell?" Quinn asked.

"Well, it's a series of spells and rituals, but yeah."

Taylor came over and pulled a chair around to sit beside Quinn. She put her phone on the table and pointed to the image of one of the Tome's pages on the screen. "This is the first of six pages which discuss the creation of the protection amulets."

Quinn examined the screen. "It looks like a list or a recipe, but in Latin."

"It kind of is," Taylor replied. "This is a collection of three specific components needed. Below that there are the six separate enchantments used in the process. The magic is addressed in more detail throughout the following pages. They show the actual process and ritual involved. The components are something else and present a problem."

"Why, is there a shortage of eye of newt?" Clark asked.

Miranda said, "No, but we don't know where they are. We think at least some of them will have to be retrieved from those who took them when the clan was destroyed. I know where one is already, we'll go back to that later. Another is some special scrying bowl I've never heard of. The third is a ceremonial dagger. I think that has to be the dagger stolen from Clark's friend by the slayers. It's needed to gather the one final thing which I think will be easiest to get. I mean, it's probably not that much more difficult to get our hands on fae blood than it used to be a few hundred years ago."

"Blood? From a fae?" Quinn asked. "What kind of rituals are involved in this?"

"It's not as bad as it sounds," Taylor said, laughing a little. "From what I can tell, we're not talking about a lot of blood. It's just a few drops, but it is required. You can't substitute something else mystical like werewolf blood, for example. It has to be fae blood."

"Not just any blood either," Miranda added.

"I was getting to that," Taylor said. "The instructions refer to what translates as 'high-born' fae blood. Miranda takes it to mean the blood of a noble. I think it could just refer to the fae in general."

Clark shook his head. "Either way, getting fae blood without killing one is problematic. I don't know how they did it when the clan was still around, but it's not like we can sneak into a blood bank and get some. Maybe they waited until a fae went rogue, and then they collected the blood during the hunt. Now that it's just us, I'm not sure what we can do."

Quinn thought for a second and said, almost off-hand, "Maybe we just ask for some."

Clark laughed. "What, walk up to a random fae on the street and ask him for a little bit of blood?"

Quinn shrugged. "I don't hear a better idea," she said. She turned and looked at Clark. "Okay, we know some fae, or you do, at least. Where do we find a fae willing to bleed a little for us, preferably a 'high-born' one?"

"You really want to do this?" Clark shook his head when Quinn nodded and ran his hands through his graying hair. "There are a few hangouts downtown we could check out. I don't know how they'll feel about us showing up asking for blood from their patrons, but it isn't the craziest thing I've done since joining this clan."

Quinn didn't miss Clark's reference to their little group as "a clan." It broadened the smile that was already on her face. "Good, then let's do this. When do we leave?"

Clark glanced at his watch. "The places I'm thinking of won't open until after dark, so we have a few hours. Let's get in a few rounds of training, and then we can shower and leave."

"I'm definitely going along on this one," Taylor said. "I've been cooped up here at home for too long."

Clark started to say something, then shrugged and nodded. "Fine, you can come, too."

"Yes," Taylor said, pumping her fist. "Clubbing with the fae. It's going to be so much fun."

"How do you know?" Miranda asked with a huge grin on her face. "You've never been to a fae club before."

"Honestly, I haven't been to many clubs, but hey, it's a fae club. It sounds like the definition of a magical night."

Clark headed to the door. "Come on, Quinn. Maybe I

can drum a little of that enthusiasm out of you in the training room."

"You can try, old man," Quinn said, winking at Taylor as she followed Clark from the room. She wasn't as excited as Taylor was, but then, she hadn't been left at home every time the others left the hideout to do something. Still, this should be an exciting evening. Her few interactions with the fae had left her with an understanding that they were nothing if not unpredictable.

Clark waited at the door to the training room. He took off his leather jacket and laid it on a chair along with his sword and scabbard. "You're going to pay for that 'old man' remark. Let's try coming up with a different counter to that new move you worked out the other day. You still haven't been able to take me consistently when I use it on you. Now's your chance to show an *old man* how it's done."

Quinn cringed. This training session was going to be a hard one, shortened by their evening plans or not. She stripped down to her jeans and tank top and picked up the wooden practice blade that matched her Bowie.

Across from her, Clark had already armed himself with his practice sword. He didn't wait for her to assume a defensive position. He charged at her with his sword raised high. Before she knew it, she was down on the mat with his wooden blade pressed against her throat.

"Well, that counter didn't work," Clark said, helping her up. "Again."

Quinn groaned as she stood and prepared to receive his next attack, trying to calculate in the back of her mind the number of bouts he could fit into a two-hour training session. The answer she came up with didn't make her feel any better. Two seconds later, after she tried a different combination to counter Clark's next attack, she found herself spinning through the air and landing hard on her back at the edge of the mat.

"Again."

CHAPTER EIGHTEEN

Quinn walked down the steps at the front of the abandoned clinic toward the car. Clark and Taylor were already there, waiting for her.

"Are you limping?" Taylor said with a chuckle. "Wow, Clark, you weren't kidding when you said she might be late. She looks more than a little sore. What did you do to her?"

"I merely pointed out the difference between the words 'old' and 'experienced.' I believe Quinn knows the appropriate uses of them now."

"Oh, man," Quinn said as she walked up to the pair. "Is it going to be like this all night?"

Clark chuckled. "At least for the beginning of it. I'm still deeply hurt by your words."

"Yeah, whatever," Quinn said as she climbed into the front passenger seat. "Are we going or not? I need to put the last few hours behind me."

"Yep," Clark said as he got into the driver's seat. "I can't wait to see how this night ends."

"If you think it won't work, why are we going?" Quinn asked.

"I didn't say it wouldn't work. I've learned at this point that you have a way of twisting events to go your way, despite everyone else's plans or beliefs. I'm looking forward to finding out what tonight's epic twist will be."

Taylor laughed from her spot in the center of the back seat. "Careful, Clark. You might fool us into thinking you're enjoying yourself for a change."

"Never." Clark punctuated his statement by stepping on the accelerator and tearing up the gravel in the lot as they drove off.

Quinn couldn't hide her smile. She was finally getting started on the steps to get her amulet repaired. She knew it wouldn't be easy, but that didn't dampen her enthusiasm. Not even the aches and pains she felt from the drubbing Clark had given her in the training room earlier would do that. They'd fade soon enough as her huntress healing genes kicked in. She was never sore for more than a few hours after training.

Clark hadn't said much about where he was taking them, only that it was a club owned and frequented by fae and other creatures living in secret alongside the humans in the city. Quinn pictured something fanciful and old, something like the striped pavilion tents she'd seen when she encountered the fae summit a few months before.

The image she conjured didn't match up with what she saw when they pulled up across from the nondescript neighborhood restaurant in East Baltimore. She got out after Clark parked on the street and looked around. She'd lived in the city all her life, and this was just like many other working-class neighborhoods.

"The club is here?" Quinn asked, laughing a little in surprise.

"Surprised?" Clark said with a chuckle of his own. "Hiding in plain sight is something our mystical friends have mastered over the centuries. You have to try. Look for the signs that are there for anyone who possesses the ability to see."

Quinn scanned the street in both directions and tried to spot anything that screamed fae. It all looked completely normal to her.

Taylor got out and stood next to her, doing the same thing, and then pointed at an alley across the street. "Ooh, it's down there, isn't it?"

"Good catch, Taylor. See, Quinn, it's not hard."

"I still don't see anything. What are you talking about?"

"Try looking at it with your other sight engaged," Taylor suggested. "It's not there for normal people to see, just those who are magical in nature."

Quinn didn't want to give herself a headache accessing her huntress abilities outside the VR world, but she felt like she had to see what they were looking at. "This is why I need my amulet back. Then I wouldn't have to risk a migraine just to see the equivalent of a fae's neon sign."

Taylor laughed. "That's pretty good. You're close. Go ahead and see what I mean."

Quinn shook her head and closed her eyes, concentrating on engaging the HUD from the VR system. The stabbing pain began again in the back of her skull. After a vibration from the scar in the center of her chest, the overlay appeared, and Quinn opened her eyes.

She wasn't sure how to see what they were looking at, but she concentrated and an icon she hadn't seen before appeared. She engaged it. Right away, a colored filter rolled across her vision, tinting everything on the street in a blue outline. Then she saw it all and her mouth dropped in wonder.

"You see it now?" Taylor asked, a broad smile across her face.

Quinn nodded. She hadn't been far off with her neon sign comment. There, at the opening to the alley, a glowing red and green rectangle floated in the air. She could see nothing holding it up. It hovered about eight feet from the ground at the mouth of the alleyway.

The orange-red lettering spelled out the name of the club. Below the word, a shamrock pulsed with a green glow.

"O'Malley's?" Quinn read aloud. "Aside from the floaty sign, it looks and sounds like the name of a typical Irish pub."

"It's anything but typical. You'll see." Clark glanced left and right and then crossed the street and headed down the alley, disappearing into the shadows as soon as he entered.

"Come on," Taylor said, tugging Quinn's arm. "I'm not missing this for anything. We finally get a night out."

Quinn smiled and followed her best friend across the street and into the alley. It was dark as they entered, as if the illumination from the streetlights out front was absorbed by something in there.

"Dammit, I need to see." As soon as Quinn muttered the words, the alley lit up again.

Taylor clutched her arm. "I can't see a damned thing."

"Can you access magic or something like you did out front to see the sign?"

"I didn't think of that. Is it the same?"

"I don't know how it'll work for you. Maybe you need to let out some of your shifter side."

Taylor shook her head. "I don't know, Quinn. I'm not in control of that part of me yet."

"Try concentrating on the eyes," Quinn suggested. "Think about seeing the world like a wolf would."

Taylor stared straight ahead for a few seconds, then her eyes widened, and she turned around to face Quinn.

The change in her friend startled her at first. Taylor's eyes had changed color—her usually light blue irises were a glowing pale yellow.

"It worked. I can see everything now. Awesome, I can see in the dark," she said. Taylor stopped and stared at Quinn. "Why do you have that look on your face? Oh, no, did my face grow hair or something?"

"No, it's not anything like that. You look like yourself, except for your eyes. They're all glowy and yellow. It's pretty cool, actually. You should see it."

Taylor stomped her foot. "I can't. There's no mirrors or glass around here."

Quinn pointed to Clark, standing farther down the alley, waiting for them. "Maybe there's a mirror in there. You can check it out inside."

Clark stood by a stairway down to the basement

beneath the Italian restaurant. A smaller version of the O'Malley's sign hovered above the concrete stairs.

Taylor skipped over to the hunter, with Quinn in tow. She smiled and said, "Taylor said my eyes are glowing. What do you think?"

Clark chuckled. "You'll fit right in. There will probably be shifters down there, along with other sorts. Both of you, try to keep your comments to yourself, though. Some of the folk in there might be prickly."

Taylor closed her mouth but didn't stop smiling. She bounced on the balls of her feet and hooked her arm in Quinn's as they followed Clark down the steps.

At the bottom, he pulled open a heavy steel door and stepped into a small foyer. The pulsing beat of a subwoofer vibrated the tiny room. Quinn couldn't hear the music that went with it through the heavy wooden interior door.

"Clark Hunter, I haven't seen you in quite a while. I thought you were dead until I heard from herself that you were kicking around. Still trying to save the world?"

The bouncer seated on the stool at the entrance had to be six and a half feet tall, although it was hard to judge with him sitting down. His head almost touched the ceiling from where he sat atop the barstool. He had a long beard that hung down to the middle of his chest. Beneath the flowing beard, he wore a white collared shirt and a green vest buttoned across his chest, although the buttons strained a bit when he took a deep breath to speak, and khaki pants.

"Just trying to survive, as always, Jonas. You know how it is." Clark hooked a thumb toward the inside. "Is she in?"

"She was earlier, but she might have left out the back way. Based on what she's said about you lately, I'm not sure she'll be pleased you're here."

"Ungrateful as always."

Jonas shrugged. "I just work here," he said, nodding at Quinn and Taylor. "Those two young ladies with you? They seem a bit young for you if you don't mind me saying."

"Eww," Taylor said. "He's just a friend. We work together, okay?"

Jonas held his hands up in surrender. "Hey, I shouldn't have said anything. As usual, my big mouth got me in trouble," he said ruefully. The bouncer pulled out a folded stack of bills from his pants pocket. "It'll be a five bucks cover for each of you. There's a live band tonight."

Clark fished out a twenty and handed it to Jonas. "Keep the rest."

"Thanks, bud. I always did like you." Jonas stood and reached for the door. He was even taller than Quinn expected. He had to duck his head as he stepped back, pulling the door open.

Quinn had imagined a lot of things on the way there about what it would look like. The scene that greeted her as she walked in was nothing like any of her expectations.

As soon as the door opened, the pulsing beat of the subwoofer became the backbeat of an old country-western song. As she followed Clark into the club, peanut shells crunched beneath her feet with each step. Roasted peanuts filled a wooden barrel by the door, with a scoop and paper bowls so patrons could take some to their tables. Behind the barrel sat a stack of fifty-pound burlap sacks containing more peanuts. She wondered how many they consumed in a night to leave the floor littered with the shells the way it was.

Clark grabbed a handful of peanuts as he passed, breaking open one and popping the nuts in his mouth before discarding the empty shell on the floor. He angled toward the tables close to the bar, avoiding the dance floor in front of the bandstand. The five-piece group consisted of four men playing instruments, including guitar, bass, keyboard, and drums. The lead singer was a woman in tight blue jeans and a white satin shirt, with a long row of fringe across the front at the level of her breasts. All five of them wore cowboy hats.

Patrons filled the open floor, performing a line dance of some sort that had them occasionally slapping their boots as they turned in place. Taylor tugged Quinn, reminding her to keep moving, and she turned and hurried to catch up.

Clark settled down at a small round table by the wall. Quinn and Taylor sat down beside him.

"A freaking honky-tonk bar? Really?" Quinn said finally, still trying to take it all in.

Clark leaned closer and shouted so he could be heard over the band. "The fae go through phases when they become obsessed with different cultures. This particular phase has stuck longer than most. That damned *Achy-Breaky* song started it with them, just like it did with the humans. The difference was, it didn't fade after a few years with the fae. They liked America in the old days when it had frontiers and lots of wild places. I think this makes them nostalgic for the past."

Quinn shook her head. It was the most bizarre thing she'd seen in a while. It was just too strange.

Taylor seemed to be enjoying herself and wasn't bothered by the strangeness of it all. "Come on. Let's go dance. There are a bunch of cute guys up there."

"No, I don't think so," Clark said. "I don't know the moves."

"It can't be that hard."

Quinn shook her head, and Taylor said, "Well, I'm not missing out on having fun, even if you two are."

She jumped up, and with a yell, jumped into the line between two tall urban cowboys, laughing as she tried to get the footwork right.

Quinn smiled. Taylor could make friends anywhere. It was one of the things that had endeared her to Quinn. She'd used that trait to get a much younger Quinn to trust her when she needed it the most.

"I can't figure that girl out," Clark said. He laughed as Taylor missed a step and tripped the guy to her left. They both laughed it off, though, and they were soon back in the mix of people moving through the dance moves.

"She's not that hard to understand. Taylor is exactly what she says she is. There's never anything hidden with her. She shows the world the person she is without any reservations."

"Not what I expected from someone who spends so much time behind a computer screen."

Quinn nodded. "I think that's why she's this way when she's out and around people. She gets lonely, even though she loves the work and challenges of programming. We really should have tried to get her out sooner than this. I've been too busy thinking about my own problems and not worrying about what she needed."

"You shouldn't beat yourself up about it," Clark said. "This is the first opportunity we've had to do anything like this. There's been a lot going on with her shifting and with us on the run, trying to regroup. Hopefully, we've started on the road to a little more stability."

"I hope so," Quinn said. She laughed as Taylor tripped again and almost took down a whole line of people.

A waitress came by the table. She barely stood taller than the surface. "What'll it be?"

"Beer for me. Two Cokes for the ladies."

"Be right back."

The woman left toward the bar, and Quinn said, "At least she's not a giant like Jonas outside."

"She's one of the owner's daughters. They don't get very tall."

"They?" Quinn asked.

"Leprechauns."

"No way!"

Clark laughed. "I didn't tell you that on the way here? I must have forgotten."

Quinn punched Clark on the shoulder. "No, you did not mention it. I think you decided to see if we noticed."

"You would have picked up on it on your own, I suspect. The owner has a long relationship with the fae. A particular fae set him up in business over a hundred years ago when he first came here. In return, he keeps a place here for his patron to hang out and be safe from prying human eyes."

"Who's this patron?"

"Filippa."

"What?" Quinn said and looked around. "No, let's go right now. That woman betrayed us and got Miranda killed in the process. I'm not dealing with her again. She's lucky I don't hunt her down just to prove a point."

Clark leaned in, his smile gone. "Watch what you say in here. These folks can be very prickly about things, especially when one of us threatens to hunt one of them down. It's like talking about bombs in an airport."

"But—"

"No. Listen to me. Sometimes you have to let past battles and losses go. The fae operate under their own code of loyalty and responsibility. You can't ascribe human codes of conduct to them."

"Aren't you pissed off about what happened? They could've warned us not to come and rescue them. We could have avoided confronting Handon."

Quinn's anger had her voice rising in volume again. Clark held out a hand to quiet her down.

"There will be a time and place where we can play that card, but not in a way that threatens a fae princess, or any other fae, for that matter."

"What, other fae like Alistair, her snooty butler?" Quinn nodded past Clark's shoulder. The fae major-domo stood on the opposite side of the bar beside a wooden door. He stared right at the hunter and huntress.

"Him, too," Clark said as he turned to see where she was looking. He stopped when he spotted Alistair. "Oh, good.

He's here. That means she's still here as well. Sit tight while I go talk to him. You're a little worked up, and the negotiations might be a little much for you right now."

"I'm fine. Let's go talk to him and get this over with. I had assumed she went back to wherever it was she came from in the old country."

"Apparently not. That could work in our favor. Keep quiet and try to follow along."

Clark stood. Quinn got up, and they went around the bar to where the tall fae butler stood.

Alistair offered a grin as they approached, but it didn't reach his eyes, which were as cold as ice. "I'm surprised to see the two of you out and about. I'd heard you were in hiding after a run-in with a certain vampire."

Quinn had promised to be quiet, but it didn't hold her back. "You have the nerve to bring that up? We were there to save your boss's life. We lost a good friend because of it."

Alistair ignored Quinn and fixed his gaze on Clark. "Is that why you're here, to level accusations?"

"No, we came for something else," Clark said. He glared at Quinn for a second and then turned back to Alistair. "I hoped we could meet with Filippa for a few minutes."

"The princess is a busy person. She is in the process of wrapping up some business so she can return home. This trip has been tiring, to say the least."

"Nonetheless, please announce us so she can make that decision on her own. I really must insist."

Alistair considered his demand for a few seconds, then nodded. "I'll announce you. I do not think that will change anything, but it is my job to serve and advise only. I'll be right back."

The fae turned and opened the door just far enough to slip through, closing it behind him.

Quinn craned her neck to try to see inside. All she saw were stacks of beer kegs and wooden crates. "I can't believe he was going to brush us off after all we did to try to help them."

"I told you to be quiet, Quinn. The fae have to be handled a certain way. They don't look at things the way we do. It has to do with their long lifespans."

"Well, I'm human and don't have a longer than normal life ahead of me. I have things that need doing now."

"Which is why we're here." Clark was about to say something else when the leprechaun waitress came over with their drinks on a tray.

"There you two are. I wondered where you'd disappeared to. Where do you want these?"

"We'll take the beer and one of the Cokes," Clark said, lifting the pewter tankard of beer from the tray and handing Quinn one of the other two glasses. "Put the last one on the table for our friend for after she's finished dancing," he said as he pulled a twenty-dollar bill from his pocket and handed it to her. "Is this enough to cover it?"

"Yeah, I'll get your change."

"Keep it. And keep an eye out. Tell our friend we're in the back chatting with the princess if she comes back to the table looking for us."

The woman smiled and nodded at Clark, slipping the money in her pocket. "If you need anything else, just send for me. I'm Juni."

She headed back to the bar to fill her other orders. The

door behind them opened, and Alistair appeared. There was no smile on his face this time. He seemed perturbed.

"Her Highness will see you. I urge you to respect her time. She has much she needs to accomplish."

Clark smiled and gestured for Quinn to follow as Alistair held the door for them. The huntress fell into step behind Clark, and they followed Alistair into the bar's back rooms.

CHAPTER NINETEEN

Quinn wasn't sure what she expected to find behind the door, but it wasn't this. Once again, she was a little disappointed. It looked like the back room of a bar should look. There were no magical enhancements or secret fae enchantments going on. It was just a long narrow room that went on and on like a long hall.

Alistair led them past stacked crates of booze and beer kegs to another door in the wall to the left. The storeroom went on farther, disappearing into darkness because the lights only extended this far.

As Quinn stared into the darkness, a twinge of cold vibrated the scar on her chest. Her hand drifted up to touch it through the t-shirt. She peered into the darkness. What was down there?

Alistair cleared his throat, bringing her back to the task at hand. Once he had her attention, he knocked twice before stepping to the side.

A muffled voice from inside said, "Come."

Alistair opened the door and waved the two of them through. Clark led the way, with Quinn close behind.

Filippa sat in a worn padded leather chair near a beat-up metal desk. Behind the desk sat a very short man. One look at him, and Quinn knew he had to be Juni's father and the owner of the bar. There was a strong family resemblance.

Clark nodded to Filippa first and then to the leprechaun. "Filippa, Paddy. It's good to see you both."

Paddy O'Malley stood and came around the desk to shake Clark's hand. "Clark, me boyo, it's been too long since you stopped in. Did you see Juni out front?"

"I did, although I didn't recognize her at first. I don't think she knew who I was."

"That tells you how long it's been since you stopped in. I know you're here for business tonight, but promise you'll come back another time and stay for a while."

"I'll do that, Paddy. Thank you. This is my protégé, Quinn Faust."

The small man turned to Quinn and took her hand in a firm, calloused grip. "You're the one that's been causing such a stir lately. Should I call you Mistress Huntress, or is Quinn okay?"

The twinkle in his eyes as he said it told Quinn he meant no harm. She smiled and said, "I answer to most anything, but Quinn is fine."

The leprechaun tapped the side of his head with a fingertip and laughed. "Can't be too careful when addressing someone with your potential. I hope you'll consider my little establishment a place you can rest and eat in peace. I don't allow the problems of the outside world inside, so you and everyone else are safe here."

Quinn didn't miss the meaning of what he said. O'Malley's was meant to be neutral ground. She was being told to keep her battles outside the bar. She wondered how he backed up the inherent threat to anyone who violated that neutrality.

"I appreciate your hospitality and offer of safety. It's welcome, and I won't do anything to violate the peace, I promise."

"Good, good, then I'll leave the three of you to your discussion. I should go out front and show my face, so people know I'm around."

He left the small office and shut the door, leaving Clark, Quinn, and Filippa alone.

The fae princess, dressed in black slacks and a blue silk blouse, gestured to the two folding chairs against the wall opposite where she sat. "Grab those and sit, please. I'm sure you have a great deal to discuss, and it'll help to be comfortable."

Quinn bristled a little at the casual, offhand manner Filippa displayed. There was no hint of remorse in her tone or indication any apology was coming. Clark opened a chair for her first and then got himself one and sat down next to Quinn, across from Filippa.

Filippa picked up her glass, filled with a deep red liquid Quinn assumed was wine, and took a sip before saying, "I'm surprised it took so long for you two to come looking for me. You humans are always in such a hurry to seek out justice for any perceived slight."

"So, you admit you screwed up," Quinn said, triumph filling her voice.

"I do nothing of the sort, my dear. I merely acknowledged my surprise it took you so long to come to accuse me of wrongdoing. Humans are usually so predictable. I've been studying your habits and your penchant to rush to judgment for a very long time."

Clark held out a hand toward Quinn to stop her from talking. "Quinn doesn't know you like I do, Filippa. She assumes you failed to notify us on purpose about your early release from Handon's custody. I know you wouldn't be so callous about our safety."

Filippa waved a hand in the air and said, "Actually, Clark, your young huntress is quite correct. Part of the agreement for our release was to tell no one about it. John didn't want people to know about our arrangement until certain business between us was completed. I'm afraid you and your companions got caught up in it by accident."

"We came to rescue you, Filippa," Clark said. His voice had a hard edge to it now.

Quinn knew that tone and smiled. Angry Clark was fun when he wasn't focused on you.

"Clark, my darling, I'm flattered you felt the need to come to my rescue, but you should know by now I'm able to take care of myself. That was all a misunderstanding. A business negotiation gone wrong, if you will."

Quinn couldn't believe her ears. "A business negotiation? Our friend died while you were negotiating your business with that beast and his minions. What did you *negotiate* while Miranda's lifeblood spilled out of her?"

"I'm afraid that's confidential, Huntress. As I said, my

brethren and I can take care of ourselves. No one asked you to come to my aid, did they?"

Quinn didn't know how to answer that. Handon's demon-kinder, using VirSync tech, had invaded the fae summit and kidnapped two of the princesses in attendance. They'd killed numerous fae attendants in the process. Why wouldn't they want Quinn and her friends to help with the rescue?

"I can see by your silence that I'm correct. There's no way I can be held responsible for your human assumptions about our needs. It is a shame your friend was injured. However, you did kill several of John's followers as well, so I guess that's a fair trade."

Quinn struggled to tamp down her anger. She wanted to leap across the office and throttle the smug woman.

Clark leaned forward and said, "Still, we did lose one of our own, acting in good faith to help you. Surely that is worth a small boon on your part?"

Filippa smiled. "There it is. You did come because you needed something from me and not just to shout at me. What is it you need, darling? Money, perhaps a safe place to stay?"

"Nothing so crass as that, Filippa. This is something only you can provide."

The princess's eyes twinkled with amusement. "You've piqued my interest. I can't imagine what you could need from me that is so personal."

"We didn't just lose our friend in the battle with John Handon. We also lost a precious item, something dear to Quinn that cannot be replaced without your help."

Filippa turned and studied Quinn.

Quinn met her eyes with a smile. She didn't think the woman would be able to guess what it was in a million years. She wanted to see the look in her eyes when Clark told her what they needed.

Filippa stared at Quinn, then glanced at her chest for a second and grinned. "The amulet. You lost your link to your newfound clan, and you need me to help make a new one. Why not just steal it back from whichever of John's minions took it? I suspect I know which one has it."

"They didn't take it from me," Quinn said. "I overused it, and it melted."

"Oh, my. That's quite an accomplishment, Huntress. I know a little something about those charms of yours, and they are quite resilient and formidable. What did you do, if you don't mind me asking? It would take quite a bit of power to destroy one outright like that."

Clark interrupted Quinn before she could answer. "How she did it is beside the point. She has the silver to remake it, but she needs certain components that aren't so easy to come by to enable the enchantment to take hold."

Filippa sighed. "The blood. I told my brethren when they helped the early hunters create the amulets and their protection magic that we should've come up with an alternative ingredient. It was always such a bother when one of the clans would come seeking to resupply."

"We only need a small amount, Filippa," Clark said. "Taylor says it should only take a few drops."

"It doesn't matter if I give you the blood or not. There are other rare components you'll need that I know you don't have. Without them, my blood is useless to you."

"I suppose you know what they are and where we can find them?" Quinn asked.

"A crystal scrying bowl, for one. I seem to remember a ceremonial dagger and a magical gemstone of some sort. Then, of course, there's the blessing of a close blood relative to enable the protection. You're an orphan, are you not, my dear? That means you—"

Quinn jumped to her feet. "I know what it means, Filippa. I grew up knowing all too well, so you don't have to explain it to me. Come on, Clark, this is a waste of time. I don't want to be beholden to this woman for anything. She can't be trusted."

"Sit down, Quinn," Clark ordered. "Now."

Quinn considered leaving anyway. She realized Clark hadn't moved a muscle when Filippa listed the components. He must have a workaround. Clenching her fists to try to control her anger, Quinn sat again and crossed her arms.

Clark turned back to Filippa. "Suppose I'm able to figure out the other components. The only thing I don't know is the whereabouts of the bowl. The one belonging to my clan was lost in the purges. It was probably smashed to bits during the fighting in the chapter house at the end."

Filippa didn't answer, although her smile broadened as she listened.

"How much?" Clark asked.

"What do you mean?" Filippa countered. The smile never left her face.

"I know who has the dagger and the gemstone. I need the bowl, and you wouldn't have mentioned it unless you knew where it was. You wouldn't tell me anything unless you needed something from us."

"See, Clark? All that time we spent together paid off. You've learned to think like a fae. You were an apt pupil, among other things."

"I repeat, what is it you need?"

"A dear friend of mine has the bowl. She acquired it at an auction in the supernatural community following the dissolution of the clan assets. At the time, there were no survivors," Filippa said. She paused and then smiled. "Well, none we knew of."

"Who has it?" Clark asked.

"If I tell you, will you promise to pick up something else of mine she has while you're at it?"

Clark and Filippa engaged in a brief staring contest as if pushing each other in a test of wills.

"I won't agree to something without knowing what I'm stealing and from whom, Filippa. I've been burned before."

"Oh, very well," the fae said, waving her hand at him and dismissing his concerns. "It's my cousin Aurora. She has a home on the Eastern Shore of Maryland, just a few hours away. It's quite a nice place, right on the shores of the Chesapeake Bay. The scrying bowl is on display at her place. It was on the mantle over her dining room's fireplace the last time I was there. She's really quite proud of it."

"And the item for you?" Clark asked.

"It's a green ceramic egg. It should be in a case in the sitting room next to the dining room. Fetch that for me, and you can keep anything else you find there. She has many collections of rare and valuable items. You could make yourself a tidy sum selling what you find. Be careful, and wear gloves when handling the egg. Skin oils can deteriorate the finish and affect its value."

"We're not common thieves, Filippa," Clark said. "We're after the bowl, and in return, we'll pick up this egg of yours, but that's it."

"Suit yourself," Filippa said, waving off the statement. "I merely thought you could use the extra money, being on the run and all."

"We are doing just fine, thank you," Quinn said. "Give us the address for your cousin, and we'll get on our way."

"Don't need it, Quinn," Clark said. "I know Aurora. I know where her country house is."

"Oh, right. You stayed with her for a while after I left for the old country."

Quinn glanced at Clark. How many old fae girlfriends did he have?

Clark stood, and Quinn joined him. "Where should we bring the fancy egg once we find it?"

"You can bring it here and give it to Paddy. He'll know how to get it to me."

"Good enough," Clark said. "Come on, Quinn. We're done here."

"I agree," Quinn said. "Goodbye, Filippa."

"Farewell, Huntress. Good luck on this hunt. I think it will be a fun one."

Quinn turned without responding and pushed past Clark to lead the way back to the bar. They had to pick up Taylor and get back to Spring Grove. Quinn wasn't sure how she felt about it, but they had a heist to plan.

CHAPTER TWENTY

Outside the small roadside motel, Quinn stood staring across the gravel parking lot at the fields. A large tractor rolled through the rows of what she thought was corn, cutting down the stalks in neat lines. Born and raised in the city as she was, she hadn't seen much of the state of Maryland outside Baltimore. Aside from a few school field trips, she'd rarely left the city.

For the last month on the run, they'd lived in the more rural suburbs surrounding the city. This was something else altogether. Here, across the Chesapeake Bay on the Delmarva Peninsula, called the Eastern Shore by most locals, it was mostly farms with scattered housing developments.

Taylor's voice carried through the open door of the room behind her. "I think I found a way in."

"For real this time?" Quinn asked.

"Hey, if you want to hack their security systems, you're welcome to try."

"Sorry, T," Quinn said. "I'm tired of being cooped up

here. It's been three days since we got here, and we still don't have a reliable way to get past the perimeter and into the house. Aside from making a direct assault and confronting the guards patrolling the grounds, we don't have anything in the way of a plan."

"Let her talk," Clark murmured from the second bed in the small motel room. He lay on top of the floral bedspread with his eye closed, as he'd done for most of the time they were here. Quinn had assumed he was asleep.

Taylor shot Quinn a grin at Clark's words. "I haven't been able to hack into the security system OS. I still can't disable it remotely, but I did find a way into their camera feed."

"I can see how that'll help in planning," Quinn said. "But how's it going to help us get in?"

"Because they'll let us in."

"What?" Clark and Quinn both echoed together.

Clark sat up, really interested now.

Taylor smiled now that she had their undivided attention. "I first got camera access yesterday but didn't say anything, because like you said, how did it help us beyond planning? Then I noticed there were a lot of vehicles coming and going and parked around the building. After a little research and hacking into the local building permit system, I found out they're doing some sort of renovation and remodel of the whole downstairs."

"So?" Quinn asked. "You want us to hide in a work truck?"

"Not exactly. I checked into the work vehicles on-site and followed them back to their business operations. I found the general contractor in charge of the job and got into his system."

Taylor pointed to a window she had opened on her laptop. "There's a whole string of messages between the contractor and this plumber. The regular plumber they use is not available, so they've hired this new guy from a few towns over. According to the emails, they don't know each other except by reputation."

Clark chuckled. "It's almost too easy. We get his gear and assume his place. You know where this other plumber is located, right?"

"Yep," Taylor said. "He's ten miles from here in Sudlersville. I have his address and everything."

Quinn looked at her friends. "Someone clue me in because I'm confused. We don't know anything about plumbing."

"We don't have to," Taylor said. "We only need to get in there long enough to find the bowl and the egg. Then we make an excuse that we forgot something back at the shop, and we leave. We can be in and out in an hour or less and do it during broad daylight."

"I like it," Clark said. "Score a win for the tech witch."

Taylor beamed, then extended her arms, hands interlaced, and cracked her knuckles.

Quinn looked at the live camera feed on Taylor's laptop. She saw the collection of work vans in the driveway. It certainly made sense, but this whole thing still bothered her on another level.

"Clark, are we sure this is a good idea?"

"What?" Clark asked. "We're doing this to restore your amulet."

"I know, but I'm talking about pissing off another fae princess and her faction working for a rival. I feel like we're just doing Filippa's dirty work for her. If we get caught or cause a major problem, she can wash her hands of the whole thing."

"We don't have a whole lot of options, Quinn," Taylor said. "This gets us the things we need to start repairing the amulet. That puts us back in business against the slayers and whatever Handon is up to. We have the VR system up and running. With your amulet and what you can do when you have it, we'll be unstoppable."

Quinn knew Taylor was right, but was the end worth the means? She knew the fae were powerful friends, and that meant they'd be powerful enemies, too.

Clark got up and ran his hand through his hair. "It's almost dinnertime. Let's go eat and hammer out a plan. Then we'll pay this plumber over in Sudlersville a visit. Taylor, use his email account to send the contractor a message saying we'll be there tomorrow. We'll borrow this guy's truck and convince him to take the day off. I have enough cash with me to pay him to pretend we drugged him and stole his vehicle to do the job."

Quinn nodded but was still uneasy. Filippa had been too quick to give up the information, as well as offering them her blood, without any apparent reservations. It didn't make sense, even if they did recover this egg she wanted.

Taylor shut her laptop and hopped up from the small desk in the corner. "Let's go to the Crab House again."

"Good idea," Clark said. "Their food is good."

Quinn groaned.

Taylor laughed. "How do you grow up in Baltimore and not like crabs? I can't understand."

"I don't like seafood, especially crabs. It's like eating giant sea bugs."

"Yeah," Taylor said. "Delicious giant sea bugs."

Clark grabbed his keys off the dresser and headed out the door. Taylor followed, and Quinn brought up the rear, pulling the door shut behind her. She checked to make sure it was locked and headed to the car. There was other food at the restaurant besides crabs, but she was tired of seeing them piled in the middle of their table, staring at her with their tiny black eyes.

At least they could be back in Baltimore tomorrow night. That would be one positive thing if they finished up the job tomorrow. No more crabs for a while, and she'd get the satisfaction of watching Filippa bleed for them. That would make all this worth it.

CHAPTER TWENTY-ONE

Quinn sat in the white panel van's passenger seat while Clark drove to the job site. He wore a tan long-sleeve work shirt with a patch over the left breast that read Joe. It matched the sign on the side of the van, Joe the Plumbing Guy. Taylor sat behind Quinn, perched on a five-gallon bucket.

Joe had driven a hard bargain, wanting more cash than Clark had with him. The hunter told him he could not only take the money and keep the job at the same time, he could also file a claim for insurance on any equipment the thieves supposedly stole from him. He jumped on it. It had cost them a thousand dollars in cash. Quinn knew it was a big part of their reserves. She hoped it was worth it.

"We're almost there, Clark," Quinn said. She'd been following their progress on her map app.

"Yes, the turnoff is just up ahead. Remember, stick to the story," Clark said. "You're both students from a local tech school riding along to learn the ropes for the semester. Call me Joe. I'll use your real names."

Quinn tugged at the work shirt she wore, borrowed from Joe. It was a gray short-sleeved polo shirt with a Joe the Plumbing Guy patch on the left breast. Joe told them he kept several on hand for when he hired part-time helpers. He was happy to loan them to the team. Quinn suspected he'd add them to the fraudulent insurance claim he planned to file.

Taylor reached forward and patted Quinn on the shoulder. "Don't worry, Quinn. This is going to be a cinch."

"We don't know where the bowl or the egg are kept. With the renovation going on, everything's been moved around. They don't show up on any of the internal security videos you retrieved. For all we know, they've been moved to a vault off-site."

"Aren't you a bundle of happiness and optimism?" Taylor said.

"I can't shake the feeling this is all wrong for some reason."

Clark said, "We'll be back on the road in an hour, two tops. A quick search of the house and we leave. It's easy." He turned into the lane on the right. The road sign read Aurora Fields Drive.

They drove about a quarter-mile down the tree-lined lane until they came to a closed metal gate and a speaker box on a post.

Clark leaned out the driver's side and pressed a button on the box.

"Can I help you?" the tinny voice on the speaker asked.

"Joe the Plumbing Guy. I'm assigned to do a bathroom install today."

There was a pause, then the guy on the other side said, "Yeah, I got you on the list. Come on in. Park with the other work vans."

The gate opened and rolled back to let them in. Clark drove to the mansion at the other end of the driveway. The concrete and iron fence extended all the way around the two-acre perimeter. A carpenter's pickup truck with several ladders stored on a rack mounted in the back was parked by the side entrance. A carpet installation van was pulled up next to the carpenter's vehicle.

"Busy day on the job site," Clark observed. He parked their van and turned to the two ladies. "Remember the plan. You two follow me in. While I talk to the guy in charge, make an excuse to find the restroom. Since we're doing an install on the one closest to this side of the house, you'll have to go farther in to find one. Be fast but efficient. Cover as much ground as you can in five minutes or so, then come back."

"I hope we find the stuff on the first pass," Quinn said.

"Me, too," Taylor replied. "Then we'd have time for one more visit to the Crab House for lunch before driving back to Baltimore."

"We are not sticking around once we get out of here," Clark said. "We are taking Joe's van back to where we left the car and leaving it on the side of the road, just like a group of thieves would do. After that, we're driving straight back home. We don't need to stick around in a place like this where everyone who doesn't live here sticks out like a sore thumb."

"Thank God, no more crabs," Quinn said.

Clark and Taylor laughed.

The three of them got out of the van. Clark grabbed a clipboard with the job notes Joe had helpfully printed out for them. The guy seemed tickled to be part of the caper. He was happy to lend a hand with things like the shirts and the paperwork.

Clark led the way through the open side door. Inside the entrance was a hallway that led to the largest dining room Quinn had ever seen. Tarps covered the floor, and the smell of fresh paint hung in the air. They followed Clark through the room until they reached the kitchen. A guy in khaki pants and a blue polo shirt sat drinking a cup of coffee and flipping through his phone.

He looked up and then stood when they walked in. "You must be Joe."

"Yep, that's me. You Vince?" Clark asked, shaking the guy's hand.

"Yep. Who are your helpers?"

"This is Quinn and Taylor. I offer internships to kids from WorWic College's tech program. I hope that's okay?"

"Sure, you're the one responsible for the quality of the work. I'm not concerned. I've heard good things about you." Vince turned to Quinn and Taylor. "Hello, ladies."

Vince reached out to shake their hands. As soon as Quinn got close enough, she caught the distinct whiff of wet dog. *He was a werewolf.* Quinn and the others hadn't counted on there being more than a few fae guards here. Now she wondered about the other contractors working at the site. Were there any other supernaturals around?

"It's good to know I've got a good reputation," Clark

said as Vince turned back after greeting his helpers. "You're only as good as your last job."

Vince laughed. "That's the truth."

Clark looked around and said, "What's the deal here?"

Vince glanced over his shoulder and then whispered. "A lady with more money than sense if you ask me. This is the third remodel I've done here in five years, not that I'm complaining. I've got two kids in college, and this is paying for it."

"I need to get on your contractor list if you've got regular work."

"Nah, just this one. The rest are piecemeal, just like everyone else. Things are slow this time of year."

Clark nodded. "Hey, why don't you show me to the job and we can get started?"

"Sure, it's right through here." Vince turned

Taylor raised her hand. "Um, Mr. Joe? Quinn and I have been on the road since we left school this morning. We need a pit stop."

"Oh, yeah. Where's the closest bathroom for the ladies, Vince?"

Vince pointed to a second hall leading off the kitchen. "There's one back that way by the home theatre room. Just be sure you don't touch anything. Stuff in this place costs a bundle, and security is watching everything on the cameras while we're here."

"Yes, sir," Quinn said. "We'll be really careful."

She led the way, with Taylor right behind as Vince took Clark down the other hall to where the bathroom installation was supposed to happen.

The hall to the theatre passed several other rooms, and they peeled off in turn to search the first floor. They didn't have to worry about the video security system. Taylor had taken care of the cameras, hacking into the cloud storage site so they showed a looped video from the day before.

The first three rooms yielded nothing, and Quinn met Taylor back in the hallway. The next room down the corridor was the theater room. When they reached it, they found eight reclining theatre seats in two rows of four facing a screen covering the entire far wall.

At the back room was a small sink and refrigerator built into a tall, floor-to-ceiling bookshelf holding video disc cases arranged in careful rows. There were also two empty shelves. One held a sizeable cut-crystal bowl about twelve inches across. On the other was a green egg about the size of a football.

Quinn walked over to the shelves to examine the two objects up close. There were tiny spotlights recessed in the ceiling to illuminate them. It surprised her that the ceramic egg sparkled so much more than the crystal bowl. The outer surface cast tiny rainbow sparkles where the light reflected from it. Quinn reached out and traced a fingertip down the side of the shell. The warmth of the outer surface surprised her. She yanked her finger back from the egg when a static spark stung her finger.

Taylor had gone on to the next room when Quinn came in here, so she had to leave the shelf and return to the hallway to get the tech witch.

"Hey, T, I found them."

Taylor came back into the hallway from the room across the way. "Where?"

"In the theater. Come on. Let's get back to Clark. Then we can return with boxes for them. They're both bigger than we planned."

The plan had been to use the plumber's tool cases or perhaps one of the cardboard boxes they'd brought to smuggle the two items back out to the van without anyone seeing them.

Taylor and Quinn headed back to find Clark. He and Vince were just finishing checking out the room under the stairs where the new bathroom was to be installed.

"There's not a lot of space to fit both the toilet and pedestal sink, but you told me you could make it work."

"That's why I get the big bucks," Clark said. "We'll get it done. Don't worry."

Vince nodded. "I'm counting on it. I have to talk to the lady of the house now and give her an update. If you need anything after that, call me. I have to go and check on another job site."

"I don't think we'll need you, but I'll call if anything comes up."

Vince left, and Clark waited until he was gone then turned to Quinn and Taylor. "Good news, I suppose?"

"Yes and no," Quinn said. "Both items are in the theater room. We just need to get some boxes in here, and then Taylor and I will grab them."

"And the bad news?" Clark asked.

"You know Vince is a werewolf, right?"

"Of course," Clark replied. "It's not unusual for people in our community to support each other's businesses. I'm sure he realized Taylor was a shifter, too. It lends us credibility."

"If you say so," Quinn said. She wasn't sold and remained on guard. She worried about the additional danger of Vince being a shifter.

Clark clapped his hands. "Okay, let's head out to the van and start bringing in the gear. Since Vince is planning on leaving soon, we'll need to make it look like we're getting started until he goes to the other site."

The two of them nodded and followed Clark out to load up the folding cart Joe kept in the back of the van. There was also a two-wheeled dolly back there to move heavy equipment around. The toilet and sink were in the rear of the vehicle as well. They decided to bring them in, too, since the three of them had to make up extra work to do until the contractor left.

It took Vince over an hour to wrap up his business and leave for the other site. During that time, Clark had started to prep the toilet for the installation.

"How do we know we're not screwing something up or doing it wrong?" Quinn asked.

"I've put a few of these in before and repaired others."

"When?" Taylor asked.

"I haven't always worked as a hunter. After the purges, when I was hiding from assassins, I took any odd job I could find. Now bring me that wax ring, and I'll show you how to seat a toilet so it doesn't leak."

Quinn and Taylor worked with Clark to get the new toilet in place over the newly installed drainpipe in the floor. The process kept Quinn's mind off her worries about why they were here.

Taylor came back from the van. Clark had sent her out

to get a small toolbox with pipe fittings for the water line to the toilet.

She set the metal box down and said, "Vince just left. The carpet guys are gone, too. It's just the two carpenters and us, and they're working out back on a new deck."

"Perfect," Clark said. He dumped out the toolbox, leaving the pile of curved pipe fittings on the floor of the new bathroom. "Will either of the pieces fit in here?"

Taylor nodded. "The egg will, I'm pretty sure."

Quinn glanced around and spotted a broad, flat cardboard box that used to have a coil of copper tubing in it. "This should work for the scrying bowl."

"Good. You girls go get the two items. Don't forget to wear those work gloves I bought you. I don't want you leaving fingerprints for an investigator if they report the theft. I'll stay here and keep working so nobody gets suspicious about nothing getting done. Hurry up. We'll leave as soon as you get back."

Quinn said, "We need to figure out if the cases are alarmed or protected by spells."

"I can do both, Quinn," Taylor replied. "We've got this. Come on."

Taylor headed off down the hallway, and Quinn followed her back to the theater. Taylor set the empty toolbox on the floor and checked out the two shelves up close. Quinn came over and helped. The two of them examined the items from all sides as well as they could. Each rested on a small padded disk.

"See any wires?" Taylor asked.

"Nope," Quinn said. "But the disks are probably pressure sensors or something. How about magic? Do you know enough to detect a protection spell or an alarm spell?"

"I think so," Taylor said. She got a faraway look in her eyes, and her face went blank for a few seconds. When it returned to normal, she turned to Quinn and said, "I don't see any magical energy around either of them. There is something holding powerful magic inside the house. I can sense it somewhere, but it's not in here."

"Good," Quinn said, checking the door. She scratched the center of her chest. Her scar itched, and she wondered if it meant anything. Pushing down her worries, Quinn pulled on her gloves and said, "Get the box ready as I lift the bowl."

Taylor joined her in front of the shelf holding the bowl and held open the flaps of the box while Quinn picked up the artifact. She bent down and placed it in the cardboard box.

Taylor flipped the flaps closed and smiled. "One down."

Quinn's scar twinged again, and she jerked her head around to check the open doorway. It was clear, and she turned back and went to help Taylor with the big green egg.

Before they even got to the egg, a voice from behind her froze them in their tracks.

"My dear Huntress, if you wanted to borrow one of my toys, why didn't you just come to me and ask?"

Quinn and Taylor turned around to face a tall, thin woman with long straight hair the color of honey draped over her shoulders. The tips of her pointed ears peeked from beneath her hair on either side. Behind the woman who had to be the fae princess Aurora stood four burly guards, each armed with black batons in addition to holstered pistols on their hips.

Quinn's shoulders sagged, and she raised her hands to match Taylor's, holding them high.

CHAPTER TWENTY-TWO

Quinn sat beside Taylor in the front row of theater seats, their hands bound in front of them with zip-ties. The four guards stood with their backs to the screen, watching the two. They made no menacing moves other than standing there, black police batons held in front of them.

The princess had left without saying anything else. Quinn hoped Clark had enough sense to try to get away. She knew he wouldn't, though.

She heard him in the distance, answering that particular question. The voices drew closer, and Quinn and Taylor twisted in their seats to see the doorway. Clark and Aurora entered together. Another pair of guards came in behind them, but they weren't detaining or holding the hunter. His hands weren't bound, either.

"My cousin likes to play these little games. It's one of the reasons I moved out of the city. I grew tired of the constant drama."

"I wish I had the luxury to just disconnect," Clark said.

"Unfortunately, I have to keep the world from descending into a festering pit of demons."

Aurora laughed, a silly, high-pitched giggle that was going to be annoying if it happened often. "Clark, my dear, the world's always descending into the pits of hell, according to you hunters. You should see things from my side. Take the long view. It's much easier on the blood pressure, I assure you."

Clark's eyes darkened for a moment. "Aurora, I'll remind you that while the fae were taking their 'long view,' my clan and all the others were wiped out. You helped create the hunters so they'd be there to protect you from the forces of evil. Without them, you're just as vulnerable as everyone else."

The princess waved a hand at Clark. "Pish-posh, Clark. You're always so doom and gloom. It's why we could never make our thing work."

"That and you're like a thousand years older than I am."

She smiled and waggled a finger in his direction. "I'm not going to be tricked into revealing my age, my dear. Sorry."

Quinn was tired of the friendly banter. She cleared her throat and held up her hands, bound by the thick plastic zip-ties.

Aurora glanced at Quinn and Taylor seated nearby and smiled. "Release them. They've learned their lesson."

Two of the guards flipped open folding knives from their pockets and came forward, cutting the plastic ties with flicks of the sharp blades. Quinn and Taylor rubbed the red marks on their wrists for a few seconds.

Quinn stood and faced Clark and the princess. "Clark,

why don't you introduce me to your friend? Apparently, despite our efforts to hide, she was expecting us."

"Oh, I wasn't expecting you, my dear. At least, not this soon," Aurora said. "However, even out here in the hinterlands of the Eastern Shore, we've heard about you. I took the time to learn a little about you and even managed to lay my hands on a photograph of you. Your high school yearbook photo, actually. It's quite nice, although it doesn't capture the fierce determination in your eyes."

"If you weren't expecting us, how did you know we were here?" Quinn asked.

"When Zephyr, my security assistant, told me the video cameras were on the fritz and he couldn't figure out the problem, I wondered if something was up. Then Vince reported that one of the plumbers was a shifter, probably a werewolf. I became sure something was going on. I know most of the supernaturals around here, and I didn't recall any who were in that particular line of work. Those with sensitive noses tend to avoid that sort of dirty work for the most part."

"That's it?" Quinn asked. "We got caught because of Taylor?"

"I don't believe in coincidences, my dear. I had Zephyr reboot the video cameras into an old system I made sure we kept around for backup. Then I watched from his command center as you all went about your little caper. It was quite entertaining. Of course, I recognized Clark right away. You were next. The only one I don't know is your friend here. You said her name was Taylor?"

Aurora walked over and extended her hand to Taylor. "I am Her Royal Highness, Princess Aurora. It's a pleasure to meet you and welcome you into my home, even under these unusual circumstances."

Taylor looked confused but took the princess' hand in hers and shook it. "It's an honor, I guess."

Aurora giggled again and said, "As I was telling Clark on the way here, Filippa and I are rivals. We constantly vie to outdo each other. I'm afraid you three got caught up in one of her little ploys to get back at me."

Clark shook his head. "People could have gotten hurt. We needed the bowl, and when she told me you'd bought it, I just assumed…"

"What?" Aurora asked. "That I'd gotten it as a memento of the long-lost hunters? On the contrary, my dear, I bought it because my seers told me to. It was never meant for me to keep it. I bought it to hold until the time came to return it to the new hunter clan they predicted would rise from the ashes of the old ones."

"Wait," Quinn said. "You mean we could have just asked you for the bowl, and you would have returned it to us?"

"Of course. I don't believe in that stupid human adage about possession being nine-tenths of the law. Ownership of mystical things runs much deeper than that. I can't imagine the bad luck keeping it for myself would have brought me. I told all this to Filippa when I bought it. It was one of the few times we found ourselves in agreement."

The princess turned to one of the two guards standing near Clark. "Zephyr, please go and get the container we had made for the scrying bowl. It wouldn't do to have it break in transit."

The taller of the two guards left, heading at a fast walk for the exit.

Quinn's anger at Filippa continued to grow. First, the woman had betrayed them, getting Miranda killed. Then she'd sent them here on this wild goose chase to retrieve something they could have gotten for free.

"Why? Why did Filippa do all this to us?" Quinn asked as she tried to sort out what was going on.

"I suspect it was to get her hands on that silly dragon egg." Aurora nodded to the large green ceramic egg still sitting on the shelf.

"Wait, a dragon, like, for real?" Taylor asked, turning to stare at it.

"Oh, yes," Aurora said. "One of the smaller ones, to be sure, but a dragon, nonetheless. Filippa made a calculated guess that this would be the year the thing would hatch finally. Whoever has laid hands on it during the last phase of the moon each year imprints the beast like a duckling. Of course, it only happens if it hatches during that next year. Once the year passes, for the month of the anniversary, another might submit to the imprinting process. It's due now as a matter of fact, which was why she sent you. Luckily, none of you touched it."

Quinn stared at the egg and swallowed hard. "Um."

Clark rolled his eyes, throwing his hands in the air. "Oh, my God. You didn't!"

"It was only for a second. The outside was so smooth, and it shone so brightly under the lights."

"Aurora," Clark said, turning to their hostess, "I assure you she'll do whatever she has to do to transfer ownership back to you."

"Well, well, this is an unexpected turn of events," the princess said. Her lips broadened into a huge grin, followed by the silly giggle again. "Oh, Filippa is going to be so angry. I can almost hear her screaming now."

"There must be something I can do to give it back to you," Quinn said. "Just tell me what to do. Magic can undo anything, right?"

"Unfortunately, not in this case," Aurora said. "Dragons utilize wild magic, siphoned directly from nature. Only a sentient being can harness the wild magic and control the dragon once it's born. That's why most of the wild un-imprinted dragons had to be killed millennia ago. They couldn't be controlled and destroyed whole swaths of land in their rampages. Eventually, we discovered how to gather the eggs and imprint them, although only a few varieties survived at that point. This is the last of the green dragons. Unless it is allowed to mate with another variety of dragon, it will be the last of its kind."

"So, I'm stuck with a dragon."

"Oh, of course not. That will only happen if it hatches while it's in your care, which is highly unlikely," Aurora explained. "You can return it to me next year, and I'll take the responsibility back from you."

Taylor smiled and said, "Don't worry, Quinn. What are the odds of it hatching on your watch?"

"Don't even joke about it, T. I don't want this." Quinn turned back to Aurora. "Your Highness, how long does it take for a dragon to mature enough to hatch?"

"My cousin and I have been passing this one back and forth for the better part of two hundred years. The odds favor your being able to return it to me intact."

"I will definitely do that. I'm putting a note in my calendar to remind me now." Quinn pulled out her phone and jotted down the message on the same date next year.

"We are stuck in one way," Taylor said.

"How?" Quinn asked, looking up from her phone.

"We can't go back to Filippa. If you own the egg she wants, there's no way she'll give us her blood to use in the ritual to rebuild your amulet."

"If you promise to return the egg to me, Quinn, I will gladly agree to come and give a few drops of my blood when the time comes to use the bowl in your ceremony. Will that suffice, or does it have to be Filippa's?"

"No," Taylor said. "The instructions merely said 'highborn fae.'"

"Then I will certainly suffice. Clark knows how to reach me when the time comes. I suppose you've already found a blood relative to contribute to the amulet blessing ceremony as well?"

"No," Quinn said. "But we're going to find a workaround for that requirement."

"There's no need to do that, my dear," Aurora said. "My chief seer was most specific in her vision. A great huntress and her mother would use the bowl to bless the beginnings of a new clan. Since you're here, your mother must be somewhere nearby." Aurora clapped her hands. "It's all sort of exciting, don't you think? Things have gotten rather boring since the hunters left us."

"We didn't leave, Aurora," Clark said. "We were killed off and purged from the records."

"Semantics. Sometimes great magic must reset itself.

The magic used to create the original hunter clans was among the greatest created by the forces of light."

Quinn didn't know how she felt about finding out her mother was alive and had survived the purges. If she had survived, why hadn't she come and retrieved her daughter? Quinn's brows lowered as anger at her parents she thought she'd dealt with long ago resurfaced.

Taylor must've noticed Quinn's reaction and said, "Let's not worry about that now. These things have a way of working out, don't they? I mean, destiny isn't just a stripper from Dundalk."

Quinns smiled at Taylor's attempt to cheer her up with an old joke they'd shared in school.

Clark stepped forward. "I agree. Let's just take the bowl, and I guess the egg, too. We should really be getting back across the bay."

Quinn got the distinct impression the two of them were trying to change the subject. She wasn't sure why but she was glad of it. She hadn't thought about her real parents for a long time, and she had no desire to revisit the hurt she'd felt as a child growing up in the system without them. If her mother was alive, Quinn wanted nothing to do with her.

Aurora seemed to get the message. "Of course, I understand. Clark, you keep in touch. I want a personal report from you on Filippa's reaction to all this. That's the only price I exact from the three of you for the affront of this attempted thievery."

"I can do that," Clark said.

"If he doesn't," Taylor said, "I'll be happy to describe it to you in gory detail."

Aurora giggled again and nodded. "I will take you up on that, Taylor. I suspect I'll enjoy your account much more. Now go. Get home and assemble the rest of the components for your ritual. I will come when you need me."

Quinn nodded and followed Clark and Taylor to the back of the room. Zephyr had brought not one, but two black cases. Somehow he knew about the egg, too. Each had customized foam interiors cut to match the shapes of the artifacts. He'd already placed the bowl in the first one. He'd left the dragon egg where it sat on the shelf and glanced at Quinn.

Quinn shrugged and walked over. She lifted the warm egg in both hands, set it in its foam cradle, and closed the heavy-duty plastic lid.

Both boxes had handles and wheels, so Quinn took the one holding the egg and Taylor the one with the bowl. They headed out to the van. Clark came along behind them, with Aurora at his side. Their caper had been a bust, but they'd still managed to land the loot.

Quinn smiled at their luck, despite the feeling she'd had earlier. She wondered what else that was required for the ritual to remake her amulet was written in the tome. She was one step closer to getting it back. Then she'd be ready to face Handon, Myles Hickman, and the rest of them. She planned on ruining their plans before they took over the world.

CHAPTER TWENTY-THREE

Given that their plan fell through at the villa, the three of them decided to return Joe's van to him. There was no need to pretend it had been stolen anymore. It made them run later than expected heading home, so it was well after dark by the time they started along winding country roads toward Route 50, the highway leading to the Bay Bridge back across the Chesapeake Bay.

Quinn thought she was the first to notice the two vehicles following them along the dark, winding country roads. She stared over her shoulder and asked, "Clark, what are the odds Aurora changed her mind and wants her stuff back?"

He glanced at the rear-view mirror. "You talking about the two SUVs tailing us?"

"How do you know they're tailing us?" Taylor asked, oblivious to what was going on because she'd been glued to her tablet.

"How do you know they're SUVs?" Quinn asked. She

hadn't been able to see anything but headlights behind them in the darkness.

Clark ignored Taylor. "I know they're SUVs because of the wide spacing of the lights and the height from the road surface. It's a guess, but I'm pretty sure I'm right."

Quinn tried to see what he was talking about. "What do we do?"

"We try to keep ahead of them and get back on the highway. They'll be far less likely to cause problems with other cars around and risk being seen by a random State Trooper or local county cop."

Another glance back, and Quinn said, "They're speeding up. How much farther to the highway?"

"Too far. I think they just made the same determination I made about their options. Hold on."

Clark stomped on the accelerator, and his old sedan picked up speed. He navigated the backcountry road with surprising ease.

Quinn couldn't see anything, but then she realized he was using his dark vision skill. Closing her eyes, Quinn muttered, "Dammit, I need to see."

When she opened them, she could see past the area lit by the headlights. She looked back over her shoulder again. While the glare blinded her just as badly, she could make out the shadowy outlines of the big SUV bodies behind the pursuing lights. They were much closer now.

"They're gaining on us," Taylor called out. "Can't you go faster?"

Clark spun the wheel, taking a sharp curve in the road. "Not if we don't want to end up wrecking this car and making it easy for them."

Just as Clark said it, the lead SUV gunned its engine and surged forward, tapping the rear bumper of the sedan. It wasn't much of an impact, but at this speed, on this winding road, it didn't have to be. The rear end of the sedan spun around.

Taylor screamed and clutched the door. Quinn shouted for Clark to watch out because the second SUV had charged past the one that struck them, and it looked like it was coming right at them.

Clark spun the wheel and slammed on the brakes, struggling to regain control. He got the steering to respond in time to avoid a direct hit from the second vehicle as it charged at them. The SUV still clipped the front passenger side of the sedan beside the wheel well.

Quinn grunted in pain, and she slammed sideways into the car door. She clutched the door, trying to steady herself as the car spun in a complete circle. Her hand caught the release handle, and the door popped open. It threatened to spill her out of the car despite her seatbelt.

For a moment, she stared at the asphalt roadway spinning past her face. Using all her strength, Quinn pulled herself back into the car as it twisted to a stop.

The two SUVs slid to a halt nearby with the headlights pointed her way, high beams engaged, blinding her. Voices shouted, and figures ran at their car past the lights, forming menacing silhouettes.

"Clark, they're coming." Quinn punched her seatbelt release, but it was jammed. She didn't wait to fiddle with it. Instead, she drew her Bowie knife and cut the nylon webbing away from her chest and waist in two quick slashes.

She bounded from the passenger side just in time to meet the first attacker. Without thinking, she boosted her strength and speed to match her opponent's, drawing down her stamina bar. Quinn winced at the instant headache it caused but charged her attacker, a female vampire dressed in a leather jacket and jeans like she was. Armed as she was with only her fangs and talons, this chick was about to learn a hard lesson about what it meant to face an angry huntress.

Quinn lunged forward and slashed with her Bowie, sure she would connect. The vampire twisted in an acrobatic move that caught Quinn by surprise, spinning from her attack into a horizontal leap, her body stretched out and forward as she raked her talons across Quinn's back.

Despite the relative thickness of her leather jacket, the talons slashed through it like paper and scored deep cuts into the skin on Quinn's shoulder blades.

Grunting in pain, Quinn let her lunge carry her forward, continuing under the vampire's attack. The move saved her from more damage, and she rolled across the asphalt between the three vehicles and bounced back to her feet.

The move carried her close to another opponent, a guy this time. Quinn recognized him from the broad scar on his neck from her blade. He snarled at her as she came within reach.

Taking advantage of the target of opportunity, Quinn ducked under his attack and plunged her blade into his chest as he stepped toward her. He let out a croaking sound and clutched the hilt of the Bowie around Quinn's hand, then slumped to the ground. She yanked her blade free, turning back to face the more formidable opponent behind her.

"Peter," the woman shouted in alarm as the huntress felled her companion. She glared at Quinn. "You'll pay for that, girl."

"I did you a favor. He couldn't handle himself in a standup fight. I should have killed him the first time he faced me."

The female let out a screeching snarl deep in her throat and charged, fangs bared and long fingers leading the way, talons extended.

Quinn needed to finish this fight so she could help her friends. She caught a glimpse and knew Clark battled two other vamps on the far side of the car. Judging from the growling howls somewhere nearby in the darkness, the stress of the attack had caused Taylor to lose control and shift. That wasn't good.

Turning her attention back to the opponent at hand, Quinn batted away multiple incoming attacks. She had hoped stoking the female vampire's anger would lead to a careless mistake. She was wrong. The woman's moves were just as precise as before, only now with the cold burning energy experienced fighters used anger to fuel. She blocked all of Quinn's attacks without much trouble, taking only a few minor wounds.

Quinn, on the other hand, had barely avoided additional injuries herself by engaging in a fighting retreat. She couldn't afford to let the vamp get her claws on her. If she did, she'd draw Quinn in for the bite that would do the real damage.

Clark shouted from the other side of the car, "They're taking the cases."

Quinn spared a glance and saw Clark was right. Damn, Quinn had thought this was an attack on the three of them. It was all a pretense to get the bowl and the dragon egg.

To prove the point, a man's voice shouted over the fighting, "Back to the vehicles. We have what we came for."

The woman Quinn fought smiled and clawed at Quinn's face with one outstretched hand. The attack made the huntress dodge backward, disengaging from the melee temporarily.

When Quinn regained her balance and came forward again, the vampire had already sprinted away.

For a moment, she considered boosting her speed even more to chase the woman down. A howl in the open field to her right stopped her. That had to be Taylor since she had run in that direction. She had shifted and was probably unable to control herself. She could easily hurt or kill someone in her current state.

"Damn," Quinn said as she stood up. The doors slammed on both SUVs, and they reversed up the road a hundred feet. Both executed spinning turns before driving away at high speed, leaving Quinn and Clark standing beside their disabled car.

Quinn counted the bodies on the ground. The first was the guy she'd killed. Running around the vehicle, Quinn found two more, one on the ground by Clark and the other lying on the pavement beside the open rear door. His throat had been bitten open, and part of his guts hung from a broad tear that had ripped his belly open. Werewolf bites could apparently kill vampires if the damage was severe enough.

"This one was taken out by Taylor before she ran off," Quinn said. "We have to go get her."

Clark pointed to the headless body at his feet. "We have to clear these bodies and hide them until daylight dusts them for us. I can't call a tow truck until we do."

Another howl pierced the night in the distance. It was farther away this time. "She could kill someone else, someone who's an innocent. I have to track her down. Maybe I can get her to regain control again."

Clark looked into the darkness in the direction of the howl. He nodded. "Go get her, but be careful. She might not be able to stop herself from attacking you."

"I'll take that chance." Quinn sprinted into the night while Clark bent down and began dragging one of the bodies off the road.

Pushing through the searing headache she already had, Quinn brought up the HUD and engaged the tracking skill. She could already see well in the dark, but that wouldn't be enough.

Right away, she caught Taylor's scent. Along with the usual smell of wet dog that went with every werewolf, was a faint hint of cinnamon and apples. The second part brought a smile to Quinn's face. That was Taylor's favorite body wash for sure.

Following the scent, Quinn raced across the field of waist-high wheat. Taylor howled again. It sounded closer, but not close enough. It looked like her friend had headed in the direction of the lights from a nearby farm. Quinn had to catch her before she got there and started into the farm animals, or worse, the farmer and his family.

She checked the stamina bar, now a pale yellow strip with only twenty-five percent remaining. Quinn hadn't realized she'd needed so much to counter the female vampire. If she drew on it to speed up, she wouldn't have anything left to fight with. Shaking her head, denying the apparent risk, Quinn pulled on the last of her remaining stamina. She charged even faster toward the distant farmhouse and barns.

Quinn caught up with Taylor as she reached the wooden fence beside a pen full of black and white dairy cows. The animals had sensed the danger, moving away from that side of the enclosure. They milled around restlessly near the barn.

Not slowing at all, Quinn slammed into the werewolf. Taylor had hunched to leap the fence, and Quinn hit her from the side, tackling her snarling friend to the ground.

If she'd been a moment later, Taylor would have started into the panicked cows.

The two of them rolled over on the ground until Taylor ended up atop Quinn, straddling her waist. Holding off the snapping jaws and claws with every ounce of strength she had left, Quinn called to her best friend, "Taylor, it's me. It's Quinn. Stop this."

The only response was a growl followed by renewed attacks by the furry form atop her. The werewolf's greater strength soon overcame Quinn's waning energy. Before Quinn could stop her, Taylor clamped her jaws down on her best friend's forearm.

Stifling a scream from the pain, Quinn reached up with

her free hand. She ignored the clawed hands that clutched her shoulders, pulling her toward the bared teeth. Instead, Quinn grabbed at the thick fur at the back of Taylor's head. Quinn held the wolf's head close while simultaneously pressing her bloody forearm deeper into the wolf's mouth.

This brought Taylor's yellow wolf eyes closer until they were just inches from Quinn's. Holding those eyes with her own, Quinn said, "Concentrate on who you are, T. You can control this. Come on. Find yourself again. Please."

The last words came out as a pleading cry as the claws tore her shoulders despite the protection of her leather jacket.

A few desperate seconds passed where Quinn thought she might have to try to draw her Bowie. Then, as she stared into the feral eyes above her, they changed, becoming less animal and more human somehow. The pressure on her forearm lessened and stopped entirely as Taylor's jaws released her.

The werewolf pushed away from Quinn and bounded away a few yards before cowering against the side of the barn. Her growls had turned to a sad whimpering.

Quinn pushed herself to her feet with her uninjured hand and stumbled over to her friend. "It's okay, Taylor. I'm all right. I'll heal."

The wolf-woman crouched by the barn. She leaned forward and sniffed the air near Quinn. She whimpered again.

"I'm fine, T. It's just a little blood, that's all. What's important is you stopped yourself."

Taylor twisted her head to the side as if questioning

what Quinn had said. She couldn't speak, but a soft wail came out of her mouth.

"I'm good, really. Don't worry about me. You know how fast I heal. If I can find a ley line around somewhere, maybe I can do it even faster, right?"

Taylor gave a short nod, which Quinn took as a good sign.

The sound of voices from the farmhouse a hundred yards away drew Taylor's attention. She growled deep in her throat.

"Taylor, look at me and pay attention to me. Don't lose yourself again. Focus on my voice and come toward me."

The werewolf looked at Quinn and then turned toward the farmhouse again, the hackles rising on the back of her neck.

Quinn took a step forward and extended her uninjured hand toward her friend. "Focus on me. Take my hand. I'll take you back to Clark and the car. Come on, T, you can do this."

Taylor choked back a rumbling growl in her throat and turned back to Quinn. A clawed hand clutched Quinn's outstretched fingers.

She breathed a sigh of relief and pulled gently on the hairy hand in hers. Taylor took a few tentative steps toward her and then a few more. Soon they both walked back into the field of wheat, letting the night close about them and leaving the farmer and his livestock safe behind them.

CHAPTER TWENTY-FOUR

Taylor woke up and groaned. Why was she in so much pain? She ached the way she had after the first two nights she'd shifted. It didn't make any sense to feel this way now.

Then she remembered, and her eyes opened wide. She sat up with a shout. "Quinn!"

"Shhh, I'm right here, T."

Taylor twisted her head around, trying to get her bearings. She was lying down in the back of Clark's car. Had it all been a bad dream?

Quinn reached back and grabbed her hand to give it a squeeze. A fresh white bandage was wrapped around her friend's forearm.

It hadn't been a dream. None of it.

"Oh, my God. Quinn, I'm so sorry."

"What? This?" Quinn said, holding up her arm. "It's nothing. A scratch, that's all. Remember, my huntress genes protect me from the worst of your bite's effects. It's already started to heal. I'll show you when we get home."

"What time is it?" Taylor patted her pockets for her phone. She wasn't wearing the same clothes she'd had on before. But then, she wouldn't, would she? What she wore last night during the attack wouldn't be much more than shredded rags now. Her phone must be in her bags in the back with the remnants of her clothing.

Clark, who drove in the front seat, said, "It's about noon. We just left the garage, where they fixed the tire that blew when the SUV spun us around. It took them all morning to get the tire in to replace it. We're lucky it wasn't worse."

"Yeah," Quinn said. "You slept through the whole thing in the back seat while he fixed the car. We told the mechanic that if he woke you up, he'd be sorry."

Clark chuckled. "He was a little nervous because of all the blood splattered on the windows and doors. I don't think he bought our explanation that we ran into a small herd of deer."

"I killed that guy. I did it with my teeth. I can feel when I crunched through…" Taylor shivered as she relived it in her mind. She fought down the bile rising in her throat. "It was like I was there and yet not. So scary. I ran away before the fight was done. Did we scare them off?"

"Not exactly," Quinn said. "They left when they got what they came for."

"They took the bowl?"

Quinn nodded. "And the egg. We're heading back to Baltimore now. We'll stop at Spring Grove and see if we can locate them. The vampires came from Handon. I recognized the vampire Clark took to the metro station. I killed him for good this time.

Clark shook his head. "It doesn't make sense. The only person who knew where we were going was Filippa. She had to be the one who told Handon's goons how to find us. We have to find her first. She made the deal that included getting the egg back from them, and it means she knows where Handon is hiding."

"How did she know we wouldn't bring it to her as we promised?" Taylor asked. "She should have waited until we got back to find out what we did and why we had to keep the egg."

Clark shrugged. "My best guess is, Filippa has a spy on Aurora's personal staff. It's pretty common among fae royalty. There's so much intrigue, you can't keep it straight sometimes. You're better off just knowing Filippa was behind it and leave it at that."

Taylor shifted in her seat as Clark drove up a ramp and onto the highway that would eventually lead them back to Baltimore.

As she watched the tall span of the Bay Bridge get closer, Taylor decided that scared her. "I want in. I want to be there when we confront Filippa and when we retrieve the bowl and egg from Handon's crew."

"Taylor," Quinn said, "I don't think you're ready for that. You can barely control your change now, and we don't know if there will be innocent people around when the fighting starts."

"I don't care. I have to exact payback for them causing me to break through and change that way. I don't ever want to lose control like that again. I'll fight them to show them they didn't control me."

"T, you don't have anything to prove to Clark or me.

You're still new to all this, and these things take time. Dameon told you when he came to help you get ready for your first full moon."

"I don't care. You guys are my pack now. That means I have to be ready to defend you."

Taylor didn't mean to come off sounding as angry as she did, but the more she said it, the more it seemed right to her. Quinn and the others had become her pack. They were more important to her than anyone else she knew.

"Clan or pack," Quinn replied. "I'm glad you're here."

Taylor smiled. She and Quinn had been through a lot together. These last months had been bad, but there had been moments in the past when Quinn had lived on the streets alone. She'd needed Taylor's help to intervene and get her a place to stay.

Now, it was Quinn's turn to give her a home, a place where she could be herself while she explored this new aspect of her nature. Taylor settled back in her seat and looked out the window at the Bay as they drove up onto the westbound span of the Chesapeake Bay bridge. She was happy to go wherever Quinn and the others went. With her pack was where she belonged.

It was mid-afternoon when they finally rolled into the gravel parking lot back at Spring Grove. Taylor climbed out and stretched. She felt refreshed and ready to get started on getting their stuff back. On the trip, they'd discussed several ways to track down the stolen items, and each time came back to the best option being to try to find the slayers online.

Taylor waved to Quinn and Clark as they got out. "I'm heading in to fire up the VR system and then trigger the tracking bots. Let's see if we can find them before they schedule the meetup with Filippa."

She walked up the steps to the rear entrance and walked inside, jumping back a step when Miranda appeared in front of her.

"God, Miranda, you've got to stop doing that. Give me a heads up before you pop in."

"Sorry, but I didn't want you walking into a trap, and I couldn't manifest outside in the sunlight."

"What trap?"

"Someone came into the building early this morning while it was still dark. They walked around as if they were searching for something. I could sense them moving from room to room, but when I got to each one to check, whoever it was had left. It's like it was another ghost."

Taylor shook her head. "Wait, you're not making any sense. Was someone here or not?"

"I'm sure I didn't imagine it if that's what you're asking. I can't tell what they were doing or why they were here, though. They left as silently as they came."

"Who did?" Clark asked, walking in, followed by Quinn.

"Tell him," Taylor said.

Miranda explained what happened while they were gone once again.

"If they didn't do anything, could they have taken something?" Quinn asked.

"Good idea," Clark said. "Everyone split up and check your rooms and belongings. We'll meet back in the kitchen when we're finished."

The three of them dispersed. Miranda floated beside Taylor, wringing her spectral hands.

"I don't know how to tell a ghost to relax, but you need to do it, Miranda. You're making me nervous, floating there with your fists clenched."

"Sorry, I worry about what I might have missed and how they avoided being seen."

"Are you sure it wasn't just another spirit associated with this hospital? There've got to be a few."

"Oh, there are a dozen or so ghosts here in the building, but they don't like to be seen. The things done to them here in the clinic make them afraid of anyone still alive who walks the halls. They mostly just watch from the shadows. I don't think it was one of them."

Taylor reached her room and looked around. She dropped the backpack of clothes and her laptop bag on the floor and checked the small dresser and the single drawer in her nightstand.

"Everything looks the same here. Let's go check the computer gear in the office downstairs."

Miranda nodded and followed her as she went to check the equipment there.

Once again, Taylor checked over everything. She fired up the computers and did a system diagnostic on the VR rig and the computers themselves. Whoever it was could have slipped a virus into her systems.

While they did that, something else occurred to her. Taylor opened the bottom drawer on the desk where she'd hidden the life tome. It was gone. The drawer wasn't empty, though. There was a folded piece of paper with Quinn's name on it. Taylor picked it up and unfolded it, and her heart sank as she read it.

"What is it?" Miranda asked.

"It's a note for Quinn."

"Who's it from?"

Taylor held it out for Miranda to see. "Her mother."

Quinn,

I hope you get this message before you seek to recover what was lost. There are those who will do anything to stop you from completing your quest to recreate the clans.

They have the bowl and the tome now. They'll try to bring the final components together soon to complete the triad needed to enact the enchantment. Their goal is to create similar charms to supplement their slayers. If successful, the slayers will become nearly invincible.

I can't tell you what to do. All I can say is to trust what is within you and tell you my heart leaps with joy when I see what you've become. You have more power than you know. Be strong in the coming storm, my brave huntress.

Mother

Miranda read the note and then shook her head. "It was her? The vampire from the museum? She came here?"

"It looks that way. What I don't get is how she found us and why go to the trouble to steal the book and leave the note? It makes no sense."

Miranda shrugged and said, "Perhaps she's limited in what she can and cannot do to counter her vampire sire. If he gave her a direct order, she'd be unable to ignore it, but she could leave a note to let us know it was her."

"Perhaps, but it doesn't explain how she found this location. I need to tell Clark."

"You need to tell Quinn, too," Miranda said. "She deserves to know about this. About everything."

"You're right. I'll bring the note. Let's go meet them in the kitchen. It's time."

CHAPTER TWENTY-FIVE

Quinn returned to the kitchen after checking her room to find Clark already there.

He looked up as she came in. "Anything missing in your room?"

Quinn shook her head. "No, nothing. Maybe Miranda was mistaken."

"Could be. We were gone for a few days. Maybe she got a little stir crazy in here alone."

"Can that happen to ghosts?" Quinn asked.

Clark shrugged. "I have no idea. I've never had a friend who's a ghost before. I guess we'll have to ask her if Taylor doesn't find anything."

Quinn walked over to the refrigerator to see what they had left that she could make for dinner. It was close enough to dinnertime that she figured they could eat early. She dug around and decided to cook fried eggs and toast for dinner. They could go to the store and resupply in the morning.

Taylor came in as Quinn pulled out the frying pan to get started.

Quinn looked over her shoulder and asked, "Hey, what did you find? Anything?"

"You should come over to the table. You need to see something."

Quinn turned off the stove and put down the frying pan. She walked to the table and sat down with the others.

Taylor sat at the other end with a single piece of paper in her hand.

Clark sat down between them. He pointed to the paper. "What's that?"

"I went to check on the VR system in my office. The computers are fine as far as I can tell. I'm running a diagnostic to be sure. But while I was doing that, I found out why they were here. Our burglar was after the life tome."

"They took it? It has to be Handon again," Quinn said.

"It was Handon, at least indirectly. Quinn, it was someone you know. They left you a note," Taylor said, handing the folded sheet to Quinn.

Quinn opened it and read the note. As she finished, she put the paper on the table and stared at it for a few seconds, then looked up at her friends. "Is this some sort of joke? This is Handon's crude attempt to get under my skin. The joke's on him, though. My mother is long dead."

"No, Quinn, she isn't," Taylor said.

"How could you possibly know that?"

"Quinn, I—" Taylor started, then closed her mouth before starting again. "We figured it out right before we left for the shore. Who your mother is, I mean. We were going to tell you. It was just a matter of figuring out how and when."

"We?" Quinn asked. She looked at Clark and Miranda. "As in, all of you?"

Each of them nodded.

Clark said, "Quinn, if you're going to be angry with someone, it should be me. I figured it out and didn't tell you either."

Quinn glared at him and turned to Taylor. "You kept this from me? Why would you do that, Taylor? I've always trusted you with everything. How could you do this?"

Tears welled in Taylor's eyes, and she blinked to clear them. "Quinn, I didn't want to hurt you. It wasn't just that we'd found your mother. It was who she is that's the problem."

"All right, who is she?"

Clark and Taylor exchanged looks, then Clark said, "Your mother is Naomi Rodriguez."

It took a few seconds for it to sink in. Then Quinn's eyes widened. "That vampire! No way. She's only a little older than I am."

"Think about it, Quinn," Taylor said. "She's a vampire."

A thousand thoughts spun through Quinn's mind. She was trying to make sense of all of it. She'd always thought her mother had left her behind and run off to live her own life. Once she'd found out about the purges from Clark, she'd assumed her mother had died with all the other hunters, and she had resigned herself to that. But this revelation changed everything.

Quinn stared at the note, trying to comprehend what had happened. "So, she surrendered to become a monster rather than die fighting. Typical of someone who'd abandon a baby on the side of the road."

"I don't think that's what happened," Miranda said.

Quinn started to object, but Miranda stopped her. "Taylor told me something about how you grew up. You always thought something lucky protected you. You thought it was your amulet, and that could be part of it."

"What? You think my vampire mother stalked me growing up and somehow protected me? If she wanted to protect me, she should have taken me back so I didn't have to deal with all those awful people in the foster system as a child. She let me live alone on the streets rather than claim me."

Tears streamed down Quinn's cheeks as her emotions overwhelmed her. It seemed like everyone she knew had betrayed her at this point—her mother first, and now her friends. It was almost more than she could bear.

She crumpled the note in her fist. "I'm going to find her and drive a stake through her heart. She has a lot of nerve dropping this bomb on me. She doesn't deserve to call herself my mother. You three can help if you want. I guess I can't stop you from coming along, but you'd better stay out of my way when the time comes."

"Quinn," Taylor said.

"No, Taylor. You of all people should have known better and told me right away. I could have killed her back at the museum, and none of this would have happened. We'd probably still have the book and the bowl. Then we'd only need the dagger and whatever the other item is. We already have a line on where to get the fae blood. Now we might as well have nothing."

Taylor said, "We're in better shape than that, Quinn. We have the scanned pages of the book, so we don't need the life tome anymore. They screwed up and don't know it. We still have what we need to do the spell once we have all the components."

"Well, the bowl and the dagger are probably with Handon," Quinn said. "If Filippa's there, we won't need to call Aurora. I can take care of gathering the fae blood we need at the same time. What about the third thing we need? Do we know what it is?"

Taylor pulled out her phone and scrolled through it. "It says something about using the heart stone. I don't know what that is, though."

Clark shook his head.

Taylor glanced his way. "Clark, do you know what the stone is and where it might be?"

"Unfortunately, I do. I didn't know it had belonged to the clan originally, though."

"Okay," Quinn said. "Don't make us guess."

"It's the Ruby Heart," Clark said. "It has to be."

"The power gem they're using to create the demon-kinder?" Quinn asked.

"It makes sense," Miranda said. "Myles Hickman and VirSync probably got it as a reward for helping during the purges. That allowed them to fuel their demonic takeover."

Quinn leaned back in her chair and shook her head. Her anger with the others was making her tremble all over. As pissed off as she was, though, she couldn't do this alone. She needed all of them to retrieve the items to create the amulet.

Leaning forward again, Quinn took a deep breath and

looked at each of them, saying, "First things first. We have to go up against the slayers, plus Myles and the others, to recover the Ruby Heart. Taylor, you have to find out where they've moved their base, and you have to find it tonight. Got that?"

Taylor nodded, and Quinn continued. "After that, we track down Handon's vampires and Filippa. If they're creating their own amulets for the demon-kinder, they're going to need fae blood. That has to be part of the deal when they turn over the dragon egg. Once we know where they are meeting to make the exchange, we'll likely find the scrying bowl, too. Clark, that falls on you. You have to figure out how to get Filippa to give up the location of the meetup. Can you do that?"

Clark met her eyes with a level gaze and said, "I can."

"Good, then you all know what you need to do. In the meantime, I'm going back downtown to have a chat with my mother."

"Do you think that's a good idea?" Taylor asked.

"She chose to reveal herself now. Well, I'm going down there to tell her now is also the time she has to choose sides. I want to know why she's done everything she's done to me. She can't have it both ways, not anymore."

"Naomi might not have had a choice in the matter, Quinn," Clark said. "The bond between a vampire and their sire, the one who turned them, is strong. If he gave her a direct order, she'd have a hard time resisting it. My guess is he told her to find and recover the life tome. The note was her way to try to reset the balance in your favor."

"Whatever her reason, she knows more than she said in that letter. I need answers, and I'm going to get them."

"We only have one car," Clark said. "I'll need it if I'm going to go rattle some cages and see if I can shake the location of the meetup loose. How will you get to her?"

"The same way we met before. Taylor can send me through the VR rig while she searches for VirSync's new operations center. I'll need to use it to stop them anyway."

"I can do that," Taylor said. "With Clark out searching the city for Filippa, you won't have any backup, though. What if Naomi is forced to attack you?"

"She's had the chance on at least two occasions, and she's resisted it," Quinn replied. "My guess is the sire bond Clark mentioned isn't strong enough to overcome what she feels for me. I'm going to use that to my advantage."

"Let's make sure we all stay in touch," Clark said. "Keep the earpieces active so we can coordinate once we get answers."

"Agreed," Quinn and Taylor said in unison.

The three of them stood, and Clark and Taylor headed out to begin their assigned tasks. Miranda followed Taylor. Quinn watched them go, maintaining her calm outward demeanor. Inside, a sense of betrayal by those closest to her threatened to overwhelm her.

She had to hold it together. Too much hung in the balance. Quinn didn't know whether she'd survive the night, but she wasn't going to give up now. It was time for the huntress clan to make their move. Her visit to Naomi was just the first step.

CHAPTER TWENTY-SIX

Quinn stared at her dresser, trying to decide what to take into VR with her. Her leather jacket had been ruined in the fight with the vampires the night before. She settled on a waist-length light blue denim jacket over a black t-shirt and jeans. Knee-high black boots finished off the outfit.

She settled the shoulder sheath for her Bowie beneath her right arm where she could reach it and pulled on the jeans jacket. It was a little tighter than her leather one, but it would do to cover her knife if she ended up out in public.

Quinn was the last to get started on her part of the plan since she had to wait until after dark to catch her mother awake. Clark had been gone for hours, and no one had heard from him. Taylor had spent the rest of the day searching the data collected by her bots over the last few weeks for any trace of the slayers.

The huntress expected Taylor to be distracted by her search for the slayers. To Quinn's surprise, Taylor already had the VR rig set up and ready to go when she got there. Quinn didn't say anything, though.

The few hours she had spent apart from the others had tempered her anger a little, but she still didn't want to talk to Taylor.

Quinn's best friend didn't say anything either, just gestured to the top of the desk, where the goggles and headset sat ready for her. Quinn let the awkward silence hang between them as she climbed up on the desk.

It was Miranda who finally broke the silence. "You two need to stop this. You're best friends, and if something happens tonight to either of you, you'll never forgive yourselves for ending it like this. Trust me, I know what it's like dying with unfinished business."

Quinn looked over her shoulder at Taylor behind the row of monitors.

Taylor glanced up and gave Quinn a half-smile, then glanced at Miranda. "I guess we shouldn't count on being lucky enough to come back as a cool ghost like you."

"Lucky?" Miranda said, raising her voice. When she shouted, she became less transparent. It was as if her anger helped her manifest on the earthly plane. "I'm freaking *dead*! You two kids have no idea what it is like not being able to DO anything. I can only offer advice and sort of float along for the ride. It sucks."

Quinn's smile broadened at the rant, as did Taylor's. Quinn said, "At least you don't have to worry about laundry and stuff like that. You have just the one outfit." Miranda always showed up in the same clothing—what she was wearing the night she died.

Miranda was speechless at first, which got both girls giggling.

Their reaction set her off again. "I don't have anything but these. That's how the afterlife works apparently. There's no BroadMart to go shopping for new outfits. What you show up in is what you're stuck with." Miranda threw her spirit arms in the air. "Thank God I didn't die naked in the shower."

That did it. The girls laughed out loud and couldn't stop. After a minute, Quinn's stomach and face started to hurt from laughing so hard.

Miranda just stared at them until they settled into occasional chuckles.

"Are you both quite finished?"

"Yes," Quinn said.

"Me, too," Taylor replied.

They still smiled, but they'd stopped laughing.

"Good," Miranda said. "Now apologize to each other for being angry. You need to make up so we can do what needs to be done tonight."

Quinn hopped off the edge of the desk. Taylor got up from her chair and came around the corner. The two rushed into an embrace.

"Quinn, I'm sorry."

"Me, too. I hate it when we fight."

"Yeah, it sucks when we're not in sync," Taylor said. "Good thing we have our ghost-mom to help us see when we're being silly."

"Our grave nanny?" Quinn suggested.

Taylor smiled and said, "Our ectoplasmama."

"Ooh, I know," Quinn said. "Our very own phantom

godmother. I don't suppose you can summon a bunch of ghost birds and mice to clean our rooms?"

"All right, that's enough," Miranda said, rolling her eyes. "All I wanted was for you two to make up. There are serious things that need doing tonight, and the only way it's going in our favor is if you two work together."

Quinn squeezed Taylor's hand and climbed onto the desk, picking up the goggles and headset.

Taylor peered over the monitor. "You want to see Naomi, so I assume it's back to the museum?"

Quinn nodded. "Put me in the attic again."

Miranda started to tap on her keyboard but stopped and looked around. "Wait, I don't have the box to disable the alarm initialized. You won't be able to shut off the security system."

"Exactly." Quinn smiled. "Let's see how long it takes Mommy Dearest to show up to check on her book babies."

Taylor shrugged. "Okay, starting the countdown now. I'll keep looking for the slayers once you're in the system. I'll be on the headset if you need me."

Quinn nodded and double-checked to make sure her headphones were in place. She propped the goggles on her forehead and slid the cups into place. She laid down and held up her thumb, then pulled the VR glasses into position.

Taylor started the rhythmic chanting of her spell, and Quinn fell into darkness once again.

CHAPTER TWENTY-SEVEN

Quinn opened her eyes and choked down the bile rising in her throat as she fought her nausea from the transition. It wasn't as bad as before. Taylor must be getting better at casting. Quinn made a mental note to thank her when she got back.

It was dark, as it had been before. Quinn concentrated on her HUD and said, "Dammit, I need to see." The attic space brightened with a faint green haze that looked similar to what you see through night-vision goggles.

Now that she could see, Quinn slid over to the crawl-space entrance and got into position to open the trapdoor and stairs again. Before she pushed to open it, she listened to the storeroom below, straining to hear if anyone was there.

She waited a good ten seconds before she decided it was clear. Placing her feet against the folding wooden ladder, Quinn pressed down just as she had the last time she was here.

Nothing happened.

She pressed harder and harder until she stood with her full weight on the inside of the trap door. It didn't budge an inch.

"Damn," Quinn muttered.

"What's wrong?" Taylor said over the earpiece.

"The trapdoor is locked or stuck. It was foolish to come in this way again. They must have added a latch or lock to the door below. Can you recall me and send me somewhere else in the building?"

"Not if we want to send you to intercept the slayers and retrieve the bowl. I used up a lot of my energy casting the spell to get you there. I can bring you back, but after that, I only have enough left for one more round trip."

Quinn cursed as she crouched and studied the edges of the trapdoor. She was stuck. They didn't have the luxury of coming back another night. She had a feeling things were going down tonight. It was now or never.

She hooked her fingers under the frame around the trapdoor and pushed down with her legs while pulling up with her arms. There was a little movement, but only a quarter-inch or so. She could see light creeping around the edges. In a few places, the thin shadows from nails showed, and Quinn understood. She smiled. Nails could be pulled out.

Summoning her HUD, Quinn tapped her stamina reserves and boosted her strength. Tensing again, Quinn yanked up while pressing with her legs.

After about two seconds, the nails that had been hammered in to hold the trapdoor closed loosened all at once. The door swung down, dropping Quinn in a fall she hadn't had time to prepare for. She landed hard on her side with a grunt that knocked the air out of her. A popping feeling inside her chest and a shooting pain in her torso told her she might have broken a rib or two.

She laid there gasping to catch her breath. Her entrance had been a lot noisier than she'd planned, and she was injured, too. It hadn't gone unnoticed.

"Well, well," a woman said nearby, her voice coming through the open storeroom door in the office next to the closet. "The boss was right. You did come back."

Quinn pressed her hands to the floor, levering herself up to a sitting position. She still felt like she couldn't breathe right. The rib was definitely broken because she couldn't take a full breath without stabbing pain in her side.

Seated in a desk chair on the other side of the office was a woman wearing black leggings and boots, topped with a gray University of Baltimore sweatshirt.

She stood and called out over her shoulder toward the stairs. "Zabe, she's up here. She came back just like the Master said. You owe me fifty bucks."

The woman turned back to Quinn and bared her fangs. "I get to kill you and collect the price Handon put on your head. This is my lucky night."

Quinn climbed to her feet and drew her knife, trying to hide her inability to breathe right. She kept her elbow down on that side once she drew her blade. Pressing the arm against her side seemed to help splint the injury.

Sneering at the vampire, Quinn asked, "If I kill you, does Zabe owe me the money?"

"Why don't you come out here and find out?" the vampire said, stepping away from the desk.

A shouted answer from downstairs and the thump of feet on the steps told Quinn she had to work fast, or she was going to be both injured and outnumbered.

Quinn siphoned more power into her speed to supplement her already increased strength and charged at the woman.

The preternatural speed all vampires possessed still caught Quinn by surprise. By the time she'd raced over to meet the woman in the center of the office, the vampire had dodged to the side in a blur of motion almost too quick to see.

Quinn managed to block the incoming attack from the vampire's talon-like fingernails, now extended for combat. She batted aside the arm and twisted to the side, bringing her Bowie around in a broad slashing attack.

The vampire had overextended herself, too confident her first attack would work.

The blessed silver blade cut deep into the woman's belly, hissing as it sliced through skin and muscle. A thin trail of smoke followed the silver-steel alloy through the wound.

The vampire's eyes widened in surprise, and she clutched the gaping wound in her stomach while attempting to back away.

The footsteps from below were getting closer, so Quinn took a chance and dropped, kicking out with her leg.

It worked.

Quinn knocked the woman off her feet, and she fell to the floor with a thud. The huntress plunged the Bowie knife into the vampire's chest and pierced the heart.

The blessed blade did its job. The woman went limp, eyes open and vacant in final death.

Quinn winced as she climbed to her feet. That last move hadn't helped her broken rib at all. Suppressing a groan, she looked up and assumed a defensive stance. Another vampire, a male this time, ran across the third floor to the office.

"You must be Zabe. You owe me fifty dollars."

"What the…" Zabe said. He took in the body of his friend and glared at Quinn. "I'm going to rip your arms off and beat you to death with them."

"Wow, that's pretty graphic. Have you seen a therapist about your anger issues?"

Snarling deep in his throat, Zabe charged at Quinn. As he got closer, he lowered his shoulders like he was going to tackle her and use his heavier body to his advantage.

Quinn raised her blade up high to plunge it down into his back as he got close. She never got the chance.

In another of those blurring vampire speed boosts, Zabe jumped into the air. At the same time, he slashed down at Quinn's raised hand with his vamp claws.

The razor-sharp nails cut into her wrist and forearm, hitting her with enough force to cause her to let go of the Bowie. Her hand flew up and the blade dropped to clatter on the floor about ten feet away.

The vampire's surprise move carried him over Quinn's head and he landed behind her. As soon as he touched down, he launched a backward kick. The attack caught Quinn in the small of her back and launched her into the air. She flew across the room to slam into a large metal filing cabinet. The sheet metal on the side of the cabinet caved in when she hit it. Quinn struggled to regain her feet, pressing against the dented side of the cabinet to steady herself.

Zabe laughed as he walked toward her. "Not so badass without the fancy pig sticker, are you. You must've got in a lucky shot to cut down Kim so fast."

"I'm sorry," Quinn said. "Did I kill your girlfriend?"

"Her? No way. Too weird for me. That girl was into bizarre stuff, and that's saying a lot for a vampire, believe me."

Quinn pressed against the side of the filing cabinet to steady herself as painful muscle spasms coursed up and down her back. Now she had a bad back in addition to her broken ribs. On top of that, she was unarmed.

Quinn made a mental note. If she survived the night, she would consider a backup blade or even two, like Clark.

Zabe blurred again as he raced toward her. He must have seen she was injured. His talons raked at her arms as she raised them to block the incoming blows.

His body collided with hers, smashing her around to the front of the filing cabinet on her knees. The earpiece fell off and rolled into the corner.

Before she could get up, he jumped on her back and wrapped an arm around her throat, pulling her toward his waiting fangs.

His voice snarled in her ear, "I've heard hunter blood is a delicacy. I'll let you know how you taste before you die."

There was no way she was dying here and now, like this. Her anger fueled her to drain all of her stamina into a last surge of strength.

"I'm a huntress," Quinn grunted through gritted teeth. "Nobody feeds on me, especially not you."

Fighting the pain, her strength surging to beat the vampire, she reached up with one hand. Quinn gripped the back of Zabe's neck and pulled down hard while sliding to the side on her knees.

Since she had no weapon to finish him, she had to improvise. Yanking open the bottom filing drawer, Quinn shoved the off-balance vampire's head in among the hanging file folders inside.

Zabe struggled to pull free from her grasp, but she kept her hand clamped at the nape of his neck. Quinn slammed the heavy drawer closed, once, twice, and then a third time on Zabe's exposed neck.

Quinn heard a loud crack on the second hit, which sent spasms shooting down the vampire's struggling body. The third blow was the charm, though. With a sickening crunch, the drawer slid all the way closed, and Zabe's headless body slumped to the floor beside the blood-smeared cabinet.

Gasping, Quinn sat back and stared at the carnage around her. She turned to crawl over to where her Bowie lay on the floor.

She'd almost reached her knife when a slow clap from the top of the stairs stopped her.

Naomi stood there. "That was impressive. Those were among the best of John's coven. He was sure they'd be able to take you if you were foolish enough to show up here again. Good work with the filing cabinet, by the way. I'm not sure I would have thought of that. Quite innovative."

"Hello, Mother," Quinn said as she worked to get to her

feet. "If you saw what I did, why didn't you stop me? You're on Handon's side, right?"

Naomi's eyes softened. "Oh, my dearest daughter..."

"Don't call me that," Quinn snapped. "You don't get to do that. Ever. You *abandoned* me."

"There are a lot of things you don't understand, Quinn. Maybe another time, you'll let me explain."

Quinn shrugged. She needed to stall for time until she could either go for the knife in front of her or for the earpiece behind her. "Why not now? It's just you and me, right?"

"We're alone if that's what you wanted to know."

"So, tell me what's supposed to convince me not to hate you." Quinn pressed her arm against her side as a muscle spasm grated the broken ribs together. She winced at the sudden burst of pain.

"You're hurt worse than you're making it appear."

"It doesn't mean I can't take you," Quinn replied.

"I don't want to fight you, Quinn. I won't unless you force me to."

"Don't you have to do whatever your sire tells you to do? I was told you are stuck under his power because you let him drink from you and turn you into this creature you've become."

"Quinn, I don't expect you to understand everything I did. Only a mother knows the desperation that fueled my decisions that night."

"Stop calling yourself a mother. You gave me up so you didn't have the liability of a baby while you tried to escape. You must've thought it would make it easier for you to get away from the purges. It didn't work out for you, did it?"

Naomi's brows lowered and she said, "You're alive right now because of everything I did that night and on many nights since. I gave up everything I loved for the chance that I could help you survive and hide from the purges."

Her voice broke as she continued, "They were killing us. All of us, Quinn. Men, women, and children, too. Nobody was spared. My sister and her entire family were wiped out in a single attack. She had twins your age. They never had a chance. It was about wiping the hunter genes away so they could never again threaten the plans made by John Handon and his comrades around the world. They killed my entire world that night, except for you. You, I managed to protect."

Quinn struggled with the things Naomi was saying. Clark had let on a little of what had happened, but she'd never thought about what it meant in terms of the human cost. Of course, they killed the children, too. They were totally evil bastards. She'd seen what they would do to serve their ends.

But Quinn bit back the sorrow she'd started to feel. She didn't want to empathize with this woman, who claimed to be the mother she'd lost so long ago. Instead, she asked, "Why?"

"Why what?"

"Why let them turn you into," Quinn gestured toward Naomi, "this? A vampire."

"I was sure I was going to die when they caught us. They killed your father right away, feeding on him while I watched, helpless. It took four of them to hold me down while they did it, and they made me watch every second of it. Two of them drank until his screams faded and he died.

I'd killed three of them in the initial attack, and I was sure the four who held me down were going to take their revenge once Brian was dead."

"Brian?"

"Your father, Brian LoFasso. My husband, although he wasn't part of the clan. I don't think he understood what happened in the end. He didn't really believe everything I'd told him about who I was."

Quinn fought down her curiosity about this woman and the man who had been her father. "So, did you plead for your life? Was that why they spared you?"

Naomi shook her head. "No, never. It never occurred to me becoming a vampire would be an option. John Handon showed up as they were ready to start in on me. He wanted to feed on me, to taste hunter blood.

She stopped for a second and took a deep breath before continuing. "That's what he did. While they held me, he fed. I was sure I would die and soon join your father in the afterlife. For some reason, John stopped. I was nearly drained, delirious, and near death when he asked me."

"He said, 'Perhaps you'd like to live on to see the aftermath of what we've wrought here with the death of the clans? You would make a suitable trophy for my collection. You must consent, of course.'"

"At the time, weakened by the loss of blood, I was thinking of the last time I'd held you in my arms. My beautiful Quintana, who'd just learned to smile. It helped me make up my mind and do something I'd never imagined I would."

Naomi shrugged. "Once I agreed, it was over quickly, and I became one of them. It took me several years to work through my blood lust and gain enough control of myself to be allowed out from under direct supervision. It took still more to work my way up into his confidence so he'd give me enough autonomy to allow me to look in on you. It was all worth it, though, because here you are, a grown woman and a true huntress."

Emotions warred within Quinn. She wanted to hate this woman, not just for abandoning her, but for not revealing herself until now. It was irrational, and part of her knew it. Everything Naomi said made sense in a twisted but logical way. Quinn couldn't say it aloud, though. That was too much for her to accept right now.

"So, what do we do?" Quinn asked. "We're at an impasse. Will you try to turn me in or let me leave?"

"Quinn," Naomi said. "I thought I made it clear. All of this, what I am now, was to help you become what you are today. I will not harm you. No order from my sire can make me do that."

"So, why are you here? If not to stop me?"

"John told me he'd sent Zabe and Kim here to wait for you. I knew there was a chance you'd show up, so I came to send them home before you got here."

"I don't understand."

"Quinn, I'm here to help you defeat John Handon. Once you do that, I will be free and can stop doing his bidding. Then I can finally die and rest."

"How can you help me if you're bound to do what he says?"

"I'm able to resist him when it comes to you, and you alone. I think it's a final bit of my hunter blood somewhere inside me. But that won't stop me from hurting or killing your friends if he tells me to. The only way I can get my free will back is for you to kill John Handon. Do that, and you set me loose from his control."

"I'm not here to rescue you, Naomi," Quinn said. "I came here to find you and get some answers."

"Did you get them?" Naomi asked.

Quinn paused to think. She didn't know if she believed everything Naomi had told her, but most of it rang true. She nodded. "For now, yes. I might have more later on, but that's for another time if it ever comes."

Naomi smiled. "Fair enough."

Quinn decided to see if Naomi was serious. She walked over to pick up her Bowie, watching the vampire. Naomi followed her with her eyes but didn't move from where she stood.

Quinn sheathed her blade and said, "I guess I need to get back and help the others find the bowl and the egg."

"You don't have to look. They're downstairs with the tome."

"Everything?" Quinn asked.

"Yes, the tome, the scrying bowl, and the dagger are all downstairs, packed in a hard travel case strapped to a dolly. They're ready for transport to the ritual. Someone will be picking them up soon."

Quinn tried to hide her excitement about getting the bowl and dagger while she was here. She didn't need the book since Taylor had scanned it. A question occurred to her. "How did you figure out our location? I mean, what's to keep you from coming and taking it all back?"

"It was a lucky accident," Naomi said, shrugging. "I placed a tracking chip in all the rare books here so they could be located in case of theft. I wish I could claim credit for having the forethought, but it was actually suggested by John's insurance company to lower the museum's rates."

"Who else knows we're staying at the old hospital? This is important, Naomi. I need to know if my friends are in danger."

"Just me. I went to check on the location alone. None of the others are aware of how I found the book and took it back. I told you, Quinn. I'll do nothing that would endanger you."

Quinn considered Naomi's words as she retrieved her earpiece from the floor beside Zabe's headless body. She stood and put it in place. Part of her wanted to believe the woman. How far could she be trusted?

Time to find out.

Quinn walked over to Naomi at the top of the stairs. "Step aside so I can go down and retrieve the bowl."

The woman paused for a moment. Quinn didn't miss the way Naomi's fists clenched and her shoulders tensed. She expected the vampire to attack. Instead, Naomi stepped aside in slow, jerky movements.

"Go," Naomi said through gritted teeth. "I can resist John's explicit command to protect the contents of this building, but only because that would threaten you. You should hurry, though. I don't know how long I can hold off the command. I'll do it as long as I can, but..." The woman's voice trailed off as her body jerked and shook while she fought for control.

Quinn understood. Naomi was fighting her master's compulsion, and it could overwhelm her at any moment.

With a single nod, Quinn limped down the steps as fast as her weakened state would allow.

It didn't take her long to find the case. It sat by the locked front door, awaiting pickup just like she said. Quinn opened the latches and lifted the lid. The book, scrying bowl, and dagger were all inside.

Crouching by the container, Quinn tapped her earpiece to contact Taylor, but nothing happened. Cursing, she realized the device had pulled out of the remote radio connection. She took it off her ears. The tiny red light was off. She pressed and held the small button in the side with her thumbnail, waiting for the light to show it had turned on again.

As soon as the light returned, Quinn replaced the earpiece and tapped the button.

A second later, Taylor came on the channel. "Oh, my God, Quinn, you're back. We couldn't contact you—"

"I'm fine." Quinn checked over her shoulder. No sign of Naomi yet, but she could show up at any time. It was clear from the way she struggled that she couldn't hold off the command indefinitely. It would only take her a few seconds to descend to the first floor once she lost control. "I'm bringing the bowl and the dagger back. Count down from ten and then recall me. I'm on the first floor by the front door."

"Got it. See you in a bit," Taylor said. She began counting down. "Ten, nine—"

Quinn lifted the crystal bowl from the case, hugging it to her with one hand. She picked up the dagger in her other hand, holding it close to her body for the return transfer. Then she looked at the book, wondering if she should take it. Deciding to try to carry it and the other two items, she leaned into the case and levered her hand under the hefty tome to pull it free.

Then she ran out of time.

A snarling scream sounded from upstairs, and pounding feet indicated Naomi was coming in all her vampire speed. In the end, she'd been unable to resist Handon's commands any longer. Quinn stood, hoping Taylor pulled her back quickly.

Quinn waited as Taylor got to one. Naomi had reached the bottom of the stairs and charged at Quinn. The change in the vampire was both stark and terrifying. The woman's eyes now shone with a red glow, her fangs were bared, and talons had extended from her fingernails. Naomi had lost control.

Naomi reached for Quinn and the huntress felt a wrenching yank as she started falling into the VR again. Then everything went black.

.

CHAPTER TWENTY-EIGHT

Quinn woke with a start, reaching for the bowl and the dagger, which were no longer there.

"Noooo," she shouted as she rolled to the edge. The rolling wave of nausea overwhelmed her. Taylor didn't get there in time with the trash can, and Quinn vomited on the floor.

When she finished emptying her stomach, Quinn sat upright and swung her legs over the side of the desk. She battled nausea and pain as she conducted a frantic search on the desktop.

"Taylor, tell me you took the scrying bowl and a silver dagger from me as I came through."

Taylor stood up, looking around. "You don't have them?"

"No. Oh, God, no. Naomi took them from me just as I transitioned back here. Quick, send me back. They're coming to pick up the book and the bowl any minute."

"I can't, Quinn. I need a few minutes to recharge, and the system has to cycle first."

JAMIE DAVIS

Another round of nausea hit her, and Quinn couldn't hold it back. She leaned over, retching into the plastic trash can this time. Each heave sent shooting pains through her chest as the ends of her broken ribs ground against each other.

Taylor held out a handful of paper towels.

Quinn took them and wiped her mouth as she sat up.

Miranda came around the desk and said, "Hon, you look awful."

"I don't feel that great either, and I lost the bowl again. Any word from Clark?"

Miranda and Taylor shook their heads.

Taylor said, "I'm worried. He should have checked in by now."

"Did you try calling him?"

Taylor nodded. "Several times. He's either ignoring us or his phone is off."

"How long until you can send me back inside?"

"At least a half-hour," Taylor replied. "Quinn, even if I get the system ready to go again, what do you think you can do in the condition you're in?"

"I'll clean up and get something to eat. That'll help me heal up some. I can't pull energy from the ley lines anymore without my amulet, so that will have to be enough. Once I've eaten, I'll feel a lot better. You'll see."

Taylor shook her head but didn't argue with Quinn.

Quinn was thankful her friend didn't push the issue. "What about the VirSync command center location? Were you able to locate it?"

"I'm running down some final leads," Taylor said. "I

252

should have an answer soon. Go and get some food. I'll try to expedite the remaining parts of the search."

Quinn hopped off the desk, careful to avoid the mess on the floor, working to hide the pain in her side. She pointed at the puddle. "I'll clean that up when I get back."

"No worries," Taylor said, holding up the roll of paper towels. "I've got it."

"Thanks," Quinn said. "Get that search done. With the bowl and dagger lost, it's even more important to track down the Myles Hickman and his slayers. They have the Ruby Heart."

Quinn started toward the kitchen.

Miranda said, "Mind if I tag along, Quinn?"

"Suit yourself, although I might not be great company. I've got a lot to figure out right now."

The ghost nodded and drifted beside Quinn in silence as she limped her way down the hall to the kitchen. When she got there, she pulled open the refrigerator to see what she could grab in a hurry.

There wasn't much, and Quinn didn't feel like heating up anything. She pulled out a jug of milk and shut the door. Turning to walk over to the table, Quinn grabbed the box of dry cereal from the top of the refrigerator and a bowl and spoon from the drying rack by the sink.

After sitting down, Quinn filled the bowl with cereal and milk and began eating.

Miranda hovered on the other side of the table, drifting lower to match Quinn's seated position. "Did she do this to you?"

"Who?"

"Your mother, Quinn," Miranda said. "Who else?"

Quinn shook her head. "No, there were two other vampires there. It was them. And don't call her my mother. She hasn't earned that title."

"She gave birth to you, Quinn. She might not be Mom or Mommy to you, but she is your mother. Did you learn anything from her?"

"We talked. She claims to have done everything so she could watch over me. I went through childhood in hell, and she thinks she somehow protected me from things."

Miranda shrugged. "It's possible for both to be true. There were some things she couldn't protect you from—anything that happened in the daytime, for example. After all, she could only get away to look in on you after sundown."

Quinn hadn't considered that part of it, and the revelation angered her. "Don't try to make this better, Miranda. Nothing is going to fix my deep-seated mommy issues, certainly not a five-minute conversation. She's a monster. She as much as admitted to killing people to feed, in the mistaken assumption that by becoming what she was, she could later justify it all by saying she did it to watch over me."

"So, what next?" Miranda asked, opting to change the subject.

"We wait and see if Taylor comes up with a location or Clark calls in. After that, I don't know. One thing is for sure; this location isn't safe. Naomi knows about it. That means we need to relocate."

"Quinn, there's no time to do that tonight. If we try to pack up and move, we won't get the rig set up again in time to send you anywhere. And what if Clark needs help?"

"I can't leave you and Taylor here alone. I mean, Miranda, you'd be all right. They can't kill you twice, but Taylor isn't safe."

"You forget that Taylor's a werewolf, Quinn. She can more than take care of herself. She might have issues holding onto control, but she'll be fine if there are any bad guys around. There are more important things to worry about right now. First of all, how bad are your injuries?"

Quinn finished the first bowlful of cereal without giving an answer. She wasn't going to lie to her friends. Instead, she poured another bowlful of cereal, dousing the sweetened cornflakes with milk. Her body still ached, and she needed the extra energy to force more healing. She felt a little bit better, but her ribs still sent a searing, stabbing pain through her side with every deep breath. She knew her body could heal pretty fast on its own. The problem was, she didn't know how much she could expect in such a short time without the magical assistance of her amulet to draw on the ley lines.

Her thoughts turned back to what they had to do tonight, trying to assess what she might face in the hours ahead. There was no doubt in her mind she wasn't anywhere near a hundred percent. The cereal might be taking the edge off her pain, but it wasn't healing her.

As for her friends and the risks they faced if they remained here, Miranda was right about Taylor's ability to protect herself. Quinn had seen what her friend could do in wolf-woman form. As much as she worried about her best friend, she had to admit to herself that Taylor would be fine on her own for now.

Thinking about Taylor gave Quinn another idea,

though. "Miranda, how good is Taylor with the magic stuff?"

"She's good enough, considering how new she is. Why do you ask?"

"I wondered if she could cast a spell and accelerate the healing process before I go back out tonight."

"That's beyond what she knows right now, Quinn. It's more than I could do before I died. Healing is a specialized skill that requires a lot of study to do more than ease the pain or take care of a minor injury."

"That's what I was afraid of. I just wish I hadn't lost the amulet. Then I could heal and be as good as new before facing off against anyone else."

Miranda shook her head. "Quinn, I think you're using the amulet as a crutch. Hunters are known to have done great things over the ages, truly impossible things. None of those accounts mention they used an amulet to do them."

"It's probably a trade secret," Quinn said. "You wouldn't want your enemies to know that all they had to do was to take your amulet away and you'd be helpless."

"You're not helpless, Quinn," Miranda said, laughing. "You're probably the least helpless person I know."

"I can do some of the things I picked up while I was in VR in the outside world, but nothing like the power of the amulet gave me. I can't pull on the energy of the ley lines like I could before."

"If you can sense them at all," Miranda said, "then the block is within you, not due to an external cause like the missing amulet. The ley lines are invisible to those who cannot access them."

Quinn closed her eyes and called up the HUD in her

mind. She opened the map overlay for the hospital. One of the reasons Clark had chosen this site was due to the ley line running behind the abandoned building.

The bright shining line pulsed as if inviting her to touch it. Quinn reached out as she had with other lines when she had the amulet. She could sense the pulsing energy through her connection, but when she pulled it, nothing happened. It was as if she strained to bend a pipe of solid steel. The two times she'd drawn on the power lines before, the magical energy had flexed as she grabbed it until she'd peeled away the power she needed.

After straining without success, Quinn opened her eyes to meet Miranda's glowing translucent gaze. "It's no use. Like I said. I need the amulet to access that kind of power."

From the way the ghost pursed her lips, Quinn didn't think Miranda agreed with her. What did she know, though? She was a spirit who couldn't use any power.

Quinn regretted the thought as soon as she had it. The guilt surrounding Miranda's death washed over her. She owed the dead witch more respect than that after what had happened in Handon's office. Miranda might be right about Quinn's abilities. For whatever reason, though, she couldn't access it tonight.

Miranda seemed to agree with her because she said, "Quinn, I think you'll be unable to access that power until you have no other choice left to you."

Quinn didn't answer. Miranda's comment wasn't a lot of help. Instead of responding, she ate the last spoonful, then picked up the bowl and drained the milk from it. Setting it down, she stood and stretched, tested her aching ribs in a couple of simple attack moves. Even a basic lunge sent pain shooting through her torso. She could move. Maybe she could fight through the pain and hold her own. Each motion she made, however, would be a test of her will to continue.

"Quinn," Miranda said, "maybe we should try to reach Clark and leave a message for him about your injuries. I can see how much pain you're in. That is not conducive to any sort of supernatural showdown. You need to be at your best, not half-beaten when you get there. Let Handon and the others have this small win tonight. You and Clark will live to fight another day."

"No, I have to find a way to stop them tonight. Naomi knows where we're hiding. She's avoided telling Handon where we are because she's protecting me. He'll figure out she's hiding something from him, and she'll only hold out so long before his compulsion overcomes her resistance. Then she'll tell him everything. We have to take a stand now."

Miranda didn't say anything. The brief shake of her head and frown told Quinn what was going through the spirit's mind.

Quinn said, "I'm going to wash up and change. Then I'll head down and check on Taylor to see if she's found anything. I think I'm as good as I'm going to get."

Miranda nodded as Quinn left the kitchen and went to her room. She felt a little better, but not as well as she'd hoped.

When Quinn returned to the office, Taylor looked up with a frown on her face. "Good, you're back. Miranda and I think we've got a problem."

"What?" Quinn asked the two of them. "Weren't you able to track down the VirSync location?"

"I got it, and that's the problem," Taylor said. She spun the right-hand monitor around, revealing a map of the city of Baltimore. As Quinn watched, it zoomed in, centered over East Baltimore. It eventually dropped a virtual red pin on the map.

Quinn leaned forward, squinting at the screen. A few seconds later, recognition dawned on her. "Oh, my God, is that the same building where O'Malley's is located?"

"Yep," Taylor said, a grim smile on her face. "It turns out a shell company of Handon's owns not just the building, but most of the whole block, including all the row homes on either side of the street. When we were there the other night, they were probably watching the whole time."

Quinn studied the map, trying to put it together with what she'd learned over the last few days and the little bit that slipped out tonight from Naomi. Since she'd started training with Clark, Quinn had learned not to trust coincidences where the supernatural was concerned. If it looked like a connection existed, it probably did.

She pointed at the map. "That's where it's all happening, and I'll bet Clark is there as well."

"Why do you say that?" Miranda asked.

"It makes sense. He went looking for Filippa, and we know she's been there in the past. On top of that, since he hasn't reached out to us or responded to our attempts to reach him, Clark's probably run into trouble. That matches what we now know about who else is lurking around that fae bar. And I think I know where to go when I get there."

Quinn sighed, and then, despite the pain in her side,

drew herself up straight. She had to go. There was no one else. She reached out of reflex to check on her Bowie. It was still beneath her right arm. The blessed silver blade and her remaining strength would have to be enough.

Taylor and Miranda exchanged glances.

"Quinn," Miranda said, "you don't have to do this. You can barely move."

"It has to be me. If I'm careful, I should be able to sneak in and break him out of wherever Filippa is holding him. If I can do that, I won't be alone. Then we can decide together what to do next."

Taylor made no effort to hide the concern in her voice. "Quinn, that is the worst idea I've ever heard. You don't look any better than when you went down to eat. I thought you said you'd feel better once you ate something?"

"I do. The pain is hardly there now. I can do this, T." Quinn smiled at her friend's concern. "If not me, who?"

Taylor started to say something but closed her mouth. Eventually, she said, "All right, keep the earpiece in place this time and call me if things get bad. I'll pull you back out as soon as there's trouble. Got it?"

Quinn nodded. Having Taylor in her ear would be helpful, and the VR system might heal some of her injuries on re-entry.

She climbed up on the desk, holding back a groan as she twisted her torso to lay down. She pulled the VR goggles and headset on before giving Taylor a thumbs up. "Where are you dropping me?"

"I think I can drop you into that back storeroom leading from the bar to O'Malley's office. Will that work?"

Quinn nodded and slipped the goggles from her forehead into place. "Do it."

There was a brief flash of pain as her body wrenched backward, the falling sensation, then everything went black. Quinn was in.

CHAPTER TWENTY-NINE

Q uinn opened her eyes. She knelt amidst the stacked crates and kegs in the bar's storeroom. Reaching out to a stack of kegs beside her, Quinn steadied herself while the nausea and dizziness of the transition passed. The steady thump of the country beat pounded through the door, not that far away to her left. The overhead lights were dimmer this time, but that might be the VR system. It was hard to tell. It seemed like she had more shadows around her, and that was to her benefit.

Concentrating on her HUD, Quinn muttered, "Mist." Instantly, the familiar haze came up around her field of view.

It was good she'd done it. The door to the bar opened, and the pulsing country music grew louder for a few seconds. Jonas, the giant bouncer, ducked through the opening.

He turned back and said, "I'll be right back, Juni. The boss is going to want to know why the wards were tripped.

I don't know who it was, but there's been an intrusion somewhere in the building."

Jonas pulled the door closed and shuffled along down the center of the extended storeroom. It surprised Quinn when he didn't stop at Paddy's office door. Instead, he pulled a small flashlight from his pocket and continued walking into the darkness beyond.

Once again, the scar on Quinn's chest chilled and set off a small vibration as she stared into the darkness. With a nod, she murmured, "Dammit, I need to see."

The storeroom still had a gloomy feel, but she could see much better, even into the near-total darkness beyond Paddy's office door. Moving slowly, careful to remain quiet, Quinn followed Jonas down the long corridor.

After she had followed the giant man for a few minutes, Quinn realized the corridor narrowed into a genuine tunnel. She saw they had passed beneath the block of row homes. Periodically along the passageway, doors led off to one side or the other.

Quinn stopped and listened at one of the plain wooden doors. When she heard nothing on the other side, Quinn opened the door and peered through. The other side seemed to be the basement of a home or perhaps a small business, based on the collection of boxes and shelves she could see from the doorway. That matched her theory about where the tunnel was going.

Closing the door, Quinn moved forward again, following the bobbing light marking Jonas's position ahead of her. The farther she traveled down the passage, the more frequently the scar on her chest vibrated and sent a chill through her. At one point, she shivered involuntarily.

Something evil or threatening was going on ahead if the residual presence of her amulet was to be trusted.

As she realized what the scar seemed to be telling her, Quinn thought again about what Miranda had tried to say to her before. Did the former witch know what she was talking about? Quinn had her doubts, but at this point, she needed any lifeline that could possibly help her survive the night. She had to stop Handon, no matter what.

Jonas's bobbing light disappeared ahead of her, although she could see a faint, fading glow ahead. Quinn picked up her pace and came to the top of a flight of stone stairs leading down. She stopped, staring down. Her scar throbbed nonstop in time with her heartbeat now.

Bringing up her map overlay, Quinn tried to see where she was in relation to the bar. If the map was correct, she was almost two city blocks away from O'Malley's. She also understood why the passage led here. The stairs led down toward a point where two ley lines crossed each other. Quinn didn't know what such a nexus meant, but the increased magical energy down there must be why her scar chilled and pulsed the way it did as she got closer.

She couldn't turn around now. She was sure Handon and his minions had brought all three components to this place. The power nexus pretty much proved it. That meant she didn't just have to find and rescue Clark, but she also had to try to stop them from completing the ritual and making evil versions of the hunter amulets.

Quinn started down the stairs, keeping to the left side against the stone wall as the stairs curved to the right. As she continued downward, chanting voices carried up to her from below. She moved down step by step, her scar pulsing so hard now it ached. The strangest thing was, despite the obvious signs of danger below, there was something about this place that seemed almost comforting to her. When she reached the bottom of the stairs, she knew why.

The landing at the bottom of the curved staircase continued about ten feet, ending in an arched doorway with two heavy wooden doors bound in steel straps. They both stood open, but Quinn could make out the symbols carved on the outer surfaces. The stylized tree and accompanying runes carved into the doors matched the symbols that had been cast into her amulet.

This place had belonged to the hunters before the purges.

It made sense. The convergence of the two ley lines would have lent their power to any magic worked here. It would have been the perfect place to create the amulets and bless new members of the clan. The familiarity made Quinn wonder if she'd been brought here as an infant.

As she stood in the shadows outside the doors to the chamber, something else was familiar. The voices inside chanted in that same guttural language she'd last heard in the cavern beneath the VirSync complex. She even recognized the cadence and many of the words being used in that language. It meant they were in the middle of a ritual to convert someone into a demon-kinder, merging the soul of a demon with a human host body.

Quinn moved up to the doorway and peered around it into the room, trying to see more of the ritual in action. Her heart sank when she saw the subject of the chanting and transference.

Clark lay bound by his hands and feet to a rough wooden table. He'd been stripped to the waist, and black runes had been painted over his entire upper body, including his face. He wasn't comatose, as the victims had been when Quinn had seen this process before. The hunter struggled, wide awake, against the leather straps securing him to the tabletop.

Myles Hickman, wearing the same black and red robes he'd worn before, stood beside Clark. He held the glowing Ruby Heart in his fist, waving it in slow passes up and down the length of Clark's body while he chanted in unison with the cluster of ten robed individuals behind him.

Beside Myles stood the demon-kinder Cindy, one of Quinn's former candidate colleagues from those first few days at VirSync. Quinn scanned the faces beneath the hooded robes behind Myles. Most were familiar, although she didn't know all their names. She recognized her former handlers, Philip and Velma, among them.

On the opposite side of the table stood John Handon. Naomi was beside him, with a cluster of ten vampires in the shadows behind them.

At the head of the table, robed in green and white, stood another figure. The new person wore a hood, and Quinn couldn't make out the face because they were turned away from her. Jonas approached the person in the green robe, bent down, and said something. The robed individual nodded, and Jonas stood up and started back toward the entrance.

Quinn moved to enter the room, keeping close to the far wall and the shadows, trying to avoid Jonas. She slipped inside just in time. The giant bouncer crouched to pass beneath the arched entrance and head back up the stairs.

Quinn kept going into the room, trying to get a better look at the green-robed individual.

A few seconds later, the green-robed figure lifted their head a little. The hood shifted so Quinn could see inside. She ground her teeth in anger as she recognized the person.

It was Filippa.

What was she doing helping them torture Clark? They were supposed to be friends, perhaps even former lovers. The look on the fae princess's face was one of ecstatic expectation as if she awaited something wonderful.

Looking around, Quinn tried to come up with a way to stop the ritual. There was no way she could take on all the people in this room on her own, especially as injured as she was.

Carefully fitted stone blocks formed extended arches spaced around the perimeter to support the vaulted ceiling. Carved stone panels, each about four feet across, appeared every ten feet or so around the room. The same angular rune and tree motif carvings covered the panels. The images comforted her. It felt like home here, although it was now tainted with decay and evil from the use to which it was being put. Anger welled within her at the way they'd appropriated this sacred space.

Hidden in the shadows next to one of the buttresses that supported the arches, Quinn pressed herself against the wall and traced one of the runes on the carved stone panels. Her mind flared with a sudden awareness of otherness, coupled with belonging and family.

"Welcome, Huntress," a woman's voice crooned in her head. "We have waited a long time for your arrival."

At first, Quinn thought it had come over her earpiece from someone on Taylor's end. She quickly realized it was inside her mind. Moreover, she recognized the voice. She had heard it twice before.

Quinn formed the reply inside her mind. "Who are you?"

"We are those who have gone before, preparing the way for your arrival."

"You-you were expecting me? How?"

"Your coming was foretold long before your time on this earth, long before any of us at rest here walked these halls. It was foretold by the founders during the earliest formation of the clans."

The woman's voice changed, taking on a sense of many others speaking in unison.

"For in time will come one who was lost.

They will restore that which was taken.

They will rebuild the clans.

Forging them into the final weapon."

"I don't even know what that means. I'm here to stop them from hurting my friend. I don't know how yet, but I will think of something."

The woman's voice returned alone again. "Trust in yourself, my huntress. You have much more within you than you believe. Trust in your power. Trust in us. Nothing made can truly be destroyed. Nothing has been lost."

As Quinn tried to wrap her head around the riddles the voice uttered in her head, a cry of anguish from the center of the room drew her attention back to the vile ritual at work there. Straining to see past the robed people surrounding the table, she took a step forward. As soon as her hand left the stone panel, her connection to the other woman ceased.

She had no time to reconnect and ask more questions. Clark had resisted as long as he could. With a cry of triumph, Myles shouted something in that same guttural language. He moved the Ruby Heart lower to hover over Clark's head. The chanting increased in both speed and volume.

The hunter now seemed to be aware of his surroundings. His entire body had tensed, and his limbs strained against all the bonds at once. His eyes were locked on the red gemstone Myles held a few inches above his face.

Quinn moved forward, realizing she was out of time. Disregarding her aching side, she drew power from her half-filled stamina bar, adding both strength and speed. She'd only have enough to maintain power for maybe a minute, but it would have to do.

Rushing forward, Quinn drew her Bowie, holding onto her shadow invisibility for as long as she could. Clark had told her that once she attacked anyone, the magical distraction of the ability would be dispelled. That meant she'd only get one chance at this.

Gliding to the table between Clark and Myles, Quinn held the knife in two hands and slashed at the hand holding the Ruby Heart. The Bowie's blessed blade cut through skin, muscle, and bone with ease, driven by the enhanced force of her blow.

Myles Hickman screamed in agony, yanking his arm back and staring at the stump of his wrist, now spurting blood into the air. His severed hand, the Ruby Heart still clenched in his fingers, fell to the table beside Clark's head.

Quinn turned in place, her forward momentum still carrying her as shouts of alarm sounded all around her. With her free hand, Quinn snatched a curved silver dagger from where it was tucked into the sash of Cindy's robe.

At the same time, with her other hand, she slashed the Bowie through the leather straps holding Clark's hands together on the table above his head.

He sat up, in control again now that the ritual had stopped. Quinn pressed the stolen dagger into his hands. He'd have to free his feet on his own. She had work to do while she still had the strength.

Still spinning, Quinn charged at the closest target— Filippa, in her green robes.

The fae princess recovered from her initial shock faster than Quinn expected and pulled Clark's blessed short sword from beneath her robe. Holding it in a guard position, she easily parried Quinn's initial attack.

Quinn, angry that she hadn't been able to make surprise work in her favor a little longer, snarled at the fae princess and redoubled her efforts to break through. It was no good, though. Her injuries kept her from moving fast enough to get any advantage. The princess was just too good.

Behind her, shouts and the sound of metal on metal told her Clark had freed himself. At least he had a fighting chance now.

Filippa smiled, sensing Quinn's weakness. In an instant, the princess turned her purely defensive moves into parries, coupled with attack combinations. Before Quinn could stop the woman, she found herself driven away from the table. Soon she and Clark fought back to back in a desperate melee against a surging host of foes.

Several robed bodies on the floor around them told Quinn Clark had managed to end a few of them before the tide turned. Myles knelt nearby, sobbing as he tried to staunch the flow of blood from his wrist.

At some point, the demon-kinder Cindy joined Filippa in front of Quinn. The possessed girl had found another blade somewhere, and she and the fae woman attacked in tandem.

Quinn somehow managed to parry the initial flurry of doubled attacks, but it was only a matter of time until they broke through. She checked her status in the HUD. Her strength boost had almost run out, and there was nothing left in her stamina bar.

The press of attackers forced her and Clark back until they stood side by side against the wall between two of the carved panels.

The blades came in all at once, and Quinn knew they were finished. Her strength faded, and weakness swept over her.

Quinn closed her eyes, welcoming the end at last.

CHAPTER THIRTY

"Stop!"

The multiple blades coming at her did not strike.

Quinn opened her eyes to see three polished points mere inches from her face. They all quivered with anticipation in the hands of those who wielded them.

"Do not kill either of them," John Handon said from across the room. "Drop the blade, Huntress, or you won't live to see the end of what I've planned here."

Part of Quinn, aching and in pain, wanted to defy him and die fighting. However, a distant part of her mind heard the faint echo of a familiar voice.

Patience, Huntress.

Beyond caring, she resigned herself to whatever came next. Her body beaten, sore, and exhausted, Quinn lowered her left hand, her grip loosening until the Bowie clattered to the stone floor beside her.

"Good," Handon said. "Now we have two hunters to join our ritual and become one with us. One will join as a demon-kinder slayer as planned, and the other as my newest vampire child."

"You've lost your chance, Handon," Clark shouted. "You won't take me by surprise again. I'll die before you have your way with me."

Quinn said nothing. She tried to put on an air of defiance, emulating Clark. She saw no way out, though, despite what the voice had told her.

Handon smiled. "We shall see, Hunter. I see your protege also doubts I can turn her. You'll find I'm very persuasive when I want to be, Huntress. I know you've met my first turned hunter," he said, gesturing to Naomi by his side. "She's proof that even one of you cannot resist my desire when it comes to creating new children for my coven."

"She's not me, Handon, not even close," Quinn said, calling up one last ounce of bluster. "I told you the last time we met, I'm something more. I'm a huntress, and that is something you've yet to defeat."

Quinn dug deep. Despite her pain and weariness, something in her refused to give up. There had to be a way out. She'd defeated this vampire once before, and she could do it again. She just had to figure it out.

She kept her eyes on Handon, but her mind reached out to the nexus of power pulsing beneath the room. If Miranda was right, she could do this without the amulet. The power lines were much closer this time than before. She was right on top of them. The power of the magic thrummed in the back of her mind. It was as if someone played a sustained chord on the lowest keys of a piano. She noticed for the first time that the room seemed to carry the vibration, magnifying it. Quinn couldn't help but think there was something there, something about this chamber she was missing.

The vampire lord nodded at Naomi and pointed at Clark, saying, "Take him. Return him to the table."

Moving in a blur of speed Quinn couldn't follow, Naomi charged forward. Somehow the woman's hunter reflexes had been magnified by the power of being a vampire, making her more than just another of the undead.

Naomi's move happened so fast, she'd batted the curved dagger from Clark's hands before he could even twitch in her direction. The blade clattered to the floor. Unarmed, he fought back with his bare hands, landing several powerful blows that shook the vampire woman, driving her backward a few steps.

She came back, though, stepping back into contact with him, striking with even more speed and power, beating Clark until he crumpled under the rain of blows and collapsed to the floor. The red-robed cultists around him piled on top, keeping him down as they continued to pummel him.

Quinn considered going to his assistance. The cultists in front of her held their ground, though, keeping their blades pointed at her. It wouldn't have mattered since she couldn't do much in her current condition. Her injured body could barely stand upright at this point.

Soon the cultists, led by Naomi, lifted an unconscious and bloody Clark, carrying him back to the table in the room's center.

Quinn feigned bravado. It was all she had. "You can't

complete the spell. I took off Myles's hand. He's your high priest, isn't he?"

"Only until the next one takes his place," Handon said. He turned to the small cluster of cultists standing near the whimpering VirSync CEO. "Who wants it?"

Philip, Quinn's old VirSync system moderator, shouted before anyone else could speak and dove on top of his kneeling boss. He pulled a short sword from beneath his robes and plunged it into Myles, running him through. The former CEO gave a gurgling cry and then fell silent.

Philip wrenched the bloody blade free and whirled to face his fellow cultists. "Anybody willing to try me, or do you acknowledge me as your high priest?"

The others looked from side to side. Seeing no takers for the challenge, they all took a step back and inclined their heads in a brief bow to their new high priest.

Philip pointed to Clark, now returned to his place on the table. "Hold him down while I complete the ritual."

He picked up the severed fist, which was still holding the gemstone, and pried the fingers open until the palm-sized ruby fell into his hand. As soon as he grabbed it, the stone flared to life again, pulsing with an inner red glow.

Taking a stance beside the table as Myles had, Philip began passing the Ruby Heart in the air over Clark's head and body in a smooth motion and chanting. The cultists behind him resumed their echoing chants to support the spell to enable demonic possession.

Handon pointed at Quinn. "Hold her there and make sure she watches. I want her to see another of her friends lose his life in front of her. I want to watch the despair and helplessness in her eyes before I feed on her."

Naomi had returned to her place beside Handon. The three cultists held Quinn at bay with their weapons hovering near her chest. She had no doubt they'd kill her in an instant if she made any move toward Clark or Handon. Two of them reached out with their free hands to grip her sagging shoulders and press her back against the stone wall.

Quinn stood still and stared at Naomi, hoping against all hope that the former hunter would find a way to resist. It was the only chance she could think of. Would Naomi somehow become the mother she claimed to be and come to the rescue?

Despite Quinn's wishful thinking, there was no sign the vampire would do anything to help. Naomi stared back at her, holding her gaze. That was all. The only sign of anything unusual was the faint twitch of one hand at her side. Everything else about Naomi stood in complete still-ness, except that hand.

Quinn glanced down, concentrating on the hand. Why was it twitching?

The forefinger extended just a bit from Naomi's left hand, moving to a slight angle away from her body. The finger pointed to Quinn's right.

The huntress's eyes shifted to the side, but she had no idea what the other woman meant by her gesture, if anything. There was nothing but a stone wall to her right. What was beside her that could help them in any way?

"Eyes front, Huntress," Handon ordered. "Do not avert them from this. Give your comrade the respect of watching him as he surrenders and becomes everything he fought against. It is fitting that he be transformed here in the place he was instrumental in betraying."

"What do you mean? He's betrayed nothing. He survived to defy you despite what happened," Quinn said.

"Didn't he tell you, Huntress?" Handon said, his grin broadening. "He sought to impress someone and told a mundane school friend all about the hidden world around them. It was forbidden for a hunter, even a child, to tell any ordinary mortal about the supernatural world, yet he did so. Unfortunately, that friend decided he was tired of being an ordinary human."

Handon laughed, then continued, "Clark probably never understood why his friend Myles betrayed him to those who stood to gain the most from the demise of the hunters. All he could do was stand by and watch as the clan's innermost secrets were laid bare by one who sought all that hidden power for himself."

Quinn turned her eyes to the corpse on the floor. Clark had known Myles? Why hadn't he told anyone? He was wrong to tell someone hunter secrets, but in the end, it wasn't his fault his friend betrayed him.

Handon smiled. "I thought it was fitting that he should escape, to believe that he'd somehow gotten away from the assassins on his own. The killers took the rest of his clan but let him live on, alone in the world. He's lurked in the background all these years, unable to do anything as we slowly took over the whole city. In the end, he could do nothing, failing to defend those who'd befriended and hid him in those early days."

"Is that why Filippa is here?" Quinn asked. "You took her into your twisted world as well?"

"Me?" Filippa asked. "I sought only what was rightfully mine. John will help me receive my due. My many cousins have long divided this continent among themselves, giving me only a paltry single share of it. I was the first to come here, and it should all be mine."

"You did this to get a bigger fae kingdom?" Quinn asked. "Won't your kindred be angry with you for siding with their enemies?"

"All will be forgiven when the terms of my agreement with John are made clear. Besides, with his power behind me, none of them will dare to stand up to me."

Quinn ground her teeth. This had been a setup from the beginning.

The chanting resumed, and Philip continued using the stone to weaken Clark's soul so a demon could come and take over.

Her eyes returned to Naomi, her hand, and that one finger.

Naomi had told Quinn back at the museum that she'd never stopped being a huntress in her heart. Did that mean she still had some sort of connection to this place?

Naomi would have come here when she was younger. After all, it must have been the ritual center of the hunter clan here in Baltimore.

Feigning a cough, Quinn turned her head to the right and spared a quick glance around. All she could see nearby was one of the carved, square panels, the same as the others spaced all around the room. She turned her head back to the front and scanned the perimeter of the room. There were panels all around the room except for several places where the panels were just plain smooth stone, not yet carved with runes or images.

What had that voice said when she first touched the panel?

In a burst of awareness, Quinn remembered, and she knew what she had to do.

It was risky. The panel to her right was about two feet away. She couldn't just reach out and touch it. The cultists stood on either side of her, holding her arms and pressing the tips of their blades against her. As soon as she moved, she'd risk injury from the nearby swords keeping her at bay.

As she considered her options, the ceremony and chanting increased in volume as Philip raised his voice and held the Ruby Heart directly over Clark's forehead. The gemstone's inner glow now pulsed in time with the chanting, gaining speed as well.

There was no time left. The spell to transfer a demon's soul into Clark's body was almost complete.

She pulled up her HUD. She had no stamina left to assist her. All Quinn had was the limited ordinary human strength remaining in her injured body. It would have to be enough.

Taking a deep breath and steeling herself to be skewered, Quinn shoved at the cultist to her right and dove toward the carved stone panel.

Her move caught those guarding her by surprise. They had gotten caught up in the ritual, chanting along with Philip. They tried to strike Quinn when she made her move, but none of their belated attacks connected.

Quinn landed on one knee, reaching out with her right

arm. She pressed her hand against the center of the carved stone, praying her guess was correct. She silently called out to the ancestors she suspected were entombed behind those panels.

A flash of white light passed through her, blinding her, and she closed her eyes. When she opened them again, pale, glowing figures stepped away from the carved panels all around the room—men and women, former clan leaders who'd been laid to rest here until they were needed again. The spirits turned in her direction and flew at the speed of thought across the room.

Her eyes widened as the first of the ghostly forms entered her. The huntress's body jerked and twitched as they each flew at her, melding their energy with hers. With each added hunter consciousness came not only strength and power but also knowledge.

Quinn's stamina bar filled in her HUD, returning to complete green status with the entry of the first spirit, and the ghosts continued filling her. The stamina bar pulsed and changed color again and again until the final ghost from the farthest tomb melded into her. The stamina bar now glowed with a blinding white light, pulsing in time with Quinn's pounding heartbeat.

She closed her eyes, inner peace falling over her along with the power. The familiar voice in her mind, now backed by a chorus of other male and female voices, said, *"The power of us all now fills you, Huntress. Go. Cleanse our holy place of this abomination."*

CHAPTER THIRTY-ONE

Quinn opened her eyes. She still knelt by the wall. The first thing she noticed was the pain, or rather, the lack of it. The aches of her earlier injuries had all washed away, although she wasn't exactly healed. Instead, she now contained so much energy that it supported her despite her injuries.

The world slowed around her, granting her a hyper-focus on every detail in the room at once. Barely a second had passed since she'd touched the panel, although it had seemed much longer.

Behind her, the cultists who'd guarded her charged at her back, weapons raised.

A grin spread across her face. Quinn's hand stretched out, calling her Bowie to it. The blade snapped into her hand from the floor as she twisted around with a blinding speed unlike any she'd had before. She moved so quickly, the friction of the air molecules burned a little against her skin.

Parry, slash, lunge, block, stab.

That fast, she dispatched the three who'd guarded her.

She stood and faced the room's center. At the same instant, the three bodies around her fell to the floor.

"End her," Handon yelled, panic in his tone.

The cultists to the right and the vampires on the left all charged forward at once—all except Naomi, who stood rigid and quivering beside Handon.

Enhanced by the blood energy they fed upon, the vampires reached her first, although the enraged cultists were close behind them.

Quinn quickly dispatched the first pair of vampires to reach her. They seemed almost surprised by the way her Bowie slashed open one's throat before transitioning to a different grip in her hand so she could lunge forward and sink it home in the heart of the other.

Her body flowed through all the combinations of attack and defense Clark had painstakingly taught her. Plus, she had the accumulated knowledge of the clan leaders in her mind upon which to draw. She began using combat moves so complex there was no way she'd ever replicate them. More of her opponents fell, dead or dying before they hit the floor. Vampires and cultists littered the ground around her, and still they came, driven by Handon's orders.

Quinn ducked under an incoming attack. She grabbed the wrist holding a sword aimed at her throat and redirected it into the chest of another attacker behind her.

She twisted out of the grasp of several who sought to tackle her to the floor, somehow remaining on her feet, spinning to elude their clutching fingers.

Quinn needed help. Even with the enhancements from

the ancestors, she had nearly been overwhelmed twice in a few seconds.

She spared a glance at Clark. He was still unconscious on the table and would be of no assistance.

Filippa had backed away and was inching toward the door, probably bent on escaping the carnage from either side.

Only John Handon and Naomi stood in the same positions. The vampire lord glared at Quinn. Naomi stood trembling beside him.

Quinn understood in that single glance what had happened to Naomi. She had been ordered to kill Quinn. She resisted that command, but Quinn realized her resistance was a finite thing. She'd seen how Handon's commands eventually overcame the woman's will.

If Naomi entered this desperate melee, Quinn was done. The enhanced vampire/hunter hybrid would be a solid match for her own souped-up skills.

Unless...

Quinn twisted, working to disengage and break away from the mob surging around her. The move left her open, and several attacks landed at once.

She cried out in pain. Her enhanced power compensated for the pain, simultaneously lessening her strength and speed a little.

Despite the injuries, the move worked, allowing her to disengage from the massed opponents. Quinn leaped upward to run sideways along the wall, clear of the mob of vampires reaching up for her.

Once past her closest attackers, Quinn dropped back to the floor and charged at the vampire lord. He didn't seem alarmed. A smile spread across his face. He reached into his black suit coat, pulling a foot-long dagger free as he turned to face her.

"You can't think you can take me, girl," he snarled. "You've none of the training needed to take on one such as me."

Quinn smiled and accessed the inner voices before she answered him. A chorus of her ancestors replied, "The girl is no longer alone, creature of the night. The might of the entire clan resides within her."

Handon's eyes widened, fear filling them for the first time since Quinn had injured him months earlier. Before he could respond to her taunting words, she was upon him. Her knife flashed in blinding attacks, seeking to break through his defenses.

Block, slash, parry, thrust.

Quinn engaged in a never-ending series of combination moves, using every defense and counterattack the vampire offered her.

Twisting and dodging, Quinn kept moving so Handon's followers couldn't get near enough to close with her while she fought their master. On several occasions, she was able to twist away in a way that allowed one of Handon's attacks to instead kill a cultist behind her.

The first of her attacks to reach him was followed almost immediately by a counter from him. That strike scored a shallow slash in her side. Her piercing attack on his shoulder had been serious, but the vampire could take more damage than she could since only a strike to his heart or decapitation would kill him.

Quinn glanced at her stamina bar. It no longer glowed

bright white. It had nearly returned to its standard green color. She had to finish this while she had the power to do it.

Taking a chance, Quinn feinted toward Naomi, who was still rooted to the spot beside Handon.

The vampire lord took the bait and lunged at Quinn's exposed back.

She twisted a hair too late to avoid his blade altogether, and it cut deep into her right shoulder. The move succeeded in overextending him, though, which had been her intent. Quinn ignored the searing pain in her back and continued her twisting maneuver, bringing her Bowie around.

With a shout of triumph, she thrust the shining silver blade up into Handon's chest, her Bowie sinking in to its hilt.

He stared at her for an instant in disbelief, then sank to his knees, the light in his eyes dimming.

Quinn yanked her blade free and spun away to avoid the continued attacks from the ten or so remaining cultists and vampires still trying to reach her.

She shouted to the still frozen vampire standing next to John Handon's crumpled corpse. "Naomi, wake up."

Two other vampires closed on Quinn at the same time, and she failed to escape their clutching talons as she tried to duck and pull away. Before she knew it, they held her between them as a pair of cultists with curved daggers charged at her. One twisted her wrist until the Bowie fell from her clutching hand to the ground.

"Naomi," Quinn called out, desperation coloring her voice. "Mother! Please!"

The frozen hunter vampire snapped out of her trance, going from total stillness to eye-blurring speed in an instant.

The vampire to Quinn's left went down, his head spinning in one direction and his body toppling in the other.

That was all Quinn needed. She pulled hard on the other arm, gritting her teeth against the pain of the talons digging in to try to stop her.

Taking advantage of the vampire's savage grip on her arm, she swung the vampire, a female, around in an arc until she collided with the two cultists rushing in. The move tripped the three of them, and they all tumbled to the ground at Quinn's feet.

She scooped up her Bowie from the ground and thrust down once, twice, and a third time, leaving a dead vampire and two twitching cultists on the ground.

Quinn straightened and spun, searching the chamber for a new target. None were close. Three cultists ran for the chamber entrance, trying to escape. Nearby, Naomi battled a pair of vampires, a third already fallen at her feet.

The huntress ran over and stood side by side with her mother as they took on the last of Handon's vampire coven together.

A few seconds later, it was over. Quinn hunched over with her hands on her knees. She gasped to catch her breath. Moving at that speed for an extended time had taken its toll on her. The power of the clan ancestors inside her had subsided over the course of the fight. There was a faint hint of a connection lingering in the back of her mind.

Quinn clutched at her side as the pain of her other injuries returned.

Naomi asked, "Are you all right? Where are you hurt?"

"It's only a few scratches from this fight. I'm still pretty beat up from the fight at the museum, though. The power that masked the pain so I could fight is mostly gone now."

"Power?" Naomi asked.

"The dead hunters entombed here. Somehow, they gifted me their energy. Didn't you see all the ghosts come from their tombs? That was how I was able to escape and take on Handon in the end."

"I saw nothing," Naomi replied.

Her answer surprised Quinn. "I don't understand. How did you know what I should do, then?"

"I'd hoped there might be some truth to the legends about the tombs in this place," Naomi told her. "There've been stories told about them since long before I was born. Ever since Handon appropriated the ritual chamber after the purges, I kept waiting for the old power to come back like the stories said it would."

Naomi turned to Quinn with a half-smile on her face. "I guess it took you to do it. I'm so proud of you."

Quinn shook her head, "I was lucky, that's all. I took a chance even coming here tonight. I just couldn't let Handon get away with what he planned to do with the ritual components."

Quinn looked down at the stone floor. The vampire lord stared at the ceiling. His wide, sightless eyes made his dead facial expression seem startled.

Naomi chuckled. "He won't get away with anything like that ever again, thanks to you."

A groan from behind them turned the pair around. She raised her Bowie, expecting a survivor to rise from among the bodies littering the floor.

She lowered the blade when she saw who it was and rushed over to Clark, still lying on the table. He rubbed at his battered head as he tried to shake off the last of the cobwebs from being knocked unconscious.

Quinn had many things she wanted to say to him. He hadn't been honest with her about what had happened to start the purge here in Baltimore. She wasn't sure she blamed him, though. It wasn't his fault Myles betrayed his trust, but he should have told Quinn and the others about it, and about his connection to the VirSync CEO.

Clark sat up and looked around before spotting Quinn coming his way. His eyes widened and he rolled off the table, trying to pull Quinn out of the way.

"Quinn, watch out behind you."

She turned to see what he was talking about, her knife coming up, ready to defend herself. She saw Naomi standing there, arms crossed.

"Clark, it's okay. She's with us now."

"She can't be. She betrayed the clan by becoming a vampire."

Quinn spun around, anger rising inside her. "You accuse Naomi of betrayal? Are you sure you want to do that, Clark? I mean, Myles Hickman used to be your best friend or something, right?"

Clark closed his mouth but didn't take his eyes off Naomi. "You don't understand, Quinn. I didn't know what he did until it was too late."

Quinn nodded. "So, there were extenuating circumstances. I get it," she agreed. She hooked a thumb over her shoulder. "Same with her. If you have a problem with that, you can leave the clan. I won't stop you."

Clark's head turned toward her. He started to say something but closed his mouth. He looked at the carnage around him and shook his head. "You did all this?"

"I did, with help from Naomi. I'm not a hundred percent sure how, but it worked out." Quinn glanced from the carnage to Clark. "I wasn't kidding when I said I was starting something new. I'm the huntress, and my new clan is open to everyone who's proven they'll fight for those who need protection, and who will stand by me when it counts."

Quinn turned to look at Naomi. "That includes ghosts, tech witches, old washed-up hunters, and you, if you'll accept the offer."

"I'm not sure I have anything I can teach you. Clark has already taught you so much, and you somehow manage to accomplish the impossible."

Quinn laughed. "I'm sure you'll come up with something. Besides, I can sometimes do the impossible, but the other stuff along the way I still need lots of help with. Maybe the two of you can team up to fill in the gaps."

Clark glanced at Naomi.

The vampire met his gaze and nodded.

He nodded in reply and turned back to Quinn. "I guess we're both in. So, what are we calling this new clan of yours?"

Quinn smiled. She decided to keep it simple. "The Huntress Clan has a nice ring to it, don't you think?"

CHAPTER THIRTY-TWO

The forge glowed white-hot as the smith pulled the crucible of molten silver from the coals. Quinn suppressed a shiver of excitement and anticipation as he turned and tipped the tongs holding the vessel until a thin stream of liquid metal poured into the clay mold.

Taylor, standing beside Quinn, put a hand on her best friend's shoulder. "You don't need it, you know. You've proven that."

Quinn smiled. "It's a promise I made to myself and to the clan. This is the first of many amulets. There'll be one for each of us. This is an important step for us as we climb back to reclaim what was lost."

"It is time, Huntress," Princess Aurora said. "My smith must complete the casting process soon. The magic needs to be completed before then."

Nodding, Quinn glanced at Taylor. "You've got this, right?"

"Miranda explained it to me, and I've read the ritual in the life tome. It's complex, but not impossible."

"So, that's a yes?" Quinn asked.

Taylor nodded and stepped over to the small table set up by the forge. The crystal scrying bowl glinted in the faint light of the forge's fire. Beside it lay the Ruby Heart and the curved silver dagger they'd recovered from the battle in the ritual hall.

"Princess?" Taylor asked, picking up the dagger and holding it out.

Aurora took the blade, gripped the hilt, and laid the sharp edge against her palm. With a hiss, she drew the dagger across her hand, closing her fingers to clench her fist, keeping the blood inside.

Taylor picked up the Ruby Heart and held it over the scrying bowl. The gemstone began to pulse with a glow from deep inside. She started chanting in low tones, speaking foreign words Quinn didn't understand.

Aurora stepped forward and turned her clenched fist to the side above the Ruby Heart. She squeezed the muscles of her hand until a stream of bright red blood spilled onto the gemstone and formed a small puddle in the bottom of the bowl. The princess pulled her hand back and wrapped it in a clean white cloth.

Miranda hovered behind Taylor, whispering occasional instructions in her ear.

The tech witch finished her chant and set the gem down in the bowl in the center of the small puddle of blood. She turned and nodded to the smith.

The pulsing glow inside the gem intensified as Taylor chanted once more. The reflected light in the blood below soon became a glow emanating from the blood. Then the

Ruby Heart's inner glow faded as Taylor lifted it from the blood. The reddish glow from the liquid inside the scrying bowl remained.

Taylor set the gemstone down and carefully lifted the crystal vessel in both hands. She nodded to the fae smith, who used metal tongs to bring over the small clay mold.

Quinn tensed. She knew from discussions with her friends that this was the most challenging part of the ritual. The smith and the spell caster must work together to ensure none of the blood spilled outside the mold.

Taylor took a deep breath and let it out slowly as she tipped the crystal scrying bowl and poured the glowing fae blood into the mold.

The smith held the clay steady until the last drop entered the hole at the top of the mold. Taylor nodded, and he moved back to the workbench and anvil beside the forge. She set the bowl down and stepped back to stand beside Quinn.

Setting the clay mold down on the anvil, the fae smith picked up a hammer from the bench. He tapped twice on the mold, cracking the fragile clay until it fell away. A small silver amulet gleamed on the dark iron of the anvil.

The smith smiled and picked up the amulet in a gloved hand, using a tiny emery board to file away excess silver, smoothing and polishing the edges. He carefully wiped it with a soft cloth from the pocket of his leather apron. Then he turned to Quinn.

She reached into her pocket and pulled out the original chain from the silver necklace her mother had left her. The fae smith carefully threaded the amulet onto the chain and turned back to the huntress, holding the necklace by both ends. The restored amulet swung in a gentle pendulum motion as he walked up to Quinn.

She nodded to Naomi, who was standing on her other side, opposite Taylor. The smith handed the ends of the necklace to Quinn's mother.

Naomi smiled and moved until she stood behind Quinn. Reaching around her daughter, she placed the necklace around Quinn's neck and connected the clasp. She let it drop into place and returned to her spot.

Quinn reached up and stroked the still-warm surface of the amulet where it lay against her shirt. She knew what Taylor had said was right. She no longer needed the necklace and its magical charm. Quinn had drawn in all the powers it contained and now held them within herself.

It had been essential to restore it, though. Its remaking signified the birth of a whole new clan. She turned until the forge was at her back. Her clan, the Huntress Clan, stood watching and waiting. The next move was hers.

Clark, the mentor, stood beside Aurora, the benefactor. Naomi, the mother, stood beside Taylor, the companion, and Miranda, the spirit guide, hovered just off the ground behind them all.

Quinn smiled. Her Huntress Clan now offered more than just a new start. It offered new hope for the whole world.

The End

When another survivor of the Hunter purges shows up in Baltimore and starts on a killing vendetta and Quinn must track them down before a full-on war between supernaturals and humans begins in Huntress Scout.

Extreme Medical Services: Medical Care On The Fringes Of Humanity

Monsters, Paramedics, and Street Medicine

New paramedic Dean Flynn is fresh out of the academy.

Then he learns his patients aren't your normal 911 callers.

With patients that are vampires, werewolves, fairies and more, will Dean survive his first days on the new job?

Will his patients?

Come along now with Extreme Medical Services, a supernatural medical thrill-ride with the paramedics of Elk City by best-selling author and real-life paramedic Jamie Davis.

Jump on the ambulance with Dean, Brynne and the rest of the team.

Get the first book in this best-selling service for free at Amazon.com.

JAMIE'S AUTHOR NOTES

FEBRUARY 17, 2020

I marvel at how my books and stories reflect back on my own life at the time I write them. If you're reading this, you've learned that Quinn's quest to build a new clan is well on its way to completion. That quest is built upon her need to surround herself with a family of her own.

Many of us are lucky and have supportive families around us who help us when we stumble or fall down. I'm one of them and I count my blessings constantly. Most of that family is related to me, but I've surrounded myself with a family of author friends, too.

Family is more than just blood. I've been let down by blood-related family members on numerous occasions. Just because you're related to someone doesn't make them reliable. The people I count on the most are the ones I've brought into my life and kept close with over the years.

First and foremost is my wife. Wait, isn't she part of your family already? Yes, but she wasn't always there. She wasn't born my wife. I met her and built up a friendship before we became romantically involved. She is undoubtedly the best of my found friends.

Others in my friend circle include friends I've made through various parts of my life. I mentioned the author friends who are there when I need help with my writing journey. This book and the whole Huntress Clan Saga exists because of my friendship with authors Michael Anderle and Craig Martelle.

Good things are created when the people you bring into your family circle collaborate. For you, it might be something as simple as a new deck, patio, or fire pit in your back yard. Friends helping friends is the cement that holds communities, large and small, together. I think it's an important lesson to remember as division and divisiveness surrounds us all on social channels.

We all have unique differences and talents. Those differences aren't a problem. They're a strength. Quinn learns to harness all the various and diverse skills of those who end up in her clan. The people in her new clan shouldn't get along and work together but they find a way to save the day, each pitching in where they can to help Quinn defeat the bad guy.

I hope you'll take a moment and thank the ones who've helped you accomplish something in your life. It may be a blood relative, or it may be a close friend you've chosen to let into your life. Whoever it is, you're where you are because of their help and support.

Until next time, thanks for reading my books. Peace.

ABOUT JAMI DAVIS

Jamie Davis is a nurse, retired paramedic, author, and nationally recognized medical educator who began teaching new emergency responders as a training officer for his local EMS program. He loves everything fantasy and sci-fi and especially the places where stories intersect with his love of medicine or gaming.

Jamie lives in a home in the woods in Maryland with his wife, three children, and dog. He is an avid gamer, preferring historical and fantasy miniature gaming, as well as tabletop games. He writes urban and contemporary paranormal fantasy stories, and LitRPG/GameLit, among other things.

He loves hearing from readers and going to cons and events where he meets up with fans. Reach out and say "hi." Visit JamieDavisBooks.com for more books, free offers and more!

My author site is: https://jamiedavisbooks.com

My Facebook group is: https://facebook.com/ groups/funfantasyreaders

Twitter — https://twitter.com/podmedic

Instagram — https://instagram.com/podmedic